THE ONE THAT GOT AWAY

A Miami Love Affair

TISHA ANDREWS

Copyright 2016 © Tisha Andrews

| Let's Keep In Touch |

Facebook: Author Tisha Andrews
Twitter: @tisha_p12
Instagram: @author_tisha_andrews or @lil_tdrew
Email: AuthorTAndrews@gmail.com

To the Readers

This is a re-release but the love is just the same if not better. This is the beginning of many stories to come which appear below. Make sure when you get a chance, check them out.

Chapter 1
2002

"What's up, shorty. Why you looking like that? All scared and shit," he said, tucking in his lower lip briefly. When he did, he showed his almost perfect white teeth. "It's just sweat."

Speechless, Iyana stared at him in awe, caught up in his large 6'2" presence towering over her small frame. His wet, golden skin, covering his toned arms, chest and firm abs looked like it had been gently kissed by the sun. His low cut, wavy fade, neatly trimmed, cascaded down into soft sideburns that somewhat softened the smirk he had on his face.

As her eyes traveled down, she quickly took notice of his long basketball shorts that hung loosely around his hips, drawing Iyana's eyes to a slight bulge and chiseled bowed legs.

Damn, he's fine, she thought to herself.

Iyana, at thirteen, saw a few boys she thought were cute, but they were nothing like Keyz. After being held back twice in elementary for fighting, Keyz, at sixteen, was much older than the boys in middle school.

She had heard of him, but never thought he would see her, let alone speak to her. Not when most days she walked around feeling invisible, that was until someone reminded her she wasn't. Either she was "darky," "black bitch" or "that lil' black motherfucker" since she was petite with dark chocolate skin.

Then if it wasn't about her skin complexion, it was about the sheltered life she somewhat lived being raised by her devout Christian grandparents who closely monitored her everyday life.

Bouncing the basketball, *the* Kaizer Paul, AKA Keyz, stood cockily with a few of his boys who had gotten together to play basketball that morning before the first day of school. Iyana could hear them yelling as he held on to the ball, as their eyes were locked in on each other rendering her almost unmovable. She shifted just a little but not enough to cease her gawking stance that seemed to take over.

"Naw, she ain't scared. She's deaf as fuck, Keyz. Look at shorty all drooling and shit. Where are those teachers that escort them dumb motherfuckers to class? The fuck she back here for anyway?" one of his friends asked, causing them all to laugh.

Keyz just smiled, now holding the ball underneath his toned, tanned arm. It took Iyana a second or two before she even realized she was the butt of someone's joke before she scurried off to get to class in a daze, never uttering a word to any of them. Once she made it to class, Iyana quickly found a seat near the back as the bell rang.

The room seemed to seat about 50 students, which was

much more than she was used to coming from elementary school. Each seat, complete with its own rack for their book bags, were neatly lined up until a few close friends began to slide them closer to each other. She silently thanked God that she remembered the shortcut her sister, Myriah, told her about, given the size of her new school.

"Now quiet, everyone. I know today is the first day of school, but I'm sure being quiet is not a new expectation. I mean, you all did successfully complete elementary school or you wouldn't be here. I am Ms. Gomez, your homeroom teacher. This is the class where your attendance is taken each day. If you are late or absent, it does not matter if you attend the rest of your classes because this class is the one that tracks your overall attendance for the school year.

Now, I see a few of you are moving around to find your friends, but let's be clear. Friend time is once you leave my classroom, so kindly place your desks back where they were before you arrived. Am I making myself clear?" Ms. Gomez stood up and asked in a snide manner, looking over her glasses that barely sat on her nose.

A few of them nodded while others said "yes, ma'am" in combination with a few groans and laughs. Ms. Gomez's eyes scanned the room before taking her seat, setting the stage as to who was in charge of her classroom.

Iyana sighed with relief having made it just in time. She didn't want detention although Myriah, her fifteen year old sister, seemed to end up there quite often for being late. She took note of her classmates pushing their desks back to where they were, but caught a few murmurs where Ms. Gomez was now "that bitch" followed by a few laughs.

As she sat there not knowing anyone, Iyana felt a smile forming as her morning encounter danced around in her head. His bold presence made her very uncomfortable, but in an intriguing way, to the point that she was a little sad she didn't respond.

He must think I'm an idiot, she surmised, knowing she couldn't be his type gently rubbing her chocolate thighs underneath the desk.

Shaking it off, she quickly sat straight up, casting away the thought of being on the arm of Keyz in any shape or form.

"Now, I need for you all to complete the emergency contact form that—" Ms. Gomez started before Keyz barged in the classroom like he knew he was already late.

"Mr. Paul. You're late," she said looking annoyed with his presence as she pointed to the clock.

"Ooooo, he late, y'all!" one boy yelled, getting Keyz's attention as he mouthed "fuck you" before responding to Ms. Gomez.

"Naw, Ms. Gomez. You're still just here. I mean, shouldn't you be retired or something? Like wasn't Moses in your graduating class?" he cracked, lightly brushing his knuckle underneath his nose as he winked at Iyana.

His comeback evoked a few more laughs, further irritating Ms. Gomez as he stood long enough for her to see he hadn't changed. Well, not his attitude which coupled with a swag although he still wore a school uniform. She frowned at the way his beige khaki shorts thung loosely off his hips, but the girls didn't. They grinned, seeing how he finished it off with red Polo top, and red and black Air Jordans looked like they were made just for him.

A warm feeling came over Iyana as she desperately tried to peel her eyes off of him until she was caught staring. Embarrassed, she quickly looked away, lightly scratching the back of her neck where her freshly permed hair fell over her hand and past her shoulders.

"Still mute, huh? I can fix that for you," he whispered as he sat down closely behind her, ignoring the ruckus he caused. Feeling sort of bold which was unusual for her, Iyana decided to respond.

"I didn't think anything was broken," she whispered, her head slightly leaning back as she took in his pretty, white teeth and full lips, unknowingly biting her own lip.

Damn, she's gorgeous, he thought before Ms. Gomez got both of their attention, clearing her throat.

"Mr. Paul, please go to the principal's office!" she yelled. "I think Miss...uh, young lady in front of him. What's your name?"

"Me?" Iyana asked, sinking down in her chair, not used to all of this attention she had just gotten.

"Yes, you. What's your name, young lady?" Ms. Gomez repeated with a slight look of agitation on her face.

Iyana wasn't too sure if Ms. Gomez saw her talking, but she was already second guessing herself once she responded to him.

"I—I—Iyana," she stuttered, looking back down while her fingers dragged up and down her neck.

It was something she did to soothe herself whenever she felt nervous or uncomfortable. She smiled as she could hear her grandmother saying, "Iyana Wilkers! Now if you don't pick yo' head up like you lookin' for cockroaches behind that neck of yours, I'ma hurt you!"

Her grandmother always seemed to have a way with words that would make sense even when they shouldn't have.

"Iyana Wilkers," she repeated adding her last name, feeling his breath on her neck causing her to squirm.

"Humph, I see," Mrs. Gomez replied, looking at Keyz who was even closer to her than he was when he first sat down.

Once he realized she could be easily unnerved, he took pleasure in getting under her skin. It also didn't hurt that he felt she was the most beautiful girl he'd ever seen. Especially with her dark, smooth complexion against the peach nail polish she had on her fingernails. Pulling his dick that was starting to swell, Keyz sat back thinking of all the things he wanted to do her, but knew she probably wouldn't let him.

I bet lil ma a straight ass virgin. Damn, he thought to himself.

"I don't think Miss Wilkers appreciates you interrupting her school year on the first day of class. Why don't you go and join *Moses* wherever he may be since you seem to know what's going on with him," she replied sternly, pointing to the door.

"Ahhhh haaaa," one of boys said, laughing and clapping his hands. "Man, it's the first day and you already getting kicked out."

"You, sir, can go with him," she said, obviously short on patience. "Mr. Paul, take your little comrade with you."

"Man! Ms. Gomez, I didn't even—"

"Enough! Now go before I call security," she yelled at his friend, snatching her glasses off her face.

"Oh, and Miss Wilkers? Run, my dear. There is nothing he

can offer you except trouble," she warned her, putting her glasses back on.

Instead of leaving right away, Keyz decided to have his own parting words with her while leaning closely to her ear. Although he was sweating a few moments ago, Iyana smiled as his spicy cologne found its way to her nose. Papa B, her grandfather, loved Old Spice which was clearly a throwback aftershave cologne. Still, whatever he wore captivated her nasal senses, causing her to feel things she'd never felt before when it came to the opposite sex.

"Meet me during lunch time at the basketball court. Don't fuck with me, *Iyana*," he demanded in a flirtatious way, tucking his lip like he did that morning.

He could tell she wasn't used to someone being so forward with her, but he didn't care. He wanted her and he usually got what he wanted. It didn't hurt that he could tell no one else had had her, making her that much more appealing to him. At sixteen, the streets were his real school that was filled with the likes of crime and hoes, and Iyana, to him, was a virgin to both. That alone made him want to get to know her even more.

Instead of her heeding to Ms. Gomez's warning, she smiled looking over her shoulder as Keyz and his friend walked out. She wanted to know more about him even though she knew he probably wasn't serious.

Hell, why not meet him during lunch? she thought, feeling bold again which was scary to her.

"Ewwww, why he whispering in her ear?" one girl said loud enough just for her to hear them.

"Who knows. Prolly feel sorry for her black ass. Look at

her smiling like he really wants her. Stupid bitch," another girl said, laughing as Iyana looked their way.

"Hoe, why the fuck you looking at us with them fake ass color contacts in your eyes?" the first girl popped off, trying to get a rise out of Iyana. "Like, do people even wear them shits anymore?"

Iyana shook her head, hating that everyone thought her eye color was fake.

"Hell naw. And look at that hair, ole homey looking ass. Like, bitch, getchu some weave," the second one said, frowning with her lip turned up as the other one laughed.

Iyana's mood shifted, as their slurs shot down any chance she thought she may have had with Keyz as they seemed to be the kind of girl he would want. Sinking even further down in her chair, she stole a quick glance at them to see what he might see in them since they so confidently shot her down.

One girl was a "dirty red" complexion while the other had a caramel complexion. Not knowing their names, Iyana chuckled to herself calling them Cherry Cola and Blondie in her head because of the color of their weave. She wasn't afraid of them. She just hated confrontation, which was something her sister and Sky, her best friend since first grade, took on with ease. In fact, she was used to ignoring the insults but frustrated that she was being judged yet again, because of how she looked.

"Girl, Keyz is so fucking fine. The other day when my mama left, he was all on my porch trying to fuck. Big dick ass," Cherry Cola said, popping her lips.

Fidgeting as she continued to scratch the back of her neck, Iyana's body language must have pushed Cherry Cola's

The One That Got Away

button. She was not even remotely interested in sex. Her sister was though along with her best friend, chase, talking about being fingered fucked by a few boys from church. She concluded if Cherry Cola was his type, she was good on him no matter how he'd just made her feel.

"Yeah, something her black ass would never know. Rightttt!" Blondie yelled, high fiving Cherry Cola.

"Do I hear talking back there?" Ms. Gomez asked, looking up to throw the next victim out of her class.

Cherry Cola and Blondie quickly shut up, filling out their emergency contact cards, which was short lived as they continued to snicker here and there albeit under their breath. Sadly, hurtful comments like theirs led to her scrubbing her face three to four times a night in the shower, hoping to make it lighter. She figured God must have hated her because short of her father, who died in a riot with her mother, she was the lonely dark one out of everyone in her entire family.

∽

"How was school today, baby?" Papa B asked her when she gave him a peck on the cheek. His scratchy beard caused her to wince just a little, letting her know he'd missed his weekly shave.

"Ah, stop that," he laughed. "Papa B just got a lil' hair fuzz on his face. I saw that look you gave me."

"Na un, Papa B," she quickly said, kissing him again on his other cheek.

Every day, whenever she came home from school, Papa B could be found reading his newspaper in the living room while watching *Judge Judy*. He and her grandmother, whom they called Nana, were community activist in the 60's which led to her grandfather's obsession with daytime judge shows.

Sometimes he yelled whenever he felt someone was unjustly ruled against, especially after her parents' deaths were ruled accidental after being trampled on by police officers during what was called a peaceful march.

"Oh, Papa B. I got a little lost, but after lunch, it got easier," she said. She, intentionally, didn't share more details about her day as she grabbed an apple.

She was tired of running to them about things she really should handle herself. Especially since Sky was at a different junior high school this school year. If she were there, she would have shut it down, mopping the floor with them just for looking Iyana's way.

Being tall and curvy, many backed down whenever Sky showed up and no matter how burly she appeared to be, she was still seen as this Puerto Rican beauty with long, curly black hair and daunting brown eyes.

After fourth grade, Iyana stopped counting how many fights Sky had, even sometimes initiating them because the kids would call her out her name. Out of guilt, she would offer to do her homework or buy her a snack with her lunch money after school, but Sky wasn't having it. She just wished everyone would get to know Iyana like she did instead of bullying her about something as trivial as her skin complexion.

"Well, I can tell you're pretty hungry," Nana spoke as she walked out of the kitchen. "Dinner will be ready in an hour or so. Where's Myriah?"

"Nana, Myriah is in high school now, but I did hear her

say something about a cheerleading meeting this morning," she said biting into her apple.

"Now watch that juice running down your chin, Iyana," Nana teased, as Iyana plopped down on the beige, leather sectional near Papa B.

After years of complaining, her grandparents had finally splurged on getting some new furniture, which was long overdue as their old furniture was covered in plastic. While sturdy, its dated presence did not make for a lot of family time in the living room.

Iyana smiled as they even upgraded their television, which only happened once Papa B's eyes started getting worse, interrupting his daily viewing of the *Price is Right, Sanford and Son* and *Good Times*. Although they lived in the 21st century, Papa B was stuck like a time capsule refusing to watch any reality television unless it was *Judge Mathis* or other judge shows.

She was glad she could now invite someone over from church without them stopping and staring at the antiquated furniture they used to have not too long ago. Outside of Sky and church folks, Iyana's life was pretty boring.

Looking over his newspaper, Papa B stared at Iyana who quickly sat before she got the lecture about messing up their new furniture. She thought they would be sitting on plastic covered furniture forever until Deaconess Maybelle told them about her son who started working at the local furniture store.

Once she came to church bragging about the plush, olive green lounge chair he got for her, Nana and Papa B decided it was time to upgrade a few things around the house, not wanting to be outdone by her. It wasn't a secret that Deaconess Maybelle had been pining over Papa B for years and would find any reason to show she was the better woman, from how she cooked to the way she kept her house if they had a church meeting in her home. Nana was a lady, but there were many days her patience ran short until Papa B scolded her for doubting his love. Here they were, almost 40 years later, still married and in love.

"Well, she better be home before dinner," Papa B snapped, folding his newspaper up. "Thought we shut all that down, Jamie? That girl thinks she slick. Won't join the choir or usher board at church, but steady joining something in them schools."

That meant she would more than likely, be later for dinner. In the Wilkers' household, dinner was on the table every day around five o'clock. Nana would remind them that it had been that way for over forty years, as their mother, Sheryl, was raised the same way.

Dinnertime proved to be a way to encourage family talk time. While Iyana looked forward to it, Myriah hated it, feeling like the lesser of the two when it came to her baby sister. There were many days Papa B would shut Myriah up for bashing her sister, most times for no reason at all.

"Papa B, I told her if she got her grades up in summer school, she could try out for cheerleading next year. You must have forgotten," Nana responded quickly.

"Yeah, yeah. She too busy worrying 'bout shake it fast, watch yo'self. Pfft. These kids ain't nothin' like us, or even Sheryl, short of that one mishap she had," he spoke, staring off into space as he thought of their only child.

Their mother was known for her outgoing personality and community activist spirit, who also was quite involved in the family's church, Mount Moriah Missionary Baptist Church. They've been worshipping there since before she was born. It was that spirit that led to her participate in a local rally where she met her husband. His name was Abraham, the high school's top school basketball player.

They were the modern day Black Panther couple of Liberty City, an inner city area located in Miami. This area, while considered poor, was rich in black pride. Sheryl's love for justice came from her parents who lived through the civil rights movement. So her falling right in line with their passion came natural.

"Papa B, please don't compare these girls to Sheryl now," she countered. "Times are different with all this technology stuff and different thangs for them to do in school. Besides, they do stuff at the church all the time—"

"Yeah, like look and play around with them lil boys!" he belted, staring over his glasses at Iyana who refused to take him on.

Before today, Iyana had never really saw herself dating anyone, but she knew he was really talking about Myriah who was ballsy and outgoing. She was still smart though, which was a trait they both received from their parents.

Myriah, however, was coined the mad and rebellious one, hating her grandparents for sucking all the fun out of life. She wanted to be free, live life a little. Not be cooped up at home or in church sometimes practically six days a week.

At 5'6", standing slightly taller than Iyana, Myriah was a natural beauty in her own right. Her skin, the color of peanut butter, was flawless, complementing her body that was shaped like a Coca-Cola bottle. That was something Papa B would say she'd gotten from their mother.

At her age, Myriah attracted the male species of all ages, including a few of the deacons at church, and that drove Papa B up the wall after being on the deacon board for thirty years. To his knowledge, it never went beyond looking, but he hated that his granddaughter drew so much attention to herself.

Almost like her mother Sheryl did, resulting in him throwing her into every activity he could to keep her on the straight and narrow. Over time, he didn't have to which wasn't working with Myriah.

Now Iyana, still growing into her shape, took after their father whose skin complexion akin to soft coal. It was smooth and blemish free with light, grey eyes. She also inherited the deepest dimples from their mother that would appear from the slightest jaw movement. Her small breasts, while still forming, sat up round and perky, complementing her washboard stomach, small hips, and firm legs she developed from dancing at the local community arts center and dance ministry at church for as long as she could remember.

If asked, anyone could easily say the Wilkers' girls were beauty's in their own right. One just used it to her advantage while the other was unaware she even possessed such beauty.

Instead of arguing, Nana went back to the kitchen to finish up dinner. Tonight they were having chicken and dumplings, white rice, freshly brewed sweet iced tea and a sour cream pound cake made from scratch. Anyone at church who ate Nana's food assumed she was a chef because she cooked for every church event if Deaconess Maybelle didn't jump at it first, but she wasn't.

It brought in a little bit of money which didn't hurt, but she said it made her feel alive at sixty-two although she didn't look a day over forty. Thinking of his wife, Papa B felt proud that even after all of this time as she moved about the kitchen, he was still in love with her. It wasn't long before his mood soured, thinking how these same deacons pinned over his wife, too.

She was caramel with a melon shaped butt that still caught the eye of men, young and old. There were days he asked God why he couldn't find a lesser attractive woman, but without Nana, he didn't see life worth living and she felt just the same.

"Now, Papa B! Stop it. That ain't fair. I mean look at our girls. They are gorgeous. They can't help them boys see how pretty they are. Ain't that right, Iyana?" she asked, smiling as she set up the table for dinner.

"I guess," Iyana softly replied, shrugging her shoulders as she got up to toss the core of her apple into the garbage. She wouldn't know if a boy was interested in her or not if she had to gauge how they drooled over Myriah.

"Now you know what I mean. Look at Iyana!" he belted sitting up in his lounge chair. "My grandbaby's beauty is in a class of its own and it's timeless…you like that Diana Ross or Dianne Carroll. Makes Papa B proud such a pretty thang came from him," he said, shaking his hips in his chair like he was dancing.

"Oh, stop all that dancing," Nana laughed. "You're embarrassing my grandbaby." Nana swatted the mitten in her hand at him that she used to bring the food out.

It was just like Papa B to make Iyana feel special. In fact, he complimented Iyana and Myriah all the time, calling them his Reese's Peanut Butter Cups, which used to tickle the both of them when they were younger. Now Myriah cringed whenever he said it while Iyana embraced it, smiling so hard, her cheeks would hurt.

He was determined to dispel that house nigga versus field nigga mentality in his household, but Myriah would secretly call her names. Iyana, eager to be loved by her sister, quietly cried, never sharing the names her sister or the kids at school called her.

"Awe, thank you, Papa B," Iyana said, jumping up to peck him on the cheek.

"Hey, Papa B and Nana. Sup, sis?" Myriah said, barging into the house like she was out of breath. She plopped down on the sofa, which was a new ritual for the both of them.

"Hey to you, too, baby. I heard 'bout that cheerleading thang. Now remember what we talked about?" Nana asked, almost done with setting the table.

Sighing, Myriah shook her head. "Yes, ma'am. I remember." She was aggravated that this was the first thing they mentioned, ready to chastise her for doing something she loved because of a few F's she got last year in school.

"So no one is going to ask how my day was? I'm sure Iyana had the floor long before I got here," she huffed sarcastically, rolling her eyes at her baby sister.

"She did because, unlike you, she came straight home right after school. Now gone wash up and come back out for dinner," Papa B replied, turning off the television as he headed to the dinner table.

Choosing to ignore him, Myriah crossed her arms and

muttered, "Fuck you and that black bitch. I swear she makes me sick."

~

SHORTLY AFTER DINNER, Iyana showered and hopped into her queen size canopy bed covered with purple and silver linen and huge pillows, as she stared at the ceiling thinking of the insults thrown her way today. Nana allowed her to decorate her room purple which she said represented royalty, although Iyana didn't feel anywhere near royal. She wished Sky were there, but even if she was, Iyana knew that eventually she would have to stand up for herself. Even if it meant fighting and getting suspended from school.

"Iyana!" Myriah yelled from outside her door.

"Ughhh. Why she yell so much?" she said to herself before she got up to open her door.

"Your lil' Mexican friend is on the phone," she said, tossing her the cordless house phone before she walked off.

"I got her Mexican ass whooping," Sky said before Iyana could even speak.

"Don't bother, Sky. She's been in a nasty mood since she came home. Like it's her that has this fabulous life while I'm the one getting picked on, but she has the right to be miserable. Just ignore her like I do."

"That's the problem. No one knocks that little Chihuahua in her fucking mouth. I got her 'yo quiero, Taco Bell' ass when I see her."

Iyana laughed so hard at that she almost fell off her bed. It was just like Sky to make her laugh and today was no different.

She didn't realize it before, but it wasn't until Sky called, did she realize she needed to do more of that—laugh.

"See, your ass always laughing when I'm serious as hell. Anyway, Yi. Tell Sky baby how school was today. I misssss you," she said in a baby voice. "I can't believe Selena's ass moved me all the way up here in fuckin' Opa Locka. Bitch," she said, calling her mother by her first name. "I will forever rep Liberty City til the day we die. I swear her ass be tripping, but it's all good because I'll see you this weekend."

"Girl, you better stop calling your mama Selena," Iyana said, not even offended that her girl called her bitch. Sky said "bitch" like it was everyone's name and if she didn't call her that, it was Yi, short for Iyana.

"Why? That's her name," she quickly responded. "Girl, run it. Tell me what happened today since them hoes ain't seen the two of our asses on the scene together. Shit, I know Tone's old fine ass was there. The one that be hanging with Julio. I will climb that nigga's pole if he keep fucking with me like he did the last time I saw him at the store," she giggled, as she talked about this dude all the girls wanted.

He used to be fat last year, but slimmed up real nicely once he joined the Optimist football team over the summer. First, no one was checking for him, but now everyone was. Especially since he hung out with Sky's older brother, Julio, who always seemed to have a fan club hovering around.

"Naw, you first. You're the one at the new school in a new neighborhood, so I know you have more to tell," Iyana said, getting cozy on top of her bed with her legs crossed.

Iyana was excited to hear about Sky's first day of school now that she attended North Dade Middle School, located in

Opa Locka, a small inner city area just north of where they grew up. Sky couldn't understand why they had to move, but Selena worked hard to purchase her children a home after living in an apartment all of their life.

Once Sky and Iyana learned that they wouldn't be going to the same middle school, they cried for days on end almost making themselves physically sick. To soften the blow, Nana and Selena agreed that Sky could visit on the weekends and attend church, as long as her grades were good. Iyana was happy her grandparents felt her pain, but Myriah hated Sky's loud and boisterous ways, which were similar to hers.

"Not shit, Yi. Same ole, same ole, honestly. Hoes thinking they cute. Niggas trying to get with the pretty, new girl. You know that's me," she said as she smirked, filled with confidence.

"Uh huh. I figured as much. So you got you a new bestie already?" she asked, somewhat in her feelings.

"Bitch, whatever. You're my girl for life. Salt and Pepa, hoe. Don't play," Sky shot back. "I mean, I met a few people that were alright, but them hoes ain't the bestie. Se puede conseguir en nuestro nivel," she said, telling her other girls couldn't get on their level in Spanish. She knew how to make Iyana smile. Especially since she understood Spanish very well since they had been best friends since first grade.

"Yeah, yeah. So what about Julio?" she asked. Julio used to have a crush on her until they got older. Then she became the "lil sis" that couldn't get any play. Iyana really didn't care, knowing that all he wanted was sex even though he still teased her from time to time.

"Yi, Julio got kicked out the first day," she laughed. "I forgot to mention that shit!"

"Dang, for real?" she asked, although not totally surprised.

"Yep, yep. The PE teacher called security to come get him after he snatched the bitch's toupee off his head. He's a straight up clownin already!" she said, laughing so hard, she was crying.

"Really? I guess it's in the air because all that clowning sounds like Keyz," Iyana replied, not realizing what she'd just said.

"Keyz as in Kaizer Paul. That Keyz?" Sky asked in disbelief, wondering how Iyana was around him on the first day of school.

Growing quiet, Iyana bit her lip, unsure if she should tell Sky what happened earlier at school. They rarely spoke about boys unless Sky mentioned one or two like Tone, but the fact that she brought up one that Sky had never mentioned made her nervous. She was hoping now her best friend didn't like him. If so, he was off limits. She may have not known a lot about guys, but she knew a lot about loyalty and friendship and a dude wasn't worth losing her bestie.

"Uh, yeah. Yeah, that's him," she quickly said.

"How you know Keyz, Yi? Shit, the only reason I know him because he hangs with this boy name Skebo that Julio chills with sometimes."

"He does? Wow, I never knew that. Especially all the times I've been at y'all house," she said, her voice trailing off thinking about Keyz at that very moment.

"Yeah, and that nigga is fine as fuck! Damn, Yi. I wish I was there!"

"Me too, and now you said he knows Julio, I might as well not even think about it. You know how he loves to play and call me out my name, Sky. Lil Miss Dark Vader," she said in a robotic voiced before she laughed.

"Fuck Julio. I personally thinks he still likes you, but what he need to worry 'bout is that micro dick I saw him sticking in pissy ass Rachel last week when Selena wasn't home. Her pissy smelling self smelled like three-day-old popcorn. Stankin' hoe ain't even wash the pussy when they were done. But forget Julio. Tell me what happened with Keyz."

Iyana giggled at the foul things that came out of Sky's mouth with ease. She sometimes wished she could be so crass when it came to expressing herself, but her grandparents would die if they heard her talking like that.

"Nothing, girl," she sighed in defeat.

"Look, I'ma have Selena bring me over there if you don't tell me. You know she would do anything for Miss Iyana. She loves you probably more than me."

"Sky, stop lying. She just trusts me, is all. I mean who doesn't? I'm kind of sick of it, honestly. I mean I can be daring and do a little something," she said remembering how bold she was earlier that day with Keyz.

"Shit, I wish you would! Yesssssss. Then maybe I wouldn't feel like such a bad influence," she teased.

"Now you know Nana and Papa B don't think that. Especially with how Myriah acts."

"Fuck that mop head Muppet. Tell me sbout Keyz," she asked, getting excited again.

Choosing to leave out her encounter with Cherry Cola and Blondie, Iyana jumped right into how she met Keyz on the basketball court and what happened in class when he got kicked out.

"Ooooo, Yi. He likes you. I can tell. That muthafucka spoke to you not once, but twice today. Hoe, my panties wet! Why are you playing?"

"Wait, you really think he likes me?" Iyana asked, looking at the phone, ignoring Sky's inappropriate comment about her body part.

"Yi, are you serious? You're beautiful. Like a natural beauty who doesn't need all of that fake shit these hoes wear," she belted. "Who you know got them grey cat eyes, deep dimples and all that damn hair? Oh, and that lil' booty you be tooting around here from all that dancing. Fuck that! Why wouldn't he?" she barked.

"Come on, Sky. You already—"

"No, I don't! Stop letting that bitch of a sister make you think she's better than you. Ugh, I hate that hoe," she grumbled.

"Sky, you do know that's my sister," she sighed.

"Yeah, I do. Remind her ass."

"Now you know she barely speaks to me now that she's discovered boys. So… so like what should I do?" she asked, changing the subject.

"Holla. Let him know what's up if you see him again. Just do something different. I mean, we're cute and smart. Who wouldn't want us? Like I know I'm not as smart as you, but I'm not dumb either."

"No, you are *not* dumb. So remember that when we start applying to Howard University or Spellman," she said, sitting up to grab her homework out of her book bag. It was already seven-thirty and she had two homework assignments in social studies and algebra.

"Okay, Yi. You're the brainiac out of the two of us, but let me get out of middle school first. So whatever happened with lunchtime because I caught you never told me that part."

"I didn't go," she mumbled.

"Ugh, whatever," Sky said, growing irritated.

Their talk about how Iyana saw herself was a constant battle and Sky had a lot of homework herself. She didn't have Iyana to help her and she didn't want her to. In fact, she secretly was glad they were at different schools so she could work on getting her grades up by herself while Iyana learned how to stand on her own two feet. She loved her bestie, but wanted Iyana to love herself more.

"Look, I have to go. I just heard loud mouth Julio reminding me to cook dinner before Selena gets here. How are we Spanish, but they're always talking about spaghetti and lasagna like we're French?" she asked seriously as she headed towards the kitchen to get started.

"Italian," Iyana corrected her.

"Asshole," she laughed, teasing Iyana for always correcting her.

"I'll be that. Add some french bread. Then you're in the right country," she shot back before she hung up.

Chapter 2

"Bitch, shut they asses up! I'm trying to sleep around here! Fuck wrong with them?" Larry, Keyz's mother's new boyfriend, yelled as he was coming in from his first day of school.

Instead of coming straight home, he hung out at the store with a few old heads that were sort of like a father figure since his biological father forgot he had a son. Although he never asked, Keyz dismissed the idea of needing one as he hung on to every word one of these men spoke anytime he came up to the store.

To some, they were old men who did nothing but sit around and drink, harassing women that came in and out buying eggs or a few things to cook for the day. That's how it was in the hood. There were no Walmart or major grocery stores where they lived. Just corner stores that carried basic grocery items and hot foods like fish and rib sandwiches or a wing special with fries and a drink. To Keyz, these men spoke on what not to do, hoping he'd do better than them. Unfortunately, Larry wasn't one of these men.

"Sup, nigga. Who the fuck you talkin' to? Stand up and say that shit to me, homeboy! Fuck talkin' to my mama like this yo' shit 'cause you can raise the fuck up outta here!" Keyz yelled, dropping his book bag on the ground.

Knowing he was a hothead, his mother quickly jumped up from the sofa bed trying to diffuse the situation. She had lost count how many times Keyz had been suspended from school for fighting, or getting into a scuffle with a dude she brought home willing to pay a bill or two.

She knew he felt like he had to be the man of the house, but she really wanted him to just be a child. In his eyes, he stopped being one the day his father left, leaving him to protect his mother and younger siblings.

Keyz was the oldest out of four, having a 12-year-old brother named Keyon and 10-year-old twin sisters, Sunshine and Shower. Keyz loved teasing his sisters about their names, but he was convinced his mama was high as a kite when she named them. His mother, Lacray, grew up in the same hood, never leaving, nor learning how to break the vicious cycle that Keyz was born into.

By the time he was fourteen, Keyz had already been arrested for burglary and petty theft, selling anything he could get his hands on from TVs to the latest Jordans if he robbed an unsuspecting tourist walking in downtown Miami late at night. He didn't own a gun, but his menacing stare earned him the nickname Keyz, because he could get his hands on almost anything.

"I—I—Kaizer, it's okay. It's okay, baby," she stuttered,

calling him by his government name as she tried to keep him at bay while he stood over her and Larry laying on a pull-out sofa bed in the living room.

With little to no help except food stamps, the most she could afford was a one-bedroom duplex. Keyz and his younger siblings shared the bedroom, while his mother slept on the pullout sofa with any dude that failed to stick around long enough to make a difference.

"What the fuck this lil' nigga gon' do?" Larry yelled, standing up in Keyz' face.

Larry was taller and bigger, weighing close to 280 pounds, but Keyz didn't scare easily and was ready to die if he had to, in order to protect his family. He didn't start many fights, but he never ran from one either. The way he saw it, he owed Larry an ass whooping from day one when he first heard him speaking disrespectfully to his mother. Most times, Keyz would just crawl out the bedroom window, taking a walk to cool off because he knew his mother wasn't about to make him leave.

Sometimes he ended up at Skebo's house, his best friend since elementary school, who lived with an aunt that collected a check from the state once she took him in. She was his mother's oldest sister who seemed to raise everyone from his mother down to anyone in the family that seemed to be displaced.

Skebo's mother committed suicide when he was five years old, and his father was unknown. Saving him from foster care, Skebo loved her to death, and wasn't beyond robbing anyone if he had to whenever his check ran short before the end of the month. As he and Keyz both felt indebted to provide for their families, hustling and robbing became their solution.

"Now, Larry. You know how Kaizer is. He just got in from

school. Probably had a long day. Ain't that right, Kaizer?" his mother asked with fear in her eyes, her hand gently touching his chest.

"Now gone in the back and see what your brother and sisters are doing. Larry has to work later tonight. The route he's on will last a few days, so he needs his rest, baby," she continued, trying to break the menacing stare Keyz was giving Larry.

"The kids came home all excited about the first day of school, so help your mama out by keeping them quiet for a few. Keyon just got in and the girls telling him the same story I heard hours ago. Pizza's in the oven. Please, Kaizer. Go on in the back. Y'all can eat in there tonight," she pleaded with him.

Keyz loved his mother, but hated her at the same time. He couldn't blame her for all the men that walked out on her. He did, however, blame her for not picking a decent man to step in their place from Francisco, a known alcoholic that would beat her anytime he got drunk, to Raymond who would drop his three kids off and leave them for days at a time.

He was tired of it and Larry was about to get all of his pent-up frustration. He expected different since he started out nice and was an older dude who drove delivery trucks for Walmart, but that was short lived once he realized how needy his mama was.

"Shut the fuck up, Lacray. I pay bills 'round this bitch! This lil fucka ain't gone do—"

Pop! Pop! Pop!

Keyz threw three, quick right punches, hitting him in his jaw and eye, and then one in his chin, causing his tongue to split in half after his teeth slammed down on it. Once blood started spurting from his tongue, Keyz dragged him to the floor, kicking him in the face five to six times before he snapped out of his dark rage at the sound of his mother's voice.

"Kaizer, baby! Stop, stop, stop! Kaizer! Kaizer! You gon' kill him! Baby, please stop!" she yelled, while his brother and sisters stood quietly peeking from the hallway.

Keyon knew the drill. He had to protect his sisters at all times, only jumping in if his brother needed help which was never, since he had been fighting almost his entire life. Grabbing Keyz from behind, his mother cried and screamed, almost collapsing against his body. She was praying the neighbors wouldn't call the law on them after being there so many times to arrest him or recover stolen property.

Larry, although alive, was barely conscious, as his tongue hung loosely out the side of his mouth. His blood seeped on an already stained throw rug. With one eye closed shut, Keyz could see Larry's other eye rolling in the back of his head.

"I hope his bitch ass dies! Stupid motherfucker!" he yelled, kicking him one last time.

"Want me to go and get Chico?" Keyon asked, looking for guidance from his older brother.

Chico was only twenty, but was like a father to Keyz. No matter how much he would beg to be put on, he would tell him no. His answer was always to stay in school like the old men did at the store. They'd met a year ago when he saw Keyz running from the police one day by his house. He whistled, catching his attention as he motioned him to run to the back of his house.

The moment Keyz hit the corner that led to the back,

Chico opened the laundry room door, quickly letting him in. The police being overly zealous, yet lacking common sense, ran through the backyard onto the next street, never once realizing he ran into someone's house.

Since that day, whenever Keyz wasn't with Skebo or at the store, he would hang out at Chico's house, or would ride with him as he picked up money from his trap spots in Liberty City, Little Haiti, Overtown, and South Miami. Other times, he would just take him to the club or the pool hall, slowly introducing him to the game, although he really wanted better for him.

Over time, he realized that Keyz was just a younger version of himself. One he didn't want to see get killed robbing a store or breaking into someone house, because that's the life he lived in his native country, Cuba.

Once he and his two sisters came to the states, life with their uncle wasn't that much better. They did have a stable place to lay their heads, but everyone pretty much fended for themselves outside of food, which his Uncle Javier brought home from the grocery store he worked at as a butcher.

Growing tired of not having enough, Chico started out in the game as a corner boy hustler at twelve, and was now at the top of the game in Miami selling anything from marijuana and pills to crack cocaine. Lacray knew nothing about Keyz' dealings with Chico, but she was about to find out today.

"Ahhhhhhh! Ahhhhhh!" his mother screamed, hitting him wherever she could until he restrained her by the wrist.

She was tired of not making ends meet and now Keyz had ran off the most stable man she had in years. She didn't care about being called a bitch or sucking his dick upon demand as long as her kids had a roof over their head.

"Ma, ma, ma. Stop, ma! Damn, ma! Stop!" he shouted, pulling her into his body where she sat and cried uncontrollably.

"Why, Kaizer? Why, baby? Why would you do this to me?" she screamed, as she patted her chest, collapsing in her son's arms.

"Ma, fuck this nigga! Fuck all them! Ma, let me take care you," he begged. "Let me do it, ma."

Keyz held his mother like a baby in his arms while Keyon ran to get Chico. He was torn, having mixed emotions about leaving school in order to go into the game full time. He knew that wasn't what his mother wanted for him, choosing different men instead to pick up the slack, but it was time. It was that, or he was going to prison for killing one of them if they ever disrespected his mother again.

"Keyz," Chico spoke, his voice booming through the room as his sisters sat in the hallway crying and shaking. Keyon stood tall and brave waiting for instruction from Keyz or Chico.

Keyz sat silently rubbing his mother's hair and kissing her face that reeked of pain, not knowing how, and who would help them now. She wasn't a whore, but she wasn't above doing what needed to be done for her kids.

"Keyz!" he yelled to get his attention.

"Let her up. We're about to drag this motherfucker outta here. Get your head right. We got business to discuss," Chico said with finality, not giving him an option.

Nodding his head, he gave his mother one last kiss before

he pulled her up, laying her back on the sofa bed. She screamed and cried for Larry who hung limply while Chico's crew dragged him out of the house. The wails of his mother were so overwhelming, sending Keyz frenzy as he stomped on Larry's face two more times before he was completely out of the house.

Furiously, he looked around like a deranged man at their tattered sofa and rickety dining room table, where four folding chairs sat from a local church that was given to them. Twin sized sheets were used as curtains throughout the house, barely giving them privacy as they walked throughout their house.

He then kicked a throw rug saturated with blood that covered a cracked linoleum floor. The more he looked, the angrier he became as he watched two mice running from behind the sofa, and a few small cockroaches scurrying around. Keyz was fed up and ready to kill somebody.

"Keyon, get your sisters in the back," he barked. "Then sit with mama until I get back. Don't leave her. You hear me?" Keyon quickly nodded his head as he pushed them in the back.

Keyz's stone cold face, splattered with blood screamed death as he approached his mother, hating what he saw.

"Mama, I'm sorry, but..." he whispered, shrugging his shoulders before he stood up tall. "I'm the man in this bitch now. So you can cry tonight, but let this be the last time a bitch ass nigga ever makes you cry or I'ma kill that motherfucker, Mama. I'ma kill 'em." He turned to face Chico letting him know he was ready to do what he was born to do.

"Blood in?" Chico asked.

"Blood in," Keyz replied.

The One That Got Away

That night after he ended Larry's life, Keyz officially became a part of the Come Up Boys crew also known as "The C.U.B. Boys". They notorious for how potent their drugs were, but even more notorious for killing anything that failed to respect who they were.

∼

"LE—LEMME SUCK YO' dick," this crackhead named Cookie hissed, scooting up on Skebo and Keyz.

The staunch smell that leaped from her body was overwhelming, but her decayed teeth, matted hair, and dirt-stained clothes disgusted them even more. Cookie was only twenty-two, but had been addicted to crack cocaine since her first year of college at Bethune Cookman University.

After a bad breakup with her high school sweetheart and the death of her mother, Cookie turned to the glass pipe, choosing a slower death in lieu of grieving and moving on.

"Bitch, you better get your nasty ass out my motherfucking face and go wash your ass. Stank hoe," Skebo spat, grabbing his nose.

They had been pushing product for almost a year now, covering a few areas in Liberty City and Little Haiti. Keyz was so ruthless, he barely had to touch any of it once Chico moved him up as his muscle, running anyone off that was dry hanging on the block, to handling anyone that came up short.

However, whenever things got slow, Keyz would jump back in, helping Skebo at the trap house, proving he earned his status in the crew. Chico observed that and loved him all the more for his loyalty.

"Ma—ma—man, Skebo," she whined, twitching and scratching, "Come on, shit. Just let me get a lil' something."

Keyz, mad at himself because that could be his mother or baby sisters, tried to ignore her because she had a family. He felt that if they didn't care, why should he? It was his dismissive thinking that kept him out there day and night, selling and killing whoever he could if it meant a better life for him and his family and he made no apologies about it.

"Na—na—hell naw!" he yelled grabbing his dick before he pushed her away. "No money, no product. The fuck you think this is? The welfare office? Hoe, look around. We're in the slum, the gutter, the got damn hood. Try that shit downtown with them crackers, lying and shit on your application to get that free government cheese."

Moving on to see if his boy, Nain Man, would look out, Cookie approached him dancing like she was in King of Diamonds. Everyone knew Nain Man would let a crack head suck his dick, so Skebo and Keyz laughed while he looked around to see if anyone was watching before he pulled her to the side of the trap house.

"Man, that's a nasty nigga there," Keyz said, shaking his head, as he watched the neighborhood kids coming across the bridge from school. He missed it because many didn't think he liked school, but he did. He enjoyed the interaction of going to classes with his friends and messing with girls, but school didn't put money in his pocket. The streets did. So corner hanging and slanging it was.

"For real, though. I see school's out. Surprise you ain't ran down there to see them hoes you love to hit then get missing on. You know them hoes love Keyz."

The One That Got Away

Nodding his head up and down, Keyz was known to love and leave them, but wasn't checking for no one except one girl—Iyana. She didn't know, but he would watch her from afar walking home or to the community arts center every day, usually by herself. She never noticed because she would walk looking down, kicking whatever her feet would skirt over on the ground. He would get irritated thinking about how she stood him up that day, but on the flip, glad she did because he was now heavily into the streets.

"Fuck them hoes," he said, lighting a freshly rolled blunt he had behind his ear.

After a few tokes, he handed it to Skebo. He didn't really smoke when he sat around the trap house, but every time he thought of her, he felt fucked up in the head, hoping that one day he could step to her pretty, black ass.

She intrigued him, from her bashful presence down to her piercing grey eyes and deep dimples that appeared when she pursed her lips together. He had never dated a girl as dark as Iyana, but he never judged a woman because of her skin color. He judged them based on how they carried themselves.

That's why he and his mother had a love/hate relationship. There were times his boys mentioned how they wanted to fuck Iyana, causing Keyz to damn near kill them even though he never gave them a reason why she was off limits. Before long, the dudes in the hood were afraid to approach her. In her eyes, she wasn't worthy since no one ever did, but in his eyes, she was too good for all of them. Even him.

"Aye, ain't that Myriah's ass coming our way?" Skebo asked, serving two fiends who took off in the same direction Cookie and Nain Man went.

"Yeah, that's her," Keyz replied, hoping she would keep going by. Unbeknownst to him, Myriah and Iyana were sisters who never hung out together except for church, and church wasn't a place he'd stepped foot in. That last time he did, he was eight years old on Easter when the twins' daddy was still around.

"And her friend with her fine ass. She'on talk as much as Myriah, but she can catch a dick for real," Skebo said, calmly gripping his penis.

Skebo was a warm caramel complexion, standing at 6'1", with thick curly hair that he sometimes twisted, brown eyes and thick lips. He was the bold and cocky one used to having his way with any girl, not caring about anything but fucking, and today was no different.

"Nigga, is that all you think about?" Keyz asked, sucking his teeth.

"Honestly?" he asked with a smile, "Hell yeah!"

Choosing to not respond, Keyz stood silently as Myriah and Chase kept walking towards them. He had to admit the two of them had to be the finest girls that attended Miami Northwestern Senior High School.

He may have not been in school, but since a few of their spots were near a couple of schools, he didn't miss much when it came to checking for hoes, a term he despised but knew was true. Although they wore school uniforms, Myriah's thick, slightly bowed-legs in her khaki shorts, and full breasts in her gold polo top, made most girls wearing the latest, look like shit compared to her, and she knew it.

Her light peanut butter skin complemented the soft curls that fell around her round, chubby face, even though it was obvious she was sweating in the hot sun. Chase, a cinnamon complexion beauty, was not as thick as her homegirl, but her firm round hips, ass and perky breasts didn't leave much to the imagination the closer they got to them.

Being sure that they were seen, Myriah stopped and spoke loudly to Chase. "Damn, Chase, girl. It's hot as fuck out here. I wish I had a few dollars on me to get something to drink from the store."

Keyz and Skebo could tell Chase was embarrassed based on her facial expression, but she went along with it. Just not the way Myriah expected her to.

"Yeah, girl. It is. We better get going then. I think my mama got some Kool-Aid at the house," she said, making Myriah upset.

"Shit, I want something now. Hey, y'all," she spoke as they approached Skebo and Keyz.

"What's up, lil' mama," Skebo spoke, while Keyz pushed up off the car he had just leaned on, subtly watching his surroundings. That move bothered Myriah as she felt Keyz missed his opportunity to speak to her.

"Nothing much. Trying to see what's up with y'all," she said, speaking really about Keyz who was ignoring her.

"You already know what's up. You trying to do something?" he asked tossing his head towards the house. The look on Chase's face was priceless, as it went from nervous to shock, causing Keyz to laugh. He was trying his best to ignore both of them, but Skebo's bluntness was hilarious to him.

"The fuck, like what?" she shot back with an attitude, her weight on one foot as she put her hand on her hip.

She do got a fat ass pussy, Keyz thought when he saw what

Myriah was working with between her legs, but he wasn't interested.

He was an observer. He didn't care if it was a dude or a female. He never gotten caught slipping and if he did, it definitely wouldn't be over any pussy he didn't have to work for. So he chilled leaning back on the car.

"Shit, I'on know. Your ass stopped to talk to me. Ask your fucking friend since she seems to know what the fuck I mean," Skebo snapped back, his nose flaring up which happened whenever he got mad.

Myriah, embarrassed that she was spoken to so rudely in front of Chase, lashed out at Skebo, hoping to win some points in front of Keyz. She loved a quiet, yet boss-like dude that said nothing but a lot at the same time, by just being there.

Skebo was loud while Keyz took the back seat, something Myriah liked since she felt boys her age talked too much when it came to who they were hollering at, no matter what level it was on.

"No, bitch. I stopped to talk to *him*," she said, pointing at Keyz who gave her that "what the fuck" look as he tried to stay out of it.

"Naw, trick," Skebo said, dragging his tongue across his teeth before he smiled. "Your ass said 'we' withcho loose pussy ass. See, even your girl know your ass lying."

Myriah, waiting for Keyz to speak, tapped her foot while Chase tugged on her book bag for them to leave. Slapping her hand, Myriah called Keyz out just to see how he would handle her.

"So your boy speaks for you or are you your own man?" she asked, twisting her neck. "His ass just mad because I ain't trying to see him. I can tell he ain't getting shit, so he pouncing on the first bitch that show up."

Keyz hated being the center of attention unless it was to set an example, but what he hated even more was a disrespectful, foul mouth woman. He hadn't fallen in love yet, but if he did, he wanted his woman's presence to speak before her mouth was heard.

Against his better judgment, he initially decided to give her a pass since he had two younger sisters at home. She was making it very hard for herself though, calling him out as he rose up off the car.

"I speak when the fuck I see someone worth speaking to," he spoke coldly, eyes unwavering as he looked directly at her.

"Now, if you about to buy some shit, do that, or go get fucked by my boy. If not, keep that shit moving. A'ight?"

Watching a few more of their homeboys gather around, Myriah was infuriated and ready to go off when she heard Chase whisper, "Myriah, come on. This is the C.U.B crew, girl. We need to just go."

Not fazed as to who they were, Myriah gave Skebo a murderous look while Chase tugged on her arm. Once she realized this was not an argument that would go in her favor, she decided to take heed to Chase's warning.

Keyz may be saying fuck me today, but I'll be saying fuck you tomorrow. eating straight from his plate, she thought before she took off with Chase in tow.

∼

THREE YEARS later

Over the years, Myriah's good looks and bold approach landed her in the lap and wallet of many dudes, but they were just faces. Faces until the next face came along to keep lining her pockets. Myriah was still in school, but nothing about her was on a high school level, from sex to gifts in the forms of trinkets and purses, to name brand clothes and shoes.

Gone were the days of serving on the corner, as Keyz and Skebo were now running the C.U.B crew along with Chico, earning them crazy street credibility throughout Florida. With more territory, Keyz was in and out of town choosing to live in Fort Lauderdale, a city just north of Miami. It wasn't too far from his mother and siblings, but it was far enough to get away from his chaotic roots. He'd never imagined three years later, the same girl he shitted on one day after school would be the same one he eventually hooked up with.

Myriah and Chase decided to hang out on South Beach where the nightlife was wild, full of tourists and local hot boys.

"Damn, he looks familiar," Myriah said to herself as they approached Keyz and Skebo. They managed to get inside a local club that allowed underage kids with a fake ID inside. Walking slowly in front of him, he sat silently nodding his head to the music as if she wasn't there. Getting a little frustrated walking back and forth a few times, she stopped, standing in his line of sight. She noticed unlike others, he was being observant in a club full of people instead of chilling and enjoying the scene.

"This nigga about to fuck me tonight," she said to herself, still not knowing who he was as she danced to the music, easing back little by little with each bounce. Chase stood nearby drinking her Pina Colada. She very much aware of what Myriah was up to, but not surprised her girl chose a street dude yet once again.

The One That Got Away

"So, I see the hot pussy express is about to take off," she whispered in Myriah's ear, who pursed her lips like "and what?"

"Alright, you got it," she said to Myriah, lightly tapping her foot as she glanced around to see who Keyz was with.

"Just be careful. These niggas not pressed for shit. I can tell, My," she said, warning her friend to tread lightly.

No matter how much Myriah said she wasn't trying to get serious with a dude, she seemed to kid not only herself, but any dude she dealt with, often trying to switch it up the moment they'd slept together.

Bobbing her head yes, Myriah continued to dance in front of Keyz who hadn't said a word the entire time she stood in front of him. He recognized her face but couldn't place where he had seen her, as he had females from all over the state. Especially in Miami, where every girl wanted to be with a dude she thought was a baller. Keyz thought of Shower and Sunshine, wondering if they threw their ass on a random dude, as he watched Myriah pop her hips to the song, in front of him.

After two more songs, she turned around damn near famished from the humidity to face him. She had never met a dude that let her bounce all on him, but never attempted to touch her. That turned her on, making her want to test his vibes after her kitty jumped on sight once she saw him.

Keyz, now 6'5", was even more toned, with two tatted sleeved arms and wild, curly black hair that was faded around the sides blending into his sideburns. Although he was nineteen, Keyz carried himself like a grown ass man, never getting excited over pussy. He didn't speak much, but when he did, he had the room, and anyone who was in there gave him nothing but respect.

Myriah could tell he had money although he didn't wear every label most hood celebrities did who came up on some money. Keyz was even smarter with his money, choosing to save up money to invest unlike most of the C.U.B. crew.

She leaned over, whispering to Chase, "Bitch, this motherfucker is fine, but look at his boy. You betta do something 'cause my ass not trying to go home with you." She nudged Chase a few times, who initially ignored her before she bounced to the beat of the music turning around to see his homeboy, Skebo.

"Mmmhmm," Chase replied, letting Myriah know he had her attention, but wasn't about to act on it. "You a bit ummm…bold, aren't you. Who's to say things will even go there?"

"Fuck, Chase. Stop with your hating ass," she gritted in her ear, still bouncing as she sized him up. "You just focus on his boy with his fine ass."

Instead of debating, Chase sipped on her drink and looked around. It was crowded and she wanted to mingle, not jump on the first set of dudes they saw.

Skebo caught Myriah looking but didn't speak, as he turned around to order another drink. He knew her and her girl was checking for them, but he had pussy for days and wasn't impressed with either of them who looked to be in high school, judging how timid Chase was.

Skebo nodded standing at 6'2", now buff and cut with tattoos adorning his entire body from what they could see. His faded, wavy hair complemented his caramel color skin his thicker build. His lips, still full lips showing off his pearly white teeth. Just like Keyz, he made sure he wore the latest, but not enough that people automatically knew he was deep in the game.

Acting like she tripped, Myriah fell against Keyz as he leaned against the bar catching her against his firm chest.

"Oh, my bad. Shit, how did I that happen? Damn, girl. You see me?" she giggled, yelling at Chase, who had now turned back around, finishing off her drink.

"Ummm, please excuse my friend," she said, gritting her teeth once she realized who they both were.

"Bitch, do you know who that is?" she whispered in Myriah's ear now recognizing them. *"That's motherfucking Kaizer Paul! You know, as in Keyz, one of the leaders of the Come Up Boys crew. And the the other is his homeboy, Skebo. Girl, they are the ones who cursed you out our freshman year after school, remember?"*

"Shit, who cares? A bitch trying to get them coins and get fucked," she snapped under her breath. *"If I'm giving up pussy, why not make that nigga pay? A bitch trying to come up, too."*

Ignoring Chase's warning for the second time that night, she began to grind on Keyz who still hadn't moved short of catching her when she tripped.

A'ight, let me see what ole girl want from a nigga since she gon' block most of the night, he thought. Deciding to cut to the chase, Keyz gave her a deadly smile letting her know he saw her. Myriah, licking her lips, stuck her finger inside of her mouth then slowly pulled it out.

"Oh yeah," he mouthed, lifting his fitted Miami Heat cap to get a better look at Myriah, dancing lustfully in her black cat suit romper with black and gold sandals. The more she tooted her full, pouty lips, the more his manhood rocked up, as she gyrated her hips in front of him. He could see her hard nipples trying to peek out, causing him to shift and adjust his swollen dick.

Gauging how intense his stare was, Myriah gripped his midsection bouncing even harder to Lloyd Banks *"Karma"* that featured Avant, sipping on a Sex on the Beach. The more his bulge grew, the tighter she held on to him, grinding her moist pussy on him.

"So, we fucking or what?" she whispered in his ear as she stopped standing on her tippy toes.

Intrigued by her how full, pink lips vibrated in his ear, Keyz laughed to himself realizing how desperate she was once she figured out who he was. He wasn't hard up for sex, but he wanted to do a test run on her mouth first, watching how her lips moved to the words to the song. Especially since his soldier was at attention waiting to go to war between her legs.

"Or what… let me see what that mouth do first," he said, surprising her that he seemed to be turning down sex.

Never one to back away from a challenge, Myriah figured why not. He gon' be screaming my name tonight any fucking way, she said to herself. Especially if that meant she could get that Coach bag and wallet she wanted from Aventura Mall.

"Chase!" she yelled to get her attention who was no longer sizing Skebo up. "I'm out."

Just like that, Myriah pulled on Keyz's jersey so she could escort him outside, although she didn't know what he was driving or where he parked.

Stepping back, Chase said, "Couldn't resist, I see. Just call me when you get where you're going."

Chase loved Myriah, but her antics were growing old as she feared getting a reputation because of how Myriah got down. She walked away before Myriah could respond, hoping her friend knew what she was doing after she had been warned.

"A'ight, nigga. I'll holla. Guess her homegirl good on you," Keyz said, dapping Skebo up, who shook his head laughing.

"Shit. If she ain't fucking, she more than good. Where you taking her?" he said, tossing his drink back before he took off.

"Shit, not my spot. Fuck her. Bitch wanna throw it, I'ma catch it and take her where she gotta go when I'm through with her ass," he yelled, not caring if Myriah heard him.

"The Shores?" he asked, which was a dip off spot they used from time to time to entertain women.

"Yeah, shit not that far. Hit me up in the morning."

"True," Skebo said, taking off to leave at the same time.

That night, Myriah's mouth assaulted Keyz thick, long 10-inch penis more times than he could count. He was amazed and somewhat disgusted that such a pretty mouth could comfortably suck on a random dick. Especially since he never gave her his name, although it was clear she knew who he was.

Once the night was over, he peeled off a few hundred dollars bills and told her to put her number in his cell, dropping her off to one of her homegirls' spot. After that, whenever he was in town, he would make his presence known solely for sex, and sex only, no matter what she felt it was. In her mind, she was winning. In his, she was just another hoe that had talented throat and some alright pussy.

Chapter 3

𝒶 few months later, Keyz was still hooking up with Myriah probably more than he should have, but she made it so convenient for him whenever he was in town. Unlike Skebo who covered Miami and now the Key West area, Keyz covered their north spots laying in Broward, Palm Beach, and Port St. Lucie as the C.U.B. territory grew.

Keyz was growing tired of the game, but he had mouths to feed, keeping his promise to his mother. Keyon was now fifteen, and the twins who were thirteen, were spoiled to no end having their hand out everytime Keyz came around. He didn't care and was glad he could instead of them fucking for money like most young girls their age.

While he kept his word to his mother, he ignored what he needed which was getting harder the older he got. He was ready to settle down, but not with just anyone. He wanted *her*. He wanted Iyana.

Every morning, he would wake up and stare at the ocean

as it hit the shoreline, strategizing his next move that would help him get out of the game unscathed. He knew there was more to life than women and money, which he had plenty of, and his strategy always led him back to Iyana. Before he could enjoy his time of solitude, he got a call from Chico.

"Sup, fool," he answered on the first ring.

"Fuck a fool, nigga. This king shit over here," Chico replied with a laugh.

"You must mean 'king bullshit' with your bullshitting ass. Where Meka because you sounding real bold early in the morning? I heard how she checked your ass with that king shit."

"She quiet with this dick in her mouth. Fuck you thought?"

"Not shit when it comes to another nigga's dick. Fuck outta here. Anyway, talk since you interrupted my morning meditation."

"Meditation?" Chico asked like he was confused. "What? You gone all spiritual on me and shit?"

"I've *been* spiritual. I know there's a God up there. Shit, this life chose me. I didn't choose it. He knows that, too. I talk to that Man everyday because I know once I step out that door, I'm about to do some shit he don't approve of, but I need to get it," he said, approaching the bathroom to take a shower to relax his mind.

Sighing, Keyz grabbed the back of his neck feeling the tension, as he thought of all the shit he had to do that day like it was a never ending hood saga.

"A'ight, I hear you. So Tone?" Chico asked.

"Yeah, what about him?"

"He say he ready, man. That college shit out of town is getting hard on his mom. Nigga's about to come home and go to school here. I say let's see what he can do. Figured we'd let him sell on campus and shit. Nothing heavy, but just to see what he's about."

"Take him to a few spots. Not our big ones. Let that nigga observe, then put him to work in one of them. Let Chello manage that shit 'cause you know he ain't friendly. All business, you feel me?"

Chico smiled with how quickly Keyz could put a plan in motion at the drop of a dime. He loved that about him, especially since he taught him everything he knew.

"I feel yo. Just wanted to run that by you to see how you felt since y'all grew up together and shit," he said. "Wait. Hold on, hold on, hold on."

Keyz laughed whenever Chico said that like he was singing. No one said "hold on" three times but Chico, with that Spanish accent coming out every time he spoke fast.

"Why, Meka? Damn! Aye, I got something for that ass when I hang up!" he yelled. "Yeah, man. This bitch," he mumbled, his voice trailing off. "So yeah, let me get at you once I scoop him up. What you got going on for the day?"

"About to shower, run through my spots right quick, then grab Keyon's lil' ass."

"Lil'? His ass taller than you at six seven!"

"Man, I'on give a fuck how tall his bad ass is, he fucking up around there and Lacray act like she scared to go toe to toe with that nigga. That's just him trying to get my attention. Lil' nigga miss me 'cause I ain't been through there this month."

"Word?" he whispered, "So you ain't holla at your girl,

Thickums?" he asked, referring to Myriah, a nickname Keyz gave her since she was a good size fourteen. Keyz never brought her around, but she called so much, the crew knew who she was.

Laughing, he said, "Hell yeah, I heard from her. She stay on my line talking 'bout shit she want, but that ain't my girl. She's just something to do."

"You cold, but I knew that. Knock 'em down and keep that shit moving. A'ight, boss, I'm out."

"Yep, yep. Let me hop in this shower."

Thirty minutes later, Keyz stepped into his walk-in closet and had a problem many wanted to have. He had an abundance of name brand items like clothes, sneakers, ties, belts, but no one to argue with him to tell him what to wear or how he needed to give her some space.

Damn, why this girl keep popping up in my head? he asked himself as Iyana crossed his mind. It had gotten worse over the past few weeks back when he saw someone who reminded him of her. Immediately, thoughts of regret crept in, remembering her before he dropped out.

Yes, he knew she deserved the best and he could be that as long as he kept his personal life separate from the street. Yet and still, he never looked for her, choosing instead to get caught up with random hoes or the likes of Myriah, because they accepted whatever he gave them. Most times it was just sex.

Staring in the mirror as he threw on some deodorant and brushed his edges, he said, "You's a pretty nigga...a pretty lonely one though. Man, that girl ain't got shit for you with her pretty, black ass."

The One That Got Away

The more he stood there, the more he doubted that if he ever did see her, she would give him a shot. A dude that had no high school diploma and was deep into the game.

"Naw, nigga. You ain't shit," he said, brushing off any thought of stepping to her.

Once he did, he grabbed his cell seeing he had a couple of text messages from different women, including Myriah. A few he even had a threesome with that included Myriah, although she wasn't too keen on sharing him. Knowing she wouldn't stop until he responded, he decided to call her before his day got away from him.

"Yo," he said flatly as he sat down to get dressed.

"Don't yo me, Keyz," she said with an attitude. "It's early release Wednesday. You coming through to pick me up?"

"What the fuck that got to do with me, Myriah? I dropped out years ago to get this money. You know that shit you don't mind asking for?" he asked, already irritated at the sound of her voice.

Keyz wasn't stingy, but the fact that she expected money every time she saw him pissed him off. He also knew that's why she was calling. Myriah wanted to curse him out, but she knew Keyz. As soon as she would pop off, he would get missing and cut her off until he wanted to talk or fuck, and she really wanted this Dooney & Burke bag she saw at Bal Harbor last weekend. If Keyz was good for anything, it was being very generous with his money and dick.

"Keyz?"

"Man," he replied aggravated.

"Keyz?" she whined.

"Man, this girl right here," he huffed, wishing he never picked up the phone to call her.

"Ugh, damn," she conceded.

"Damn is fucking right. Now have your ass outside five minutes after that bell ring. I got shit to do today and you wasn't on that list."

"Thank you, Keyz," she cooed like he was a baby.

"Thank me when you taking this thick ass python down your throat."

"Alright, baby," she replied, smiling as she got her way.

"Naw, never that. Respect the name… yeah," he said hanging up.

Keyz did not intend to see Myriah or anyone else for that matter that morning. All he was focused on was getting his money right and keeping his promise to his mother. To be his age, Keyz had little time for distractions like petty antics from women that could never be wifey. He knew early on Myriah wasn't it, but she served her purpose until he was ready to settle down.

～

"Iyana, if Nana or Papa B ask about me, tell them I had a student council meeting after cheerleading practice," she whispered in her ear before she ran to jump in Keyz' truck.

"Oh… okay. Got it," she said, looking past Myriah to see if she recognized the dude she was leaving with.

Hmmmm, he looks familiar, she thought, trying to place where she had seen him before until Sky interrupted her thoughts.

"Iyannnnna!" Sky yelled as she ran down the sidewalk to

The One That Got Away

where she was. After junior high, Sky auditioned for the dance magnet program at Miami Northwestern and got in with Iyana. Now the duo was back together again, even going to the community arts center until Sky's mother picked up her every evening.

It was also the first time since elementary school the two of them went to the same school. Myriah was a senior hoping to graduate if she stayed focused. Ironically, she would ask Iyana for help even though she was in the 9th grade. Especially since most of her classes were Honors classes when she was in middle school.

Catching up, she asked, "Damn, girl. Why are you daydreaming? We only have twenty minutes to get to the community arts center but you're standing here like your brain is in slow motion." Instead of acknowledging her, Iyana was stuck on the back of Keyz truck as it drove off, wondering why he looked so familiar.

"Hello, earth to Iyana," Sky yelled, waving her hand in her face.

"Uh, yea. What's up?" she finally asked now that his truck had turned the corner.

"The community arts center? You still going today? You know how crowded it gets now since they hired Ms. Singer," she said with an attitude, hoping they made it on time.

Sky was right. After the community arts center hired Ms. Singer, the buzz got around that there was a new dance teacher from New York. Bronx, New York to be exact. Unlike Ms. Carolyn who was born and raised in Miami and approaching age fifty, Ms. Singer was a hot, fiesty 27-year-old teacher whose fearless dance moves mesmerized her students.

It didn't hurt that she did some choreography for a few major TV shows in New York and music videos for Missy Elliot, Diddy and Usher.

She was dark skinned just like Iyana, with multiple piercings in her nose, ears and lips; and on any given day, her hair could go from purple to fiery red almost matching her mood. Now, Ms. Singer never tried to hurt anyone's feelings, but she called it like she saw it.

If you couldn't dance or didn't have any rhythm, she told you straight up, no chaser. She found that approach to be the formula that got her out of the hood and into a major dance studio at an early age.

Focused on being the next Ms. Singer, Iyana became excited almost instantaneously once she realized what Sky was talking about.

"Yeah, I'm going. Oh, and today we're working on that piece from Ciara's 'Goodies' video. Yesssss," she laughed, gyrating her hips with her tongue hanging out of her mouth.

"Girl, you know Papa B gon' beat that ass. Yessss," she yelled, popping her butt up and down on Iyana's hip. "But you be doing that shit, Yi!"

"Na un, I'm not that good," Iyana said, no longer dancing as she blushed, pushing Sky off of her.

"Girl, bye. Come on so we can show them hoes how we do it," Sky yelled, pulling Iyana's arm as they ran towards the community arts center.

∽

Two months later

"Myriah, hurry up. Coach will be looking for us. If we late, we getting laps. I don't know about you, but those laps mean we miss the after-school bus and I'm not catching the city bus," Chase, whined.

"Then go, Chase. Damn! I can pee alone," she said, sucking her teeth as she walked to the bathroom while being followed.

"All you doing is being nosey."

"You are correct. I am. I am also staying to remind you that lies have short legs. I don't know how many times I begged you to tell Nana that you were having sex or at least thinking about it," Chase shot back, not caring if Myriah was aggravated with her or not.

"That's you being judgmental," she belted, pointing her finger in Chase's face.

"Oh, I see where this is going," Chase sighed with hands on both hips.

"Yep, 'cause it always does. So just say it," she quipped in a whiny, baby-like voice.

"For the record, I am not judging. I am trying to be a *friend* and this has nothing to do with Iyana. It's about you accepting the shit *you do*, Myriah. Hell, why are you not protecting yourself anyway?" Chase spat back.

"Why are you not protecting yourself, anyway, Myriah?" she mocked Chase, winding her neck with a frown.

"But you know what? You're right. You are NOT Iyana because unlike you, she would probably listen to someone else besides that delusional ass voice you got in your own head," Chase snapped back.

Myriah became aggravated, thinking back on that one

night she drank just a little too much. The details were fuzzy after a few drinks she had right after the high school football playoffs. That night, Miami Edison Senior High School played Booker T. Washington High School, the notorious rival school in Overtown. Her school lost against Miami Edison and was no longer in the playoffs, but the hood came out in droves just to see who would go to the state championship.

Instead of getting dropped off at home, she told her grandparents her coach was having a overnighter for all of the girls on the cheerleading team. She had planned to spend some time with Keyz, who never called her back from earlier that day. After a stern lecture and a reminder to be safe, Myriah took off with her girls, Peaches and Tookie, leaving Chase behind. Chase was still her girl, but Myriah hated all that preaching she did, killing her vibes.

"Sup," Keyz said, picking up his cell after the fourth ring.

"Where you at?" she asked, knowing he hated to be questioned.

"Why, Myriah? Nigga tired," his told her, his voice dragging due to exhaustion.

"Okay, Keyz. Damn, I told you I wanted to see you."

Yawning as he rubbed his head, Keyz sat up with a pounding headache. He had been drinking all night, getting more than his fair share of lap dances and his dick sucked by Lollipop, the only stripper he'd even let get close to his dick. They met a few years back when he first got in the game. He could tell she wasn't like the rest, which got Keyz's attention after hearing how she started stripping.

He hit it over time, but kept it real casual for the most part, letting her know he was married to the game. Lollipop was from Gainesville, but started stripping to pay tuition for school. After getting addicted to fast money, she dropped out but took care of her mother and five siblings back home.

Though he'd never wife her, he understood her dedication to stripping was more about her need to help her family, like his need to steal was motivated by the same thing.

"Talk. I just told you a nigga tired and my head fucked up," he said seeing it was 3:30 in the morning.

"I bet it is. So, ahhh, I'm about to leave Bayside. We came to get a few drinks and wings from Hooters after Booker T kicked their ass thirty six to nine," she replied casually like it was daytime.

"Myriah, it's kinda late to still be out and shit. Betta get home before your peoples start tripping," he told her, hinting that he was going back to sleep.

He really didn't care if she got in trouble or not, but that was another sign she wasn't what he needed in his life. She was sneaky as fuck and loose. Over the past month, he started weaning her off by ignoring her, but she was persistent.

"Oh, so you don't want company?"

While Myriah knew Keyz wasn't her man, he rarely turned her down once he answered her calls. It was a game they played that she usually won, and tonight was no different.

"If you coming through, come on. Trying to see what's up with Skebo in a few hours. So hurry your ass up," he said, hanging up.

After all this time, he finally took her back to his place in Miami, but not his main spot in Fort Lauderdale. After one too many drinks at the strip club with Skebo and Chico, he decided to crash there. Especially after being up for almost three days handling a situation because a few drops came up short. He had his own muscles for that, but sometimes he handled it personally to remind the streets who he was.

He sighed, lying back down, as he shook his right leg—something he did whenever he was tired, which helped him relax. He decided to unlock the door, shooting her a quick text to come in when she got there.

Thirty minutes later, Myriah showed up, wasting no time as she mounted Keyz's thick penis, sitting up hard and ready. Taking him in her mouth, Myriah glided her tongue up and down his veined pole the moment she snatched it out of his boxers.

"Yo…yo…girl. Wait! Ahhhh. Shit! It's like that?" he asked, losing the fight to her warm mouth now consumed with his manhood.

Watching her mouth as she feverishly attacked his penis, Keyz woke up ready to murder her pussy after she sloppily topped him off. No, Myriah wasn't the most experienced fuck he had, but what she lacked when it came to sex, she made up for it when it came to orally pleasing him.

"Ahhhhh. Ssssss. Sssss," he hissed with both hands on top of her head, pushing his penis to the very back of her throat holding it there.

Unlike most girls, Myriah relaxed her mouth and throat, increasing her gag reflex ability, while Keyz let loose, fucking her mouth uncontrollably. The more her saliva coated his dick, dripping down his shaft and nuts, the harder he lodged himself down her throat. Right when he was about to cum, Myriah began to gag, snatching her head from his hands, but quickly replacing her mouth with her small hands, jacking him while tugging his balls.

"You like that shit, baby?" she asked, sucking and biting her lip as she jacked him off.

Keyz tried to ignore her, choosing to concentrate on his pending eruption that was building up. Then his eyes popped open once she jumped up, sliding down on him, swirling and grinding her hips as she gave him the ride of all rides since they'd linked up.

He wasn't sure what had come over her, but he was glad to be the recipient of it. Keyz had never had unprotected sex with anyone, but seeing

Myriah on another level turned him on even more. He rendered himself unable to stop her the harder she went, coating his pole with her juices.

"You...you think you slick, Myriah," he grunted, meeting her thrust for thrust, holding her tightly so hard by the hips, he could see his fingerprints in her skin.

He devoured her breasts that bounced up and down once he sat up to suck and lick on them, pushing himself deeper inside of her. He stretched her ass while his curved penis hit her G spot, as her fuck face showed nothing but intense pleasure everytime he hit it.

Hmmmmm, I got to get her ass off of me now, he thought, once his balls started tightening up on the verge of exploding inside of her. Myriah was cool, but she wasn't about to trap him with a baby. She was a good fuck and he wanted to keep it that way.

"Damn...wait...wait," he said, trying to pull out, but it was too late, as she held him down, gripping his neck before they both came together.

"Ahhhh. Mmm. Fuck. Fuckkkk," he yelled, jerking inside of her while she collapsed on top of his body, her walls still quivering.

Breathing heavily while he tried to collect his thoughts, Myriah began to gently rock back and forth on his semi-limp penis until he was hard again. Knowing he shouldn't, Keyz, once again, tried to get her off of him, but failed miserably as she now sat up squatting and bouncing on his dick.

The sight of his release running down her thighs made him rock up even harder. Keyz shook his head, smiling, because no one had ever done that before. With his manhood on the line, he rolled over with Myriah now on her back pounding her with no mercy as her center tightly gripped him with each stroke.

"Didn't you say you was on the pill?" he asked right before he came again, slapping one of Myriah's thighs that bruised easily whenever he spanked her.

Nodding her head yes, Keyz pushed her back down, creating an arch. He then gripped her face after lodging his fingers on both sides of her mouth, stretching it wide open. From the front, it looked like he was trying to kill her with her head pulled back by her mouth.

Myriah wasn't used to this position, but she took it like a big girl not wanting him to stop. Once he came, Keyz let her face go, dropping his body on top of hers, where he slept until they woke up a few hours later.

It wasn't until he woke up that he realized what he had had done a few hours earlier.

"This bitch bet not be fucking other niggas raw they way she hopped on this dick," he muttered to himself before rolling over to shower, leaving her in bed. He was late, but he needed to clear his head before his meeting with Skebo and a few developers.

While he jumped in the shower, Myriah grabbed her cell phone to check her text messages only to find one that spooked her. Before she could respond, out walked Keyz with a "ah ha" look on his face letting her know he didn't trust her ass.

"Bitch, you calling me delusional?" she snapped with an attitude. "Matter fact, just go 'cause a nigga like Keyz wouldn't fuck Iyana's black ass with his homeboy's dick! Now gone!"

Myriah wasn't really upset with Chase. She was upset with herself hating that she was being compared to her younger sister once again, especially now. Her period was two months late and she was panicking. Instead of comforting her, Chase reminded her why she wouldn't be in this predicament if she took life just a little more serious like Iyana.

"Keep thinking that. Pfft!" Chase laughed, disgusted with Myriah's dig at her baby sister before she took off for practice.

One thing for sure is Iyana wasn't unattractive. In fact, Chase loved Iyana's Hershey colored complexion and often complimented her on it, although she didn't seem to think it was genuine. She also hated how much Myriah teased her, calling her names whenever she came over to hang out with them. Iyana loved her sister, but it was clear to Chase that Myriah wanted nothing to do with her over something she was born with—her skin color.

Once she left, Myriah sucked it up, squatting on her first pregnancy test. After three minutes, the results made her feel even worst knowing she wasn't 100% truthful with Keyz about being on the pill.

"Damn, it's positive", she grumbled, throwing the pregnancy test in her book bag.

For the next two hours, Myriah was distracted at practice, starting each routine late and forgetting most of their moves. By the time practice was over, she was ready to cry. On one hand, she was excited about having a baby from Keyz, but who wouldn't be? On the other hand, she knew it would break her grandparents' heart who worked so hard trying to give her and Iyana a good life.

"So I take it its positive?" Chase sympathetically asked, approaching her after practice.

Afraid to speak, she nodded her head, wiping the tears that escaped her eyes with no warning. She knew Keyz would think it was a setup because he usually strapped up. That night, however, when she sucked his dick, he didn't follow his one rule. That was to never raw dog a girl who wasn't your girl.

He could blame it on the alcohol, which lessened his desire

to fight her off, but he really was caught up in her amazing, fellatio skills that could now alter the rest of their lives.

"So what now then? I mean, you gotta tell him whether you keep it or not, Myriah," Chase said, pressuring her to tell her more.

"Look, I know. Just give me a minute to get my stuff together," she said as they went to the locker room to retrieve their clothes and book bags in order to head to the school bus.

She decided to call him from Chase's cell phone just to see if he would answer as soon as they found a seat. She'd been calling him over the past few days and he either wouldn't answer or he would rush her off the phone. She really was about to cut him off until this happened, making her feel like this was the "good Lord", as her Nana would say, giving her a sign.

"Yo, who this?" Keyz asked, picking up on the first ring.

"Who this?" Myriah asked, looking at the cell repeating him.

"Speak man, before I hang this shit up," he snapped. He hated going back and forth with random females that called him, especially from numbers he didn't know.

"Fuck," she muttered. "This Myriah."

"Yeah, what's good?" he asked in a calmer tone, but it hit him this wasn't her number. "Aye, why you callin' me from a number I'on know?"

She could tell he was driving when all she heard was Tupac's "All Eyes on Me" all loud in the background. Keyz didn't care what hip hop artist was hot at the time, he was a diehard Tupac fan.

"So, turn that down. Like for real, Keyz," she replied

almost on the verge of crying again. She hated he was riding around sounding like he had no care in the world, when hers was falling apart.

"It's Chase's number," she huffed. "So don't call this number back."

"Yeah, a'ight. Trying to handle some shit. Sup with you?"

Trying to remain calm even though his dismissive attitude pushed a button, she decided to give it to him straight. *Shit, if he mad, fuck him. That makes two of us,* she thought.

"So I took a test... today," she said, building up her courage.

"And?" he replied, trying to figure out why she was calling him about a test. "The hell a test have to do with me. You's a simple motherfucker sometimes, girl."

"This a rude ass nigga right here!" she heard Skebo yell in the background.

"Man, fuck you. She on her shit today," he said loud enough for everyone in his truck to hear.

Aggravated that he was so callous and disrespectful in front of his boys, she spazzed out on him.

"No, you on your shit today. Matter of fact, let me tell you what's not simple. This positive pregnancy test this *simple bitch* just took," she spat with Chase in her mouth hanging on to every word.

Keyz got completely quiet, in shock, as he shook his head. He was lucky he didn't lose control of the wheel, feeling like his life was ruined behind a piece of steady, mediocre pussy. After three years, she finally got him, and he felt like she fucked him with no Vaseline, finding a way to be a permanent fixture in his life.

"Hey. You still there?" she asked. She looked at the cell even though she still heard them laughing and cracking jokes in the background.

"Yeah," he managed to get out.

"Oh, okay."

She knew he wasn't happy but his silence was eerie. Even if he was mad, she needed to know where his mind was because hers was gone.

"Look, let me holla at you after I drop these niggas off and run by my mama's house. Keyon acting up again."

"Oh, okay," she sniffled, feeling defeated. She was tired of begging for his time and attention and that move right there proved their situation was not a priority for him.

What bothered her even more was how she planned to explain this to grandparents. A baby and no high school diploma or husband? Her grades weren't the worst, but they weren't the best either. To make matters worse, she was late putting in college applications, thinking she still had time for a few in-state universities like University of South Florida in Tampa.

She was ready to leave home and Tampa seemed to be a good place to go to school. It wasn't as fast as Miami, but it wasn't too slow like Tallahassee. Plenty of girls went off to college with a baby, but at this point, she wasn't so sure if she would graduate on time being pregnant and all, let alone leave with a baby. Her heart broke, shattering into pieces as she felt like another girl who was having a baby from a man who didn't want her.

Detecting she was upset, Keyz figured he needed to smooth things over so he could talk her into getting rid of it.

He was prepared to kiss up just to get on her good side, but he knew Myriah. If this baby was a way to finally be together, she would use it. So he had to go about it a different way in order for her to go along with it.

"Naw, I'm serious. We gone talk and shit. Nigga heard what you said. Just give me an hour," he said, trying to patronize her.

Keyz felt like if it wasn't one thing, it was another. First Myriah, now it was Keyon who was acting up more and more. Lacray, who had joined the church and kept a part-time housekeeping job to stay busy, was growing weary reaching out to him to step in.. He even moved them to the Pinecrest area, a more upscale community where Dwayne Wade used to live, offering his siblings a better lifestyle.

Since Keyon was the only male in the house, Lacray would have to get on him about doing homework and keeping little girls out of the house, while he focused on policing Shower and Sunshine. Especially since he was the star point-guard on Miami High's junior varsity basketball team. If they weren't calling all times a night, Lacray was catching them in his closest or watching them climb out the back window.

Keyon was feeling himself being the talent of the team and Keyz was loving it, but he drew the line when it came to disrespecting their mother. It also didn't hurt when Keyz and his crew were there, sometimes having to leave the game early before they caused a riot. Either people were loving the crew or hating on them.

Either way, he made sure he was there, front and center, being the father to his brother that he didn't have. The hustle was worth it, and he knew Keyon was definitely going into the NBA once the college scouts started showing up to his games.

"Here," she said, tossing Chase her cellphone.

"So what happened? He's in town?" she asked, showing concern as she rubbed her shoulder. "Come on, Myriah. Talk to me."

Throwing herself back into the seat, she growled wanting to hit something, anything to feel better than what she was feeling right now.

"Humph. What I expected. Nothing. Like everyone else comes fucking first. His boys, his money, his family, them hoes. Need I say more? Shit, I hate his ass," she snarled, giving Chase her back as she curled up in the bus seat.

"Okay," Chase mumbled, deciding to leave it alone.

She knew her girl was hurt, but it wasn't like she hadn't warned her all these years. She just hated that she didn't listen, making Papa B and Nana's worst nightmare come true—becoming a baby mama, instead of a wife.

Chapter 4
2016

"Iyana, what time does your show start tonight?" Myriah asked as soon as she picked up the phone. "I think Ish coming down with a cold or something and it looks like it's about to rain."

Myriah was hoping he would have gotten better so the two of them could get out of the house. She had a long week at work trying to prepare her students for a standardized test, which seemed to be tailored to fail most kids in school, especially African American students. After he came home sniffling and sneezing, she knew it was a no go.

"Awww, auntie's baby sick again?" Iyana asked, missing her nephew who was ten going on eighteen. "I'm telling you, Myriah. He needs go to a specialist. I was fine in D.C. Now that I'm back in Miami, my allergies stay acting up."

"Girl, sometimes he be playing, but I think you're right. My baby's nose all stuffy," she mumbled in her baby voice, stroking his soft, curly hair. "Then with this bullshit ass week I had at school prepping these students for this test has been draining."

"Ugh, I hate that, but they got a bomb ass teacher in you, girl. You can get them in shape," Iyana said, encouraging her sister.

Myriah smiled hearing those words. She knew she wasn't the best sister to her growing up, but she was glad they had a chance to make up. Well, she was trying to although some of her petty ways still existed. Especially since Sky wasn't around as much due to her job giving her more time to spend with her sister.

Her petty now was targeted at women who were stuck at home with kids or had no education, while she secretly struggled to understand why she was the way she was. Sadly, even she and Chase weren't even that close anymore, but Myriah didn't care. Her focus was on her baby sister who grew up to be amazingly stunning in her chocolate skin.

"Thanks, sis," Myriah said softly. "You know I don't deserve a sister like you, right?" she asked feeling sentimental and guilty simultaneously.

"Myriah, stop. We all have our issues. Let's just focus on the time we have now with Nana, Papa B and Ish. Cool?"

"I will, sis."

Myriah smiled thinking about her son. He was the bright spot in her life created during the ugliest times. The secrets she kept around her son gnawed at her day in and day out, but she tucked them away trying to be a better person. If she wasn't at an awards ceremony of his, she was putting him in any activity he mentioned, from basketball to things at church.

"So what's up with your dating life or the lack thereof?

The One That Got Away

Still messing around with Mr. Magoo?" she teased, bringing up Myriah's last guy friend.

"Hell no," she laughed. "He was just something to do. I got my eye on someone but honestly, Iyana, I don't think love is in the cards for me. You know?"

"Lies. All lies. It's time to get back out there and let mystery man know you wanna do something on another level. Ayyye," she teased, winding her hips as if Myriah could see her.

Iyana was the Jamaican winding queen as her friends and family would chant "her milkshake brings all the boys to the yard" whenever she got hood at a family gathering or birthday party. It was funny how her confidence would shoot through the roof whenever she danced, but wavered outside of that.

Yes, her self-esteem was much better than the days of old, but she still struggled nevertheless. Now as far as Elijah was concerned, her college sweetheart of five years, he didn't want her attracting anyone's attention. He would cuff her all night or sulk in a corner, nursing a cup of alcohol whenever he couldn't. It was times like those that her friends and family despised him. But until Iyana was fed up with his antics, they all accepted his presence in her life.

"Sit your dancing little ass down," she laughed. "Ishmael, your auntie is on the phone! Come talk to her before she heads out."

Running with excitement out of his room, Ishmael couldn't wait to speak to her. He'd been lying down most of the afternoon, but he loved his auntie Iyana. Almost as much as he loved his mother.

"Auntie?" he whined slightly out of breath, sounding nasally.

"What's up, Auntie's lil' man? You sound so stuffy. Wanna come spend a weekend with me once you're feeling better?"

"Ummm, let me ask my mom," he said afraid to leave his mother alone, even though he loved staying with his auntie. Even at ten, he was very protective of his mother— a trait instilled in him by Papa B the older he got.

"Boy, you can go. Stop that," Iyana heard Myriah say in the background. "Mommy will be fine. Plus, Nana and Papa B wanted to see you too. Maybe, just maybe, we can get Iyana to have *us over*, huh? You know, so she can whip up one of those gourmet five-star meals."

"Uh huh, I hear her. Tell your mama I got y'all although I don't know anything about a gourmet meal. I just cook, but Auntie will make your favorite shrimp pasta," Iyana she told him, smiling when she thought of him.

"Mmmm, Auntie," he said, licking his lips. Whenever she made shrimp pasta at home, she cooked two pans, dropping off one to her sister's house just for him.

"Uh huh. See, you're feel better already."

"I am," he chuckled.

"That makes me happy, baby. Well, Auntie needs to finish up around here so I can head out for my show. Once you get better, call me so we can set up our family dinner. And, Ish?"

"Yes, Auntie?" he said quietly, laying his head on his mother's lap as she rubbed his soft curls.

"Is your mama really okay? I'm worried about her," she whispered, making sure Myriah couldn't hear her through the phone.

Iyana and Ishmael had a bond like no other, even though he was a mama's boy. Whenever Myriah would shut down or get missing, Ishmael would always let Iyana know how his mother was doing.

It started once he was old enough to use the phone without help, which was her senior year in college. It was even him who first told her that Papa B had been diagnosed with Dementia. While she didn't birth him, Iyana loved him as her own.

"Yes, Auntie. Call me tomorrow and let me know about the show. My head and throat hurt. I'm going to lie down now. Okay?" he said sounding stuffy.

"Okay, baby. I will check in with you tomorrow. Between me and Nana, we will get some footage of the show and a few pictures. Love you."

"Love you, too," he said handing his mother back the cellphone.

"You mad? If so, you shouldn't be because you haven't cooked a real meal for us since you've been back. You know Nana gave you that magic cooking touch I missed."

"Yeah, yeah. She did, but I try to prepare a few meals and drop them off over there whenever she's tired from dealing with Papa B. But I need to do a sit down dinner for the family. You've been that way?"

Groaning, Myriah dreaded talking about her and Papa B since they'd never really gotten along. The good thing is Papa B loved Ishmael to no end, somewhat keeping the lines of communication open between the two of them over the years. As Myriah got older, she wanted to confront her grandparents for that secret they'd kept from her, even until this day.

Yet the guilt she carried for how she treated them when she was younger, just wouldn't let her. While everyone questioned why she was so hateful and promiscuous, it was her only way to get back at them for lying to her all these years. Even at twenty-eight, only one person knew why and even he didn't know how damaged she was behind it.

"Naw, not like I should, but I will soon. I promise. Look, I have to go. Ish's daddy will coming through in a few," she slipped, realizing she'd said more than she should have.

"Ish's daddy? Since when has that started happening? And why haven't you told me? So when will we meet him? Is he coming around consistently? How is Ish taking all of this?" Iyana rambled one question after another in straight panic mode.

"Damn, sis. Relax," she sighed, trying not to get overwhelmed. "I guess I was trying to avoid it, but not tonight. Please don't be mad at me, Iyana, but we are finally starting to work on co-parenting. Let me work on that before I involve him with the family. Ish is good, so that's all that matters right now and please, pretty please, don't question Ish."

Myriah hated lying to Iyana but it wasn't a total lie. It was hard enough trying to keep all of her own lies together without adding more to them by introducing Keyz, let alone anyone to her family. Feeling defeated, Iyana decided to table that conversation for another day.

She loved Myriah and was glad they were doing better, but she also knew that old habits die hard. The Myriah of old would lie to God about Jesus being the son of Mary even though they read the bible more times than they could count as kids. So believing anything that just came out of her mouth was hard sometimes. The pain she used to feel began to creep its way back in, bringing Iyana to tears. They were doing so well and she didn't want to push it.

"Okay, as long as Ish is good, I'm good for now. But you need to let us in one day. We love you. Even Papa B," she replied tearfully.

Yea, right. I can't let those judgmental, self-righteous old assess know my business right now, Myriah thought getting mad as she looked over her life.

Shortly after giving birth, Nana and Papa B were on her about going straight into college at Miami Dade College as soon as Ishmael was born. She hated their fake smiles as she waddled across the stage smiling with the biggest hole in her heart knowing she had disappointed them. Life could have been easier, but she chose to tell Keyz that she got rid of the baby, ducking and dodging him, which wasn't hard the deeper he got in the game.

After two years, she transferred to Florida Memorial University, an HBCU in Miami Gardens, were she got her bachelor's in Education. There she met a few single mothers who would help each other out from time to time. In fact, unlike her wild high school days, Myriah began to take her studies seriously and was now a fourth grade teacher and had been nominated for Teacher of the Year twice.

If asked, Myriah quickly shared Ishmael's father was a one-night stand choosing not to have an active role in his son's life. Her family barely listened to her most of the time and if she told the truth, she still got the 10th degree, so she figured why bother. Ishmael had more than enough love, so unless she had to, things were staying the way they were.

"Love you, sis. I—"

"Mmmmm," Elijah moaned lightly, gripping her ass while kissing her neck from behind. She'd almost forgotten he was there until she felt him massaging her firm butt from behind.

"Wait. Are you fucking while I'm on the phone?" Myriah asked, almost squealing in a high-pitched voice, but glad the topic was off of her.

Pushing him off of her, "Girl, no. That's Elijah just getting up. I almost forgot he was here he was so quiet. You would think he doesn't have a job with the way he lounges around here sometimes."

"Well, let me let you two get back to that non-fucking I hear in the background," she joked.

Iyana loved having him there, but Elijah was a slob. He was highly intelligent, but as spoiled as they came being that he was a mama's boy just like her nephew. So although he worked her body out pretty good sexually, he also treated her like a slave when it came to keeping a tidy house.

"I do have a job. She's just jealous because my job allows me to work from home," he yelled in the cellphone trying to talk to Myriah.

"Uhhhhh, Elijah stop," she whined, pushing his face away from hers. "Sis, let me go, and we are not finished! You are not off the hook."

"Girl, bye," she said, hanging up.

"Yeah, let me stop before your sister hears me put it on this ass," he whispered, still grinding her backside her from behind. "Besides, I need to pick up Angel. So it looks like that's three of us not going tonight."

"What? Come on, Elijah!" she yelled. "I've been talking about this for weeks now. I thought you were coming."

"Calm down. Damn, girl," he whispered, ignoring how irritated she was as he held her tightly, kissing the back of her neck.

"I was, but Sasha needs me to watch Angel tonight. She calls herself dating and let's be honest, don't we both want her to find a man?"

"Ugh. Yeah, whatever. It's at the community arts center. Why can't she come? I mean, it's full of kids because it's a play, Elijah," she whined although not meaning to.

"Because Sasha and I, her parents, are not comfortable with that. Iyana, baby, come on. You know I love everything about you from that sexy, fat ass," he said, turning her around to kiss her, "to your soft, full lips that fucking melt in my mouth. Shit girl, I'm about to fuck you in a coma if you keep poking them lips out at me."

Iyana smiled as soon as the compliments spilled from his mouth, a behavior he often did to quell her anger if they had a dispute.

"Elijah," she whispered. "I know what you're doing. I've never tried to be her mother, but one thing I do know is the world will call her *black*. Those little white girls and mothers Sasha hangs out with call her black. Hell, she's black. Don't make her have to choose because you won't."

Deciding not to argue, Elijah jumped up to shower before he headed out. Within a few minutes, she watched him dry off, looking for something to put on. Although he didn't live there, he had half of the closet and two drawers of clothes that

Iyana found herself washing the more he hung around at her house.

"Fine, then," she said, lightly adding foundation and some blush to her cheeks.

When they'd first met, she didn't wear makeup. But she did once she got older, and especially whenever she performed or had a show. Elijah hated it, always being the first one to say that her natural beauty was astonishing in his eyes like Lupito Nyong'o. He sometimes called her his Tootsie Roll, referring to how petite she was in size. Together, they looked like a modern day interracial couple as Elijah's skin, in spite of being biracial, was extremely pale.

"Come here," he whispered as he stood near her cosmetic table in his boxers, his bulge bobbing underneath, causing Iyana to stare.

Elijah may be biracial, but his penis was the size of a black man, easily nine inches long and quite thick. Dabbing her eyes that began to tear up, she shook her head no. She hated how easily she cried, especially when it was about race or skin color. Elijah knew that was a sensitive topic, but he went there anyway while trying to seduce her at the same time.

"Baby, come here… please," he begged, luring her away from her cosmetic table as he pressed her against his firm pole. "I told you already. You don't need that. Any of it."

Iyana shrugged finding comfort in her makeup, which complemented her prissy side, something else Myriah would tease her about. Right after high school, she became consumed with beauty products buying makeup, body scrubs, and lotions, to even scarves and wraps. She would also cringe if her feet touched the bare floor. Because of that, she had the softest feet and hands with tons of footies or funny looking socks in her drawer. All these little quirks, while birthed from insecurity, still didn't take away from who Iyana was whenever she showed up. She was "dope" as Ishmael would say when asked about about his auntie.

Focusing on her upcoming performance allowed her to take her mind off of fucking Elijah. He could be suck a prick at times. Especially since he'd just insulted her. Yet and still, she hated how her body craved him when he was the classic asshole most days, but he knew her body like no man did, using it to his advantage.

"I'm sorry," he said, kissing the top of her head from behind.

"Mmhmm," she said, smelling his body wash that found its way into her nostrils.

"Okay... I guess." She hated that she gave in so easily. Pulling away, she tried to avoid having sex, making her late for her own show.

"Well, you better get going before the carjackers catch you," she teased, although she was in the decent part of twon called Coconut Grove, living in a two-story townhome.

It was mixed community just south of downtown Miami. It wasn't the hood, but remnants of mom and pop stores could be found throughout the area. It was a nice compromise since they agreed not to live together just yet. In fact, he chose to live closer to his daughter, which was in a predominately white community. Iyana knew that was the reason although he would never admit it.

"You trying to be funny," he asked, biting her on her ear lobe, slowly grinding his pelvis into hers.

"Stop, Elijah," she laughed. "No, but it's getting dark and let's face it, you know you wouldn't live in this area, even if it was free."

He smirked, attempting to deny it before Iyana gave him that "don't try it" look. "You still check your car door three to four times before you walk off," she reminded him.

Years ago, he may have had a point about her neighborhood, but the area had changed, now filled with a few farmers markets, a high-end retail stores, a movie theater and different eateries ranging from Menchies, a frozen yogurt smoothie shop, to the Cheesecake Factory. Even the few mom and pop stores they remained there weren't the same.

"What?" she asked when he got quiet, still staring at him in his t-shirt and loose boxers, his thick manhood dangling against his thigh.

"Nothing, baby," he said shaking his head.

"You know," she said crossing her arms, "I would have never thought you were so concerned about the hood since we did meet at Howard. Like, you do know it's in the hood?"

"Yes, I did, but it was something my father wouldn't compromise on. He was an HU alum and wanted his son to be one. Good thing I did because I wouldn't have met my chocolate princess with this fat, little ass," he said, gripping her butt, causing her center to thump between her legs.

"Gosh, Elijah. Is that what caught your attention? Or the fact that I could be of help to you?" she asked frowning, her head titled to the side. "You know, the more I think about it, your behind was stalking me," she said poking his chest.

"Well, I mean I needed to get into this class for the School of Engineering, so the trip to the registrar was a must, but I can't lie. I saw you around campus," he replied smugly, grabbing her by her waist with a smile. "I would see doing your thing with your sorority sisters, but it was just something about you. I don't know what. Maybe because you weren't a showoff like most of them. You know how you Deltas are all loud, but not you. Not, my princess," he said.

"Boy, stop lying. We were never showoffs. We are ladies of distinction," she replied, swaying back and forth in his arms.

"I know, I know," he laughed, nuzzling his nose against hers. "So once I found out you worked at the registrar's office, I took my chances on getting your attention there, and here we are. So, I think it worked."

"You were not that interested," she shot back. "You were being your usual manipulative, charismatic self, hoping I would find you attractive and help you out by sliding you in a class you *should have* registered for on time. Besides, I was so confused, trying to figure out why this Drake lookalike only wanted me to help him. Every time somebody asked if you needed help, you told them 'she got me', pointing at me. That sort of weirded me out," she laughed.

"Because this Drake lookalike knew what he wanted then, and now," he said grinning as he turned her around. "And stop that, Iyana. Every dude in there was checking for you. I should have ran after you kept mean mugging my ass every time I said it."

"They were not. You're lying!" she squealed, her dimples tugging at his heart as he kissed her on the cheek.

Gosh, she's so got damn beautiful, he thought gazing at her while guilt kicked in about tonight.

He figured he would make it up to her another time like he

always did, but he could tell she was growing weary. He figured by now, she'd be over this power to the people movement working in the inner city, but it was clear it was embedded as to who she was as a person.

Strangely, her commitment to that is what he loved and hated that about her, which was why he was still there trying to get her to see things his way. He knew she struggled with her self-esteem and why. He just couldn't understand why she kept giving to a race that rejected her, when she could come and live in his world, leaving all that hood and ghetto loyalty behind.

"Man, I wasn't leaving until I had your number, even though you made me work hard for it. Now gimme a kiss," he moaned, pulling and biting her bottom lip before he kissed her. "Baby?" he whispered.

"Hmph?" she replied, his lips still on hers.

"I swear I'd do it all over again, Iyana," he whispered, smelling her coco butter body lotion. "Fuck…you smell good."

"Mmmm, you do too," she muttered, enjoying the taste of cinnamon mouthwash in his mouth.

"Just stop overthinking it, okay? We'll be fine, because one day you're going to have my babies and you will see how I feel, right? You're going do that for me? Have my babies?" he asked in between soft pecks on her lips.

They continued to rock and sway as she soaked in how she felt when he said that. This was typical Elijah trying to get into her head, and she was falling for it. Before she could push him off, his hands were all over her, gripping and pulling on her ass and thighs. His tongue pushed roughly into her mouth, not wanting to let her go.

The One That Got Away

"Mmmm, I don't know about that," she said in between kisses. "But I do think you're trying to make me late."

Pulling back, Elijah lifted her chin, watching the sadness in her eyes. He hated hurting her feelings and was doing his best to make it up to her before he left. Angel would love the performance, but it was a done deal. He wasn't exposing his daughter to that environment. Yet and still, he'd do anything to soften the blow.

"Now you think I went through all of that if I wasn't in this forever? As if you would not bless me with a house full of kids? Don't you want to make me happy?"

Iyana nodded, but what she also knew is that he'd never once mentioned marriage. He was perfectly fine having babies, just not getting married. She tried being understanding, hoping things would change, but he was scarred and she knew why. Especially after he took her home to meet his family in Ocala, Florida. It was a small, racially mixed community where racism was still very much alive. It was then that she learned he was partial to not only African Americans, but his own father.

"Junior," his father's voice boomed, calling him by his family nickname.

"Honey, don't call him that. You know it makes him feel like a kid," his mother Sarah said, patting her husband on the shoulder.

"Sarah, sweetie, he is a kid."

Elijah, fuming from the way his father belittled him in front of Iyana, chewed his food quietly. His tense shoulders and facial expressions gave away his discomfort in his father's presence.

"Elijah here is about to graduate with his Master's in Electrical Engineering, almost at the top of his class with a job offer already to work

for IBM. I think that's pretty amazing. Right, EJ?" she asked, choosing to call him by his other nickname he also hated.

"With a child out of wedlock, Sarah. Or did you forget that? Iyana, is it?"

Iyana, afraid to respond, had been stealing glances here and there at Elijah's father. He was a handsome, burly, toffee-colored man, with dark brown eyes and a wide nose. His face, complemented by a freshly lined haircut and mustache, maintained a stoic look the entire time throughout dinner. Although large, he was fit and tall, standing at 6'3", owning the entire room as he smoked his cigar at the dining room table.

"No, Dad. She hasn't, and neither have I," *he scoffed, stabbing his cauliflower.*

Iyana looked around at the spread on the table and humbly ate, although she wished there was a bowl of freshly made collard greens with smoked turkey, oxtails, cornbread and pigeon peas and rice. She knew his mother was white, but with an African American husband, she had hoped their Sunday spread would reflect some of that. Sadly, she ate her duck, cauliflower, and yellow rice quietly. She felt the tense energy in the air, this time because of the topic his father just raised.

"Iyana, sweetheart. How do you feel about this baby with another woman? Be honest, because I didn't raise my son to go around and multiply outside of marriage."

Standing up infuriated at the disrespect in front of his girl, Elijah yelled, "Why not, Dad? Isn't that what black men from the hood do? Or did you forget I know about the sister I have that doesn't belong to Mom? Fuck you, you judgmental fuck!"

"EJ! How dare you speak to your father like that! Apologize right this instant!" *his mother yelled, rubbing the back of his father's neck to calm him down.*

"For what? And you," *he yelled, turning his anger towards his mother.*

"Mom, you're just weak! You think Iyana would allow me to just walk all over her? Hell no! She is not my ugly secret!"

"Baby," Iyana whispered, standing by his side. "It's okay. Come on, baby. Let's just sit down and finish dinner."

"No, let's not. Since he brought it up, let's talk about my daughter. For one, Sasha got pregnant before Iyana and I became a couple. I never hid that from the day she made a commitment to be with me. Never! I even went as far as to making sure Sasha knew Iyana was here to stay. Isn't that right, baby?" he asked, grabbing and squeezing her hand.

Uncomfortably, Iyana nodded her head yes as she watched Elijah Senior stand to his feet. His booming presence made her want to shrink into the floor, but Elijah never flinched.

"No, you just fuck her into submission making her think she's lucky to have you. Don't think I don't know why you went and chose the darkest woman you could find to bring home. It's to remind me that I'm a black man who chose a white woman, a woman you just called weak.

Well, fuck you! I gave you and your mother the best of me. Fuck what you think I did in those streets because whatever I did, it stayed there. I never brought it home to your mother. She has never once been asked to raise my child like you trying to do with her," he sneered as Sarah latched on to his arm.

"That's enough, Elijah," his wife said, rubbing his lower back standing next to him. "We have company. Let's try to enjoy the time we have with her."

"No, Mom! He can't tell me how I feel about her!" Elijah yelled. "I'm in love with this woman! She don't have to find out shit about me in those streets, as you put it."

"And you should, because if I were her, I wouldn't give your biggity ass the time of day. Iyana?" his father said to her. "My son hates he has a black father who he feels is hood and ghetto, but it was my hood and ghetto *lifestyle that paid for that college education, fancy car and clothes this motherfucker wearing right now, but no more. Now he says he's in love. Make sure he proves that shit day and night. Don't let him make you feel you ain't shit because he ain't shit."*

"Okay, honey. That's enough," his wife whispered.

"Oh, I'm not shit alright. Angel is good and Iyana is my fucking world. She's knows better than to believe that bullshit ass hate you're spewing out of your lying mouth. Mom, I love you. Iyana, let's go," he said grabbing her hand.

"EJ, please! Don't go!" his mother cried.

"Don't you beg his ass to stay in my house. Now sit so we can finish dinner."

Taking her seat, she dabbed her tears with a cloth napkin. Iyana felt awful watching them tear each other down in front of a woman who loved the both of them.

"No, Ma. It's okay. In a few weeks, I will be a real man after I graduate and I won't need a dime from him. Neither will Angel. She has a mother and a father."

"But she's our grandchild, EJ," she cried.

"Is she? Or maybe some other man may raise her one day like dad has someone else raising my sister," he shot back.

That night, Iyana and Elijah found a hotel, staying until it was time to fly back to D.C. True to his word, Elijah graduated and never spent a dime of his parents' money. He went as far as requiring Sasha to move to Florida with Angel to prove he wasn't a deadbeat father although Iyana, at times, felt they were in a polygamous relationship. Sadly, she never questioned him about the events of that night, but deep down she knew she was in love with a man that was ashamed to have a black man's blood running through his veins.

So why am I with him if I know he rejects his own kind? she asked herself, her mind and body went to war staring at his long, thick penis she wanted inside of her mouth and body. It was hard not to get caught up in him, standing 6'2" with curly, jet black hair, caramel eyes and a lean body with defined muscles.

"Says who?" Iyana replied, squirming, as she tried to get away from him.

"Oh, you're going to have my babies because Angel will need a brother or sister. And this is mine," he growled, continuing his quest, his hands firmly gripping her tight ass after he picked her up. He loved how light she was to carry, weighing just a little over 110 pounds.

"Uh huh. So, will my babies be able to come to the community arts center or other areas that are not so safe?" she asked, lightly bouncing up and down on his rock hard pole she felt underneath her ass. She was playing dirty, but she didn't care.

"Baby, you know I support everything you do, but I'm not taking my daughter or our kids anywhere unless I think it's safe," he replied, quickly changing the mood.

"Oh boy, here we go," she mumbled.

"Yes, here we go," he said, not missing her sarcasm. "You see those kids getting shot in drive-bys week after week on the news? Don't act like you don't because Pookie and them won't think twice about shooting in a crowd full of kids. Damn right, I'm going there," he said in his usual condensing tone.

Iyana slid down his body, shaking her head. There was nothing she could say at this moment to change his mind and, truthfully, she just didn't care anymore. He had pissed her off and she needed to finish getting ready.

"Fine, Elijah," she snapped even though she was still aroused. "Let me finish getting dressed."

"Fine," he said, raising his hands in surrender as he backed away.

Grabbing her tights, Iyana sat down, roughly putting one leg through at a time.

"Fuck!" she yelled, snagging them on her Pandora bracelet before she snatched them completely off.

She hated she allowed him to get under her skin, as he walked around busily, getting ready to leave to get his daughter. She was pretty close to telling him not to come back, but she knew she didn't mean it, sniffling as she tried to compose herself.

"Hey, it's just a kids' show, baby. Don't mess this up for us," he said kissing her on the forehead. "What's up with all this crying?"

"Oh, for real?" she asked in disbelief. "Well tell me how you really feel, Elijah."

"Baby, I thought I just did. You know what? Look, never mind," he sighed, as he threw on his jeans and hooded pullover.

It was fall and a little nippy, so he figured he'd grab that until she did his laundry over the weekend. Before he walked out, he turned around, catching her as she washed and dried her face, her eyes a little puffy. Yet and still, she was still beautiful to him.

"Look, I'm tired of arguing and you're late. I don't want to fuss. I just want to be with you. I'm sorry, okay," he said, approaching her from behind, kissing her shoulders and neck, her body flinching from his touch.

"Fine," she said with a defeated look.

Picking her up, he sat her on the dresser, her legs in between his, trying a different approach.

"Okay, how about this? The next show you have, if you can schedule it for a Saturday afternoon, like maybe three or four o'clock in the afternoon, I'm coming and bringing Angel. Cool?" he asked, lifting her chin, his eyes fixed on hers.

"Sure," she spoke barely above a whisper, as he leaned down, kissing her softly. Instead of pushing him away this time, she embraced him, welcoming his tongue in her mouth.

"Fuck, you see him?" he asked, pointing to his erection. "Can I have some pussy before you go so this motherfucker can go down, or are you going to send me away like this?"

Spreading her legs, she let him in allowing him to explore the warmth that was trapped between her legs. She wanted to hate him. She wanted to hop down and walk away instead of allowing him to toss her on the bed towering over her, smelling her sex between her legs.

She hissed as he slipped his fingers in between her legs, pushing her thin g-string to the side. When he did, her slickness revealed how much he was pleasing her.

"Shit, I may have to tell Sasha to cancel that damn date," he growled, licking his fingers coated with her wetness.

"Elijah, baby," she moaned as he crawled on top of her.

"Iyana, baby. Please understand my crazy," he begged, searching her eyes, while his erect dick pressed firmly against her center.

"My shit is hurting, baby. You feel that?" he asked as he got up on his knees in front of her, admiring her wet pussy.

"Pull it out," he demanded.

Eager to please him, she quickly sat up and unzipped his jeans, pulling out his thick veined dick. The pre-cum that hung from his mushroom head enticed her so much, she pulled him into her mouth, relaxing her jaws so she could take him all in. She was the best he'd ever had, compliments of Pornhub, PornMD or Xvideos.com. So their sex life was anything but boring as he'd come to know every inch of her body over time.

"Damn, Iyana. Fuck, baby," he groaned, lightly holding the back of her neck, while his member went in and out of her mouth. With each pump, he fell in love all over again steadily holding her head until he was nearing an eruption.

Wanting to please her too, Elijah yelled, "Okay, baby. Your turn. Let me eat that pussy, baby."

He knelt, admiring her velvety chocolate, smooth skin against his, causing him to rock up even harder.

"Down, boy," he said, stroking his dick. "Let me take care of my girl. You see this dick, baby?"

Iyana nodded her head yes, wiping her wet lips with the back of her hand.

"You can get him next time. I'm about to eat that pussy," he huskily growled.

"Hmmm, baby. She pretty as fuck," he whispered, diving into her glistening center like an animal. His tongue, so stiff, Iyana felt like he was fucking her as her hips bucked up and down on his face.

"Uhhh. Uhhhh. Uh. Uh," she groaned, while he lifted her ass off the mattress.

"You so fucking nasty," she gritted, pushing his tongue deeper. "Now suck my ass," she commanded.

With no hesitation, he stretched her anal opening and set it on his mouth, where he licked her clean, alternating up and down not wanting to neglect her pussy. All that could be heard was licking and slurping, until Iyana's cries overpowered the room, turning Elijah on even more. With his free hand, he stroked and pulled on his shaft that was aching to feel her.

"Baby, I lied. I need some of this pussy," he declared as she fell apart in his mouth.

Elijah latched on, feeling her walls quiver around his tongue, driving him even more insane, as he snatched her off the bed, sitting her back on the dresser. He wanted to fuck her into submission for going against him earlier instead of letting him take her like he was about to do.

"Don't you move either," he said, daring her to talk back before he thrusted himself inside her.

"Nooooo, Elijah! Ah—" she screamed, her legs jacked up over his elbows.

"Damn, this pussy biting, Iyana," he whispered, looking down as he went in and out.

Like the nasty freak he knew her to be, Iyana tightened her vaginal walls, lightly bouncing and winding her hips up and down before she grabbed his face to kiss him, biting and pulling on his lips.

"That's right. Fuck mommy real good," she hissed.

"Fuck, girl," he huffed, hitting it even harder. "You're trying to get me to marry you *tonight* if you keep this up," Elijah replied lustfully. After four or five more strong strokes, Iyana felt him releasing inside of her, his hot fill running down her ass.

"Shit, girl," he panted, staring in her eyes that seemed to mesmerize him, especially during sex.

"Mmmmmm. Shit, what?" she grinned, knowing she had messed his head up.

"My ass going to *every* performance after tonight. Damn," he laughed pulling out of her.

"Uh huh. Whatever," she mumbled, getting down off the dresser. "Now you know I can't go like this," she stated, her skirt jacked up around her waist covered in their juices.

"Hurry up then," he grinned, smacking her firm ass.

Within five minutes, Iyana had showered and got dressed, this time wearing an African print leotard and long, flowing skirt. She felt better about his promise, although she knew he only said it in the heat of the moment.

Chapter 5

"Excuse me, excuse me! Can you hurry up and move!" Iyana yelled out of her window, growing frustrated at the truck. It was blocking her way into the parking garage near Target, hitting and resting on her horn for a few seconds.

Although she enjoyed her sexual tryst with Elijah, she knew it left very little time to run to the store.

"Ugh, I'm so mad," she mumbled to herself, wondering why she chose to go to Midtown anyway on a Friday night. The happy hour cliques were now in full swing as the bars turned into club like settings.

The show started at seven, giving her only twenty minutes to run in, then sparing her ten minutes for the commute.

Instead of moving, Iyana watched the driver emerge from his truck with a scowl on his face. Her body froze from shock realizing that Mr. Asshole was none other than Kaizer Paul.

"Oh shit," she mumbled, his presence unnerving her, even fifteen years later. His hair, now wild and curly, was faded around the edges, giving him a bad boy look in his True Religion jeans and button-down top.

Panicking, Iyana rolled up her window afraid that he might recognize her. Not much had changed except she now wore her hair natural, mostly in Bantu knots or braids like a braided Mohawk, unless she wanted a softer look. Then, she would flat iron her thick, long mane that fell past shoulders. Tonight, however, she wore an African wrap, which matched the theme of their play, "The Lion King," hiding her hair.

Tapping on her winder, Iyana started shaking, quickly looking in the opposite direction. She hoped he'd go away, but she wasn't so lucky.

"Hey!" he yelled, tapping on her window again. "I really don't give a fuck if you're a female. Why the fuck are you hollering and shit like you don't have no fucking patience?" he barked, growing even more agitated by the second.

One thing Iyana did not tolerate was disrespect from a man using profanity when speaking to a woman. That was a pet peeve she developed after being called a "black bitch" or "mutt ass hoe" over the years by guys when she rejected their advances. Iyana wasn't stuck up, but she certainly wasn't pressed for a date no matter how much she struggled with her self-esteem. Even Elijah had an expiration date as for as she was concerned.

"Oh, no he didn't," she grumbled, rolling down her window. "Because I don't, and who do you think you're talking to like that? A bitch? Wait, a hoe? One who don't know correct English. Yeah, *that part*. So excuse me for ignoring your disrespectful rant when a real woman, something you know

The One That Got Away

nothing about, is in your presence!" she belted, her neck swirling as she gave him attitude.

All Keyz could think of the entire time she spoke, swerving her neck, was the day he met this flawless, petite, chocolate beauty that was going to be his girl. The more she talked, the more she pulled him in under her spell. When her dimples caved in, so did a tug on his heart. A heart he never knew it existed outside of loving his mother and siblings. Her grey eyes, so clear from the reflection of the moon, were almost magnetic-like, reeling him in even more.

Damn, I can't believe who this is, he thought and smiled, rubbing his chin as she rambled on. He hadn't heard a word she said, admiring her African garb that complemented her skin. She looked so sexy to him that he wanted to violate her right then and there.

"Oh, so you're mute now?" she quipped, almost using the same line he used on her fifteen years earlier.

He chuckled once he realized she was trying to boss up on him. Gone was the passive and timid thirteen-year-old girl that had no voice. In fact, not only had she found it, but she used it effortlessly trying to rip a hole in his behind. Any other woman would have gotten cursed out by now for real. But he was too amused, wanting to take her on to see what would happen next.

So he leaned down, his face close to hers, imagining all the things he wanted to do to her. He was so close, he felt her breath lightly dancing on his face intriguing him all the more. There was no way he was letting her get away this time. No way in hell.

"Naw, but I guess you're *still* deaf," he chuckled, realizing too she used his words on him. "A motherfucker tired of waiting by that basketball court. Shit, how long it's been now?" he grinned, flashing his signature smile, while he lightly dragged his tongue across his teeth.

Wow, he does remember me, she said to herself thinking about the first day they met. At a loss for words, she sat with her mouth unknowingly open in disbelief this was even happening.

"Fifteen years, in case you forgot," he whispered slowly approaching her before his lips gently pressed against hers. It wasn't long, but its sensual nature made it hard to pull away from him.

The sound of a loud, honking horn brought her back to reality. Here she was caught up in her past almost forgetting she was in a relationship. Her thoughts were all over the place watching his wet, pink lips stretch into a mischievous grin, unnerving her like the days of old before she fought back.

"How... how dare you try to play me, Mr. Paul!" she yelled. "Yeah, I said it, and I remember who you are. And another thing, I am not *that* girl! In fact, I actually have a man."

Her eyes shifted up and down her body, getting aroused as he still felt his lips on her mouth. The fact she told him after the fact, let him know she gave no fucks about this man of hers. Especially, since she'd gotten all worked up behind a kiss.

It was too late anyway to have second thoughts, waking a sleeping beast ready to take what he felt was his. The way he saw it, her man needed to worry about him, laughing at how flustered she looked.

"Naw, you are exactly *that* girl. Shit, my girl, so fuck your man. Gotta a nigga on hold all this time, but I'ma take care of that," he replied smugly, winking his eye.

"Now see, you... you really got me—" she yelled, frustrated that she wanted him right then and there.

She knew it was just a kiss, but it was something she'd only dreamt of before tonight. She'd never tell him that, but he could see it all over her body, her chest heaving up and down, showing her hard nipples he couldn't wait to put in his mouth.

"Naw, I'on have you yet," he drawled, resting his elbow inside of the driver's window. "But I promise, *Iyana Wilkers*, I'ma make it up to you. Love on you, make sure that body know it's loved, give you the world, worship you. Shit like that," he said with ease.

She was in shock he actually remembered her name, first and last, damn near speechless once he confessed his intentions all these years later.

"It's cool. You'll get used to it. You know, me taking charge, letting you know what's up. Give me your number and when I call, your lil' ass better answer," he demanded, slipping his cellphone into her hand.

"Why—" she started before he interrupted her.

"Shhh, just dial it from my cell," he instructed her, pulling her face close to his by the chin.

"But—but—"

"*Cheeks*, dial it," his voice booming in a serious tone.

Before she could even ask why he called her that, he said, "Because of them damn dimples. You're about to have a nigga wanting to wife you today. You know you still pretty as fuck," he said, relaxing his smile once it hit him this could be it. No more random hoes, hook ups, no one else but her.

Pursing her lips which deepened her dimples, Iyana nervously dialed her number from his cell. The moment he saw it light up on her passenger seat, he smiled.

"Good girl," he told her.

With time standing still, they almost forgot about the cars waiting behind them until they angrily started blowing their horns again aggravating Keyz.

"Man, fuck that horn and answer your cell," he said, waving off the cars behind them.

"He—hello," she softly stuttered.

"Hey, Cheeks," he said pecking her on the mouth one time before he jogged back to his truck. "Because of those fucking dimples. Like perfection."

To that, she giggled, dropping her eyes. Pursing her lips once more, they appeared, warming his heart.

"Hey, Kaizer," she smiled, feeling giddy like a child that was just told a secret that couldn't be contained.

"Naw, only my mama calls me that. Call me Keyz or daddy, but you know what's up if you calling me daddy."

By this time, security had come out to see what was going on walking towards them about to give them a ticket. Cars were lined up off the main road leading into the shopping plaza. Iyana hated confrontation but this one was different. It was a welcomed one, wondering if he could be the one—would be the one. The one that got away, coming back for her out of all people.

Jumping in the truck, he said, "I'll call you in a few hours, Cheeks. Make sure you don't make Keyz wait. A'ight?"

Before she could respond, he hung up, pulling into the parking garage, leaving her in the middle of the road. His son was sick and he promised his mother he would bring him some cold medicine. Even though she ruffled his feathers calling him an asshole, she made his night and he couldn't wait to hear her voice later on.

Smiling at her new nickname, she tightly held her cellphone forgetting why she was at the shopping plaza until security tapped on her window.

"Sorry!" she yelled, smiling before she pulled off now en route to the community arts center.

"Yo, Keyz? You're getting creepy as fuck. Who was ole girl you were back there hollering at? We're late and you got to get Ish his cold medicine," Skebo said, watching Keyz with a lovesick grin on his face.

"My future," he said, cheesing hard flashing his pearly white teeth.

"Your future?" Skebo repeated, wondering who replaced his best friend. "Nigga, the hell you smoking on," Skebo asked, him wondering if he should take the blunt that Keyz's had just fired

"Bro, really?"

"I'm just saying, a female have you like that?"

"Shit...I guess. Naw, on a serious note, I can't believe I finally ran into her after all these years. Like I'm stoked and shit and that doesn't happen that often with me."

"Ran into who?" Chico asked, furrowing his brows as he sat in the backseat. He'd been on his cell the entire time, arguing with a female he was feeling that was giving him a hard time.

"Cheeks!" he laughed. The name just came to him after

she started yelling at him, her dimples deeply emerging in her cheeks.

"Man, stop playing. Who in the hell is Cheeks?" Skebo asked.

"Iyana, nigga. Iyana Wilkers," he said more so to himself, grinning so hard that his own cheeks began to hurt.

"I'on know her, but she got your ass grinning," Chico said. "Just be ready tonight after you and Skebo rap up y'all meeting. My ass is tired. Trying to slide up in somethin' before I knock out."

"Why? Shona or Meka clocking your ass?" Skebo asked.

Shona was one of the girls on the team. She was used in many ways, but mostly to get to know new dudes that popped up on the drug scene in Miami. She also managed the girls that cut and packaged their product—her and her younger sister, Kaleela. Chico never told anyone, but they all knew he was hitting Shona while he went home to Meka every night. If asked, they all would venture to say he was in love, but Keyz hoped not. Shona as too valuable to their organization to allow a situation they all could have avoided getting in.

"No fucking body puts a timer on my time," he lied, nowing damn well the love of his life did. The one none of them knew anything about—Myriah, still thinking about the day they'd met. He was beyond in love. He was obsessed with her.

Damn, who is shorty walking down the street like this all late at night and shit? The C.U.B crew had just brought in a few new recruits to handle the areas they were expanding. After identifying everyone's new role and who they were reporting to, Chico, Skebo and Keyz left the meeting, feeling good about how fast their territory was expanding. The entire time,

The One That Got Away

Keyz sent Myriah to voicemail after she tried to force him to spend time with her. He figured after a couple of years of just sex, she would move on, but it was clear she had not.

"Hola, hermosa. Es buena?" Chico probed, calling her beautiful, and asking her was she good. He'd just was pulled up near the bus stop she was sitting at near 79th Street Flea Market shortly before midnight.

After all the high school games ended, most of them went to the McDonald's, either across the street from the school stadium or further ahead near the flea market.

"Speak English, motherfucker," she shot back, mad that she was stuck once Keyz didn't pick up when she called. Chase and her girls had taken off after she told them that Keyz was coming to get her. No, she hadn't spoken to him, but she knew his schedule, and Thursday nights were usually the nights he came in town.

"Quiero chupar ese coño gordo y ver si sigues hablando inglés," he chuckled, askign her in Spanish if he could suck on her fat pussy to see if she would still be speaking English. He only did it to annoy her, smiling the entire time.

Myriah continued to ignore him as she searched through her purse looking for her Metro-Dade transit bus card that she rarely used. She was so upset that she didn't realize once Chico parked in the McDonald's parking lot next to the bus stop, walking up on her.

"Fuck! Shit! You scared me!" she screamed with panic in her eyes.

"Lo siento, mami," he apologized, this time not even realzing he said it in Spanish. His sisters spoke in Spanish, so he natually did when he was speaking to woman...a woman that made him feel and for some reason, Myriah did. "Just trying to make sure you're good. It's late and motherfuckers on this side of town ain't nothin nice. You know what I'm saying."

Myriah was feeling his swag as he stood in front of her chewing on a toothpick. His mouth was iced-out as the bottom showed nothing but miniature diamonds on them. His all-white Versace t-shirt, jeans and sneakers made him look like a hood knight in shining armor, as she got caught up in the tattoos that laced his neck and arms. He wasn't that tall, but he was tall enough. His soft brown eyes, lightly tanned skin and low-cut wavy fade barely hid his Hispanic background, although Myriah knew he wasn't black.

Shit, shit, shit, girl. This fine ass ese' doing it, she thought as she looked at his all-black Lamborghini. In that instance, she didn't care if Keyz called her back or not. She wanted whatever her newfound friend was offering.

"Changed your mind?" he asked, noticing that she was admiring him and what he rode up in.

"What? Huh? No, please. I'm used to shit. This bitch ass boy I was dealing with just wanna play tonight. So, it's whatever. I don't live that far anyway," she spat, playing it off.

"Where 'bout?" he asked, smilin, with his iced-grill on full display. The C.U.B crew all had them except a few like Skebo and Keyz. It was their signature look, but Skebo and Keyz thought the shit was tacky like people who weren't used to having money. Chico, proud to be the head of C.U.B, however, wore it like it was meant to be.

"Where 'bout, what?" she asked.

"Where you stay, unless you coming with me?"

Chico's dick got hard the longer he stared at Myriah's coffee-colored thighs barely covered in a mini, acid washed jean skirt with a white Bebe t-shirt with silver rhinestones. Her curly, black hair was pulled up into a ponytail at the top of her head, with several tendrils hanging down on each side of her face.

On her arm, she was carrying a Louis Vuitton bag similar to the one he had just copped Meka last month. After surveying her wardrobe and

The One That Got Away

bag, Chico knew she wouldn't play tough too much longer. Besides, he was really feeling shorty playing tough, knowing she migh sit another hour out there. His conscience alone wouldn't allow him to leave her.

Standing up, Myriah pulled her skirt down her thick thighs that Chico wanted around his face immediately.

"Come on, mommy. It's late and shit. Let me help you help me," he said, reaching for her small hand that quickly found his.

In that moment, Chico felt a warmness from her. It was like he could tell her tough act was just that, an act. Not even in that moment, but who she was as a person. Instantly, he wanted to know more about her instead of just fucking. So they'd spent the night doing nothing but just talking.

He learned about how her parents died when she was six and how she was being raised by her strict grandparents. She also told him about a deep family secret her grandparents didn't think she knew about, which was why she rebelled against them.

That night, Chico had given Myriah his heart without even knowing it, and his life would never be the same because of it. Before long, she was not only in his bed, but she was the reason he could no longer love Meka or even fuck with Shona.

Ironically, as Chico reminisced about how he met Myriah, Keyz's mind drifted back to his first encounter with Iyana and tonight she hadn't disappointed. In just that brief moment, her smell, taste and exotic look was etched in his mind. Just as quickly as he got excited, that feeling dissipated when he thought of how his lifestyle may conflict with hers.

No, he wasn't a street corner hustler, he was worse. He ran one of the most notorious drug empires in Florida. The only way to soften that reality was by having legitimate front businesses, a cigar lounge named On the Way Up, and Smokies, which was his hookah bar, both of which were doing quite well.

He figured he'd leave the game in a few years, but a girl like her may not wait for that nor did he expect her to. He just remembered the days of being hungry and refused to ever be hungry again. After dropping off Chico, he and Skebo decided to drop off his son's medicine before heading to his meeting. One thing Keyz took seriously was his role as a father.

"I'm outside," he said, hanging up the phone.

"Dang, nigga. You not going in there to see your lil' man?" Skebo asked, shaking his head.

"I'on trust her ass. She always making lil' comments about us or wearing lil' shit so I can see her ass or some pussy. I'll see him tomorrow though. She's dropping him off to my mama. If he's feeling better, I plan to take him and my nieces and nephews to Miami Seaquarium. It was the beach, but Ish a lil' brainiac. At ten, my shorty be saying shit to me I ain't never even heard of," he laughed.

"Man, I still can't believe your ass got a baby with fast ass Myriah. She still trippin' off you meeting her folks?"

"Pfft. Fuck them and her. Long as my lil' man know me, that other bullshit is not of my concern. Look at her ass coming outside like a nigga wanna fuck or something," he said as Myriah walked out wearing a pair of denim booty shorts and a white, racer top showing her hard nipples.

Rolling down the window on Skebo's side of the truck, he said, "Here. Have him ready tomorrow morning at nine. Mama making them all breakfast before we head out for the day if he's feeling better."

"And if he's not?" she asked with a scowl on her face, taking the bag from him.

"Then my shorty will spend the day with me and his cousins at the crib. Fuck you think, Myriah? Ain't you a school teacher? They ain't passing out common sense with them degrees?"

Keyz didn't care for Myriah after she lied about getting an abortion and cutting him off. He only learned about Ishmael through Keyon when he was about two years old. Keyon was actually dating Chase in college, who was now his wife. They linked up after running into each other at the University of Florida his freshman year, while Chase her was in her junior year.

She was considered one of their baddest cheerleaders, wanted by all the dudes on campus with her caramel complexion, dark brown, chinky eyes and pretty smile, looking like a darker version of Nicki Minaj. Although Keyon was a few years younger, Chase saw the man he became after Keyz left, and he won her over. Now they were the proud parents of their twin six-year-old sons, Keyon Jr. and Kelon.

Sadly, her relationship with Myriah wasn't the same, who seemed to avoid her after she went off to college. One holiday, she ran into Nana in the grocery store and Ishmael was sitting in the grocery basket. Shocked, Chase told Keyon and the secret was out.

"Yes, I am. The shit you do keeps me from letting you know my damn family. You're disrespectful and act like your shit don't stink, and I'm sick of it," she spat.

Deep down, Myriah was over Keyz but was tired of being looked at as the thirsty baby mama he never wanted to be with it. She hated how he shamefully talked about her to everyone, especially Chico, who loved her for who she was. Yet and still, she always felt the need to prove to Keyz that he had it all wrong. That maybe if he loved her just a little, she could have learned how to love herself.

"Man, fuck you and your family. A nigga not trying to be affiliated with your scandalous ass in the first place. Raped a dick with that mouth while I was drunk, then hopped on it. Don't fuck with me, Myriah," he snarled, pointing at her.

"Dealing with you is what got me in this situation anyway! Just get your shit together so you can spend *consistent* time with your son!" she yelled, not caring if the neighbors heard her.

"Fuck you mean consistent? I see my son every week, sometimes more when he's with my mother. Your ass just mad because you can't get this dick no more!" he snarled, pulling off and leaving skid marks in the road.

It pained her that they couldn't be cordial, as she looked back to see if Ishmael had witnessed their verbal brawl after a few neighbors stepped outside. Now embarrassed, Myriah quickly ran in the house avoiding the judgmental stares. She also feared Chico hearing about it, because he felt like she never fully gave herself to him, waiting instead on Keyz to see value in her.

Chapter 6

"Tyana, baby. That was a wonderful show. That boy you chose to be Mufasa did such a good job," her Nana beamed.

"Shoot, Nana was so scared every time that lil' boy opened his mouth," she smiled, clenching her handkerchief to her face as she spoke.

"Awe, Nana. Thank you. Jerome did great. I'm telling you he was terrified when he got that part, but he committed to it, and now look at him," she smiled, watching him as his mother hugged and kissed him.

"Harry Belafonte in the making!" her grandmother shouted. Nana loved Harry Belafonte, making Papa B crazy every time she brought him up.

"Nana, Harry Belafonte? Where is Papa B?" she asked, shaking her head.

"Yes, ma'am! Oh, he down there talking to folks about the

show. Look at him being friendly," she said, smiling as he chattered away.

"Oh boy. You better get him. He's still a good catch, Nana," she said, hugging her Nana who waved her off.

Iyana hated to ask, but she did, watching Nana get teary-eyed. "So, how is he? Did he really enjoy the show?"

"Of course! That's all he talked about this week whenever he wasn't acting up. I'm telling you, the more I keep him active, the more stable he is," she said, dabbing her eyes.

"Oh, Nana. Come on, before you start me," she said, poking out her lip. "Let's enjoy the moment. Look at him over there dancing." They both laughed as he shimmied in his seat like he heard music. It was like he was his old self.

"Nana's just happy that he's in a good mood," she smiled, patting Iyana on the shoulder. "And because you're home. Shoot, I know how mean those kids were to you, not to mention your sister, but look at you. My grandbaby has growed up nice and pretty and is very smart. Got your own dance thang and all. Nana just happy for you," she said, looking down before she caught Iyana's eyes that appeared to be sad.

"Hey, lady," she said shaking it off. "None of that. Life could have been worse. Like we could have ended up on the streets or foster care, but you and Papa B gave up retirement to raise us. My mama would be proud. So now it's my time for us to take care of the two of you. So don't let me hear you say that again, okay?"

"Alright, baby," her nana replied, getting teary-eyed. "Let me go and get Papa B. I see he's out there being fresh and then will play like the Dementia got him acting that way," she teased, giving her a hug.

Feeling proud, Iyana looked in the auditorium of the community arts center, as many parents celebrated with their kids. It was just like yesterday when she danced at this same center. Her heart swelled thinking about this place that was her sanctuary to get away from all the ugly hate of being the black girl. So, once she took over, she put in a lot of work building up the program, which included theater instead of just dance class.

There were many days parents the parents thanked her for giving their kids a place. Without it, they'd be on the streets afterschool. It was this part she wanted Elijah to see, hoping it would soften his heart.

"Iyana, wait!" she heard Nana yell, pulling Papa B to the stage.

"Oh boy. Let me brace myself," she muttered to herself. One thing Papa B didn't lose was his bluntness, but Iyana wouldn't change it for the world.

"Hey there, Papa B's Reese's Peanut Butter Cup!"

She smiled and was in shock he remembered the nickname he'd given her and her sister. Whenever he said it, if both were around, they answered, which was the joke of the house when they were little.

"Hi, Papa B. You liked the show?" she asked, straightening up his jacket and dusting off imaginary lint. It made her feel closer to her grandfather, attending to him whenever he was around after being gone for so long.

"Yeah, that boy sho nuff did a number with that part,

baby. That Mufasa boy," Papa B said, handing her a bouquet of roses. "Your Nana almost forgot to give you these."

Iyana laughed, looking at Nana because he was the one with memory issues. They knew it was a dig he'd taken at her, but they all shook their head at his joke.

"That he did. Oh, Papa B. I'm so glad you came. You look good, really good."

Staring around like he smelled something that stank, Iyana began to look around too. It was just like him to check out of a conversation while the one he was in wasn't even over.

"Where that boy at? You know the one that calls himself being my Reese's Peanut Butter Cup's boyfriend? I should slap that sucker for not being here. Papa B's old, but I can still kick some ass. Ain't that right, baby?" he asked Nana, who stood by shaking her head.

"He got tied up, Papa B. But he promised to be here next time," she said, not wanting to get him worked up since he was doing so well.

"Hmph," Papa B said, throwing his hand at Iyana before walking off.

"Now you know how he is, baby. You're still his lil' girl and any man that don't treat you like that, is just not the man for you in his eyes," she said, rubbing Iyana on her shoulder.

"I know, Nana. I know. Well, thanks for coming, again. I plan to host something in a week or so with Ish and Myriah, if you all are up to it. You know Ish is sick again. That's why they didn't come," she said.

"Yeah, I know, but Myriah baby's him or makes excuses why she doesn't stop by regularly. So I keep my distance until she wants us to baby sit. Just let Nana know what you want me to cook. A family gathering should be mighty nice, baby."

"Well, you know Myriah. She has her own mind and is very strong-willed. Has been from day one, but she was actually excited about it, so let's see," she said, giving her grandmother some hope, as she grabbed her keys and purse to lock up.

"Strong-willed my behind. Poor boy needs a strong father figure around to get him out more doing thangs men do. Now I try, but Papa B done got up there. Myriah keep him all up under her like he can't be around family unless she's there front and center. I'm telling you, he will be a lil' fruitcake if she keeps it up," she replied.

"Not the fruitcake, Nana!" she laughed.

"Awe, hush!" she huffed before finally walking off to catch up to Papa B.

∽

Tossing her keys on the table when she walked in, Iyana began to disrobe, throwing her leotard and wrap skirt over a nearby chair. If Elijah were here, she would never do that, but he wasn't, so she enjoyed her time of no rules when it came to how she kept her house.

Funny thing is she was pretty neat, but was always picking up his stuff off the floor. It was one of those things she felt he did to determine if she was ready to be his wife. Like the more domestic she was, the sooner he'd wife her, which was far from the truth and she knew it.

She decided to make a fresh pot of tea, dropping a combination of chamomile and lemongrass tea bags in the water once it began to boil. After putting it on low, she took her cell phone and placed it on the charger near her bed. It was almost one o'clock in the morning. Keyz hadn't called, but she didn't really expect it. She just *hoped* he did.

After drinking tea, which always seemed to relax her, Iyana jumped in bed naked as the day she was born, except for a pair of socks. She hated wearing pajamas to bed, only putting them on if she had overnight company or if it was that time of the month. Strangely, just like the freak she was, she felt free lying in her bed naked. Dozing off, she was jarred out of her sleep when her cell phone rang loudly, falling off the nightstand when she went to grab it.

"Hello," she said, after grabbing it off the floor, her heart racin.

"That's what's up," he smiled, feeling himself, after she answered on the first ring. He knew it was late, but he didn't care. *Shit, it's him,* she thought, straightening her wrapped scarf as if he could see her.

"What? Huh?" she said, trying to catch her breath. She was secretly excited— her crush was calling her late at night like she was in high school. She hated and loved all the things she felt right now, afraid to let him in, but also afraid to let this moment get away.

"I said that's what's up," he said.

"K—Keyz, it's after one o'clock in the morning," she stuttered out of sheer nervousness, scratching the back of her neck.

"And that should tell you how bad a nigga wanna talk to

you, *Cheeks*. What? You thought Keyz was playing tonight? Or ever? Man, hell naw."

Smiling as she felt all giddy, she asked, "Why do you call me that?"

"Call you what? Cheeks?"

"Yes, that. It's sort of... different."

"Shit, I'm different. So what are you saying? Your man can't call you that?"

"Pretty much...since you're not my man," she told him, enjoying the little banter they were having about this nickname he'd given her.

"Like hell I'm not," he snapped, then it hit him. *She really doesn't know just how beautiful she is*, he thought to himself. He knew then he had to come at her differently. Changed how she saw herself and about their future.

"I have the rest of my life, Cheeks. You're worth it. I swear you are," he said, catching her off guard. She swallowed, her words stuck in her throat. "You're still there?" he asked, praying she was.

Keyz got quiet for a moment, looking at his cell phone.

"I am."

"But with me?" he asked, feeling like a kid. He was lowkey embarrassed, like he was begging for her to vibe with him, but he meant what he said. She was worth it. Then out of nowhere she spoke, suprising him.

"I need to see you," she said, that boldest she possessed those years ago returning. Then instantly, she regretted. *Shit, he's going to think I'm a whore or something.* "Nevermind, I—"

"Naw, ain't no nevermind," he sat up with a scowl on his face. They were too close to turn back now. "I want you."

"Keyz, this is crazy. You know nothing about me. I know nothing about you. You have a whole life, a life filled with women at your beck and call. A life I can't compete with. I wouldn't even know what to say, how to act, how to...you know," she said, cursing herself silently for rambling. "I've only been with one man...what can I offer you that another woman can't."

"Shit, that's easy," he said and smiled, exhaling. He wasn't sure where she was going with that, but now he understand. She not only felt unworthy, but inexperienced too. "You can offer me you. Your time, your conversation."

"And no sex?" she whispered, praying he agreed. To that he laughed.

"Hell yeah, I would want to know you like that, but that's not a priority. Pussy comes to me leaving, Cheeks. I'm not bragging. Just stating facts. Because it does, I'm not eager to have it. I enjoy it when I do, but as I get older, I need more. Shit, I want more."

"I fit that bill of more?"

"Come over and see."

"Okay," she whispered before she hung up.

∼

IYANA CHECKED the address three or four times to make sure it was right. Looking closely at the address, she saw he lived off the water near a few hotels and high-end shops.

"You can do this," she mumbled, her nerves all over the place. As soon as she turned on the radio, she heard Beyonce's "I'm Sorry" laughing about how this could apply to Elijah.

The One That Got Away

The more she sang the lyrics, the more she felt her nerves dissipating, remembering Keyz's soft lips on hers earlier.

After parking, Iyana took a few deep breaths as she approached the door leading into his condo. After dialing the code he'd given her, she was immediately buzzed in, waking up a mad security guard. Once she walked in, he sat up, staring her at with popped eyes, admiring her petite build.

He had to be in his 60s, close to Papa B's age, which unnerved her, but she jumped on the elevator quickly before he spoke to her. After reaching the 21st floor, she stepped out looking at her cell to see which condo was his.

"202, 203, 206..." she whispered, feeling every nerve in her body tingle the closer she got to his condo.

"212," she mumbled to herself, looking down at what she threw on.

Since Iyana was a dancer, her wardrobe was saturated with tights, wrapped skirts, tanks, bodysuits, and dance shorts. Not wanting to look too desperate, she threw on a red tank and long paisley printed skirt. Her Bantu knots now showing, reinforced her natural look.

Before she could alert him she was there, Keyz slowly opened the door, tucking his lip under his teeth as he towered over her. Iyana stared at all of his tattoos that covered his toned arms that were now bigger. With no shirt on, she admired his bare, golden skin from his chest and six-pack, leading down to that V-shape right above his genital area. His hair was soft, thick and curly.

He wore red and white basketball shorts, something he didn't have on earlier that hung halfway down his hips. His wild, curly hair was untamed, short of his edges that were neatly trimmed low around the side of his head.

His lips, full and wet from licking them, woke her up followed by his killer smile he threw on her once they made eye contact. He was fucking her up before he'd even touched her and he knew it. *Fuck,* she thought dragging her hands down her skirt as her G-string quickly became immersed with vaginal moisture. There was no need to wear a bra as her tank easily held her size B breasts. Her hardened nipples were on display due to the cold chill she felt when he opened the door.

"Sup, Cheeks," he said cockily, starring at the natural look she was rocking. He wasn't one to care how a woman wore her hair, but her Bantu knots made her look naturally exotic, tugging on her grey eyes that looked tight and slanted, especially when she pursed her lips.

"Kaizer," she said before he stopped her from walking in, lightly placing his hand on her stomach. His touch immediately sent chills down her spine, her eyes fluttered trying to assess what had just happened.

"Remember, only my mama calls me Kaizer," he said smiling, still blocking her way into his condo, his legs slightly separated.

His bulge lightly bouncing against his shorts made her feel warm, as she reached for the back of her neck trying to calm down as her body seemed to have a mind of its own. Keyz chuckled remembering how she scratched the back of her neck the day he winked at her.

While he enjoyed unnerving her, he wanted her to get past that so they could really get to know each other. To make sure they weren't interrupted, he turned his cell off, hoping to talk.

The One That Got Away

That was until he saw her causing him to question if he could restrain himself.

Looking her up and down before his eyes rested on hers, he said, "I guess we forgot that name part, huh?"

"Sorry," she said, a nervous laugh following as she watched him undress her with his eyes. He was close to talking her panties off with his eyes without even knowing it. It was as if they'd stood at that door for hours when it had only been a minute, as she shifted her feet trying to get herself together. Wanting to save her before she passed out, Keyz gave in not wanting to be a jerk.

As soon as he closed the door, he pushed her body against it, searching her eyes to see if she felt what he did.

"Fuck, I swear I'm trying," he told her, the sincerity in his eyes told her it was true, but the urgency in his voice told her he couldn't help it.

"Don't then." She was like, fuck it. She'd already done the most, coming over here anyway. It was now or never. She just had to remember to breathe.

Keyz wasted no time swiftly dragging his nose up and down her neck, her rapid heartbeat driving him insane. *Fuck, she smells so good*, he said to himself, imagining coating her chocolate skin in something sugary.

She felt his swollen manhood pressing against her stomach taunting and begging her to feel the inside of her, but fear paralyzed her as she stood against the door. He sensed it, hating that she was unsure of how much she turned him on, how much he wanted to be inside of her, making her feel good.

"I'm daddy, Cheeks. Say that shit for me," he lightly

moaned, kissing her neck then swirling his nose in and around her ear. Her chest heaved up and down as he cupped her shoulders, lightly massaging her to get her to relax.

"Come on, Cheeks. Just relax for ne," he pleaded, as her shoulders slowly collapsed. Her mouth opened widely, waiting to be kissed.

Unable to fight it, he kissed her then slid his right hand underneath her wrapped skirt. He felt her toned, yet soft thighs tighten around his hand as he wiggled his fingers, finding her soft flesh that was wet and warm. Instantly, the need to be in more than just her body began to tug at his heart.

He wanted her soul and her heart, if only she would trust him. With delicate swipes against her budding nub, Keyz softly kissed her, willing her to just let go.

"Daddy..." she moaned, catching on quickly. She tugged and pulled on his hair, while their tongues wrestled. She squealed in his mouth when he dipped his fingers inside of her, slowly working her mound. Her walls clenched his fingers tightly, causing his dick to swell up even more while her body shook uncontrollably.

"Fuckkk," he groaned, slowing down as he felt her pussy erupt, coating his fingers with her love. "Shit, I need to taste this pussy. Feel it, too."

No, no, no, she quickly thought as Elijah popped into her mind. His fingers nestled deep inside of her, Keyz sensed the change in her body. Not wanting to be selfish, he rested his forehead on hers waiting for her to tell him to stop, but she never did.

Like an animal hunting its prey, he forcefully took her

mouth again, her cries muffled while their tongues wrestled. With one knee, he pushed her legs open, feeling her juices run all down his hand.

"Can I, Cheeks? Can I taste this pussy, baby?" he asked, feeling her muscles contract, teasing him even more. His eyebrows furrowed like he was in pain waiting for her to say yes.

Relaxing her thighs, she nodded yes, no longer thinking about Elijah. After pulling her g-string down, he dropped to his knees slowly, placing both of her thighs over his shoulders. Her slick warmth greeting him as he dragged his nose up and down her center, becoming familiar with her scent that covered his nose.

"Hmmmm," he moaned, taking in the sweet smell her pussy emitted. He could taste her before his mouth even found her swollen bud.

"Now when daddy starts sucking on this pussy, I want to hear you scream out his name. You listening, Cheeks?" he spoke, his voice vibrating against her sensitive clitoris.

Nodding her head, Keyz's nose separated the lips of her vagina, caught up in her smell. It was different, intoxicating, and sweet. So sweet, he dove in without warning.

"Yeah, yeah, yeah. Uh, uh, uh…daddy," she called out, pleasurably wincing as all of her vaginal nerve endings started going wild.

Keyz replaced his nose with his thick, long tongue that slowly crept inside of her, her outer lips giving way while her inner lips welcomed him. With both hands now gripping Iyana's ass, Keyz went deeper and deeper into her tunnel, her juices running down his chin. He felt her quaking and shivering just that quickly, but he wasn't easing up. He was in his mode, being the pussy savage he was, but even madder someone else tasted her before him.

"Mmmm. Mmm. Mmm," he moaned repeatedly, hungrily sucking and swallowing her nectar that almost covered his entire face.

"Ahhh. Ohhhhh. Uhhhh," she uttered, pinching her nipples that ached, waiting to be sucked.

She did this until she felt the muscles in her stomach tightening again while her vaginal walls clenched his tongue.

His ass trying to kill me. Got damn, she cried to herself, tears falling down her cheeks as she fell over his left shoulder, gripping his back. Her nails were digging and clawing the more he tortured her repeatedly.

"Iyana… baby," he barely got out, feeling his skin break the more he attacked her. He tried to stop, but her slick nectar was just that good to him.

She continued to groan, mumbling unintelligibly the more his tongue created magic between her legs. He was relentless and her body was paying for it.

"Ouch! Shit, baby!" she screamed, holding on to him, unsure of what he was doing to her.

"Yeah, that's it," he growled, latching on to her exposed pinkish, brown pearl that peeked at him when he pulled back the hood.

"Uhhhhh. Ahhhhhh. Ahhhhh," she groaned, almost in pain, as she tried to will her blooming orgasm away.

How does he keep doing that? Shit! she thought to herself.

Iyana squirmed just thinking about his dick inside of her.

Just like that, her stomach tightened, welcoming another orgasmic eruption.

"Cheeks... baby," he said, breaking her down even more emotionally and physically. "What's my name? Tell me, baby. What's my name?" he asked repeatedly, raising her ass up as he licked up and down the crack of her ass. Almost to the point of insanity, Iyana screamed and cried as she rode his face.

"It's okay to cry for daddy, but talk to me, Cheeks. Let me know if daddy is pleasing you," he demanded, slurping and humming on her entire pussy.

"DADDDYYYYYYY!" she screamed for about ten seconds, spent, as she collapsed on his shoulder, while his stiff tongue remained lodged inside of her.

"Uh, uh, uh, uh. Fuck, baby," she panted, lying almost lifeless.

Hearing her call him baby, too, did something to him. His animalistic instinct to chase and conquer his prey had now subsided. Yes, he wanted to please her, but not hurt her as guilt crept in, feeling the weight of her tiny body on top of his.

"Iyana?" he whispered still between her legs. "Did daddy hurt you?"

"Un unnnn," she moaned, shaking her head.

Pleased with her response, he laughed, then kissed the inside of her thighs before he lifted them off his shoulders, placing her feet on the floor in front of him. Iyana felt loopy as he steadied her in his arms.

His soft curls and face were wet with sweat like the first time they met, causing her to chuckle as he smiled back at her. They stood silently, admiring each other. She felt free, while he felt emotionally naked, realizing what he had been missing out on all these years.

"You are so beautiful, Cheeks. You hear me?" he whispered, pulling her chin as she smiled.

No matter how many times he said it before, she never grew tired of hearing it leave his lips. Her dimples quickly emerged, making his heart race every time he looked at her. He remembered the murmurs about how dark she was, mad that it seemed to affect how she felt about herself once she finally broke eye contact with him.

"Cheeks?" he spoke authoritatively. "Don't do that. Look at me."

Iyana lifted her head, her grey eyes filled with sadness almost, breaking Keyz's heart. Without warning, he picked her up, rushing her to his bed wanting to fix it immediately. He knew what he had done or said wasn't the answer, but he felt like it was his mission to break those walls down that she poorly hid, no matter how much she pretended to accept herself.

"What... what... what are you doing?" she breathlessly panted as he dropped her on the bed, pushing her knees back against the bed.

Luckily, with her being a dancer, her agility allowed her body to bend at almost any angle with ease. Impressed with how agile she was, Keyz stopped and stared at her with her thighs spread open being held firmly by his large hands. She looked nervous and scared, but she never moved, trusting him to have his way with her.

"Marking this pussy. And the next time I say your ass is beautiful, believe that shit. I'on give a fuck what anyone else has to say," he said, dipping his face back down between her legs.

"Ahhhhhhh," she wailed before Keyz shushed her by sticking his fingers in her mouth. She could taste her sweet honey that was all over his fingers. Instead of fighting back, she wound her hips and twisted her nipples as he went back in to taste of her. The more she wiggled and grinded on his face, the more he went in, trying to outdo his earlier performance.

"Just wait until I get up in that pussy, Cheeks. Just wait," he declared in between sucks, as he assaulted her swollen pussy for the next two hours. Iyana was sore, but happier than she had ever been in her life, with no thought of Elijah or anyone else for that matter.

Chapter 7

Iyana left Keyz's condo, frantically driving home after missing seven calls and four text messages from Elijah. Keyz, unbothered every time her cell phone chirped, never once questioned who was trying to get in touch with her. Instead, he buried his face deeper and deeper, drowning the sound out with her moans.

Whenever she tried to take a peek at her cellphone, he would latch on to her sensitive nub, yielding her helpless under his spell. If that wasn't enough, he would push her thighs back even more, knees touching the sides of her head, as he slid his tongue up and down her tunnel to her ass.

It was like he was determined not to lose to whoever was calling her this late at night, now that he had her. By the time he was done, Iyana fell asleep on his chest, only waking up after he placed a warm washcloth between her legs, cleaning her sore and swollen vagina. She walked out promising to call him when she got home, as he got ready for his day.

Keyz, nigga, just go in and out, he said to himself as he pulled up to Myriah's house. Every now and again, he felt it was his responsibility to see how his lil' man was living even though he never questioned Myriah's parenting skills. It didn't hurt that she was getting almost five grand a month in child support either.

Myriah opened the door with a scowl on her face, only to be interrupted by Ishmael's excitement when he spotted Keyz at the door. Ishmael, when Keyz's was around, instantly became a daddy's boy.

At first, Myriah's feelings used to be hurt, but now she was over it. The only part she wasn't over was being labeled and rejected by Keyz like she was a disease, based on the way he treated her. She'd admit that they never said they were exclusive or in love, but deep down she always had hope, wanting to give Ishmael a loving, two-parent home.

"Daddy!" Ishmael screamed, throwing his arms around Keyz who lightly shoved Myriah to the side to embrace his son.

"Dang, Ish. 'Bout to knock your ole man down," he said, ruffling his wild curls on top of his head before he kissed him on the forehead. "You're good?"

Nodding his head yes, Keyz walked into the living room with Ishmael's head tucked underneath his arm. It was times like these he was glad she kept the baby, because this was a time he wasn't Keyz, one of the heads for C.U.B.

He was just Kaizer Paul, father to Ishmael Paul. At ten, he had expected him to be just a little taller given his own height by that age, but he was definitely going through a growth spurt since the last time he saw him. He smiled, looking at his soft, light brown eyes, wondering why his were so light, but understood genetics.

Having never met Myriah's family, he chalked it up to them coming from his mother's side of the family which was a still a sore spot for the both of them.

Yeah, this bitch living good off my money like a fucking Asian millionaire, he thought, glancing around at their Chinese theme living room.

It was adorned with gold and red, Chinese-like vases and miniature trees that sat on the marble tiled floor. The living room, equipped with an 85-inch theater style television, two maroon lounge chairs and a leather sectional sofa that comfortably sat ten people, set the atmosphere for movie watching and family time.

Then the walls, filled with pictures of Myriah and Ishmael at different points of his life, tugged at his heart, as there was none of him with his son. For a brief moment, he wondered how life would look if he did settle for less just to be with his son every day.

"Sup, Ish. You getting big on me, huh?" he said, kissing and rubbing him on the top of his head.

Just like his, Ishmael's soft curls were wild with a soft fade around the edges. Ishmael begged his mother to let his hair grow out wild and untamed, although his was a finer texture than Keyz' hair. It was not an easy decision as Myriah fussed but gave in, as they both loved the idea of them rocking the same hairstyle.

Sometimes Keyz would pull his up in a ponytail whenever he played basketball, but he wouldn't let Ishmael do it because he had that real pretty boy look that made him look soft at times. After a few scuffles, Keyz made sure Ishmael was good with his hands, even getting into a few fights at the park or in school to prove himself over the years.

Yet and still, he was still called a pretty boy and now that he was older, he enjoyed the girls that seemed to flock and follow him around. Myriah knew it was inevitable, but she told Keyz to start thinking of how to have that father and son talk men would have with their sons.

She wasn't so sure, but she thought she saw him more than once, wake up with a hard on. So far, he never asked but she knew it was coming.

"Naw, Dad," he grinned. "I've been big. Watch me pass you. Shoot, you better ask all them girls."

"Look here," Keyz said grabbing his chin. "I'll still beat that ass though. Don't play, and leave those fast behind girls alone. It's about books and ball. Later for that."

Ishmael knew his father was teasing as they started play boxing while Myriah went to the kitchen to finish cooking, but Keyz was serious about school. He refused to allow his son to follow his footsteps, let alone know what he was into.

"Gone get your stuff while I holla at your mama," he said before he ducked off into the kitchen to see what she was really up to, given what she had on.

"Alright, ole man," he laughed before he took off to his room.

Walking in, he watched Myriah with some booty shorts, juggling between the fruit she was cutting up on the kitchen island while she sautéed what looked to be tilapia, onions and bell peppers on the stove. Just like the living room, she spared no expense on the stainless-steel appliances, wine rack complete with red and white wines, and a few other things like a coffee expresso machine.

"Hungry?" she asked, raising her left eyebrow like "yea, I'm trying to be funny."

"Yea, but I figured Ish and I would grab a bite to eat and catch up before I make it to my mom's crib," he replied, choosing to ignore the sarcasm and that ass she had hanging out. "The twins and Ieasha been waiting on him. So, I figured I'd spend some one-on-one time with him before we get there to see what's up with him. His grades good and shit?"

Keyz never had to worry about his grades or behavior in school that much, but he remembered how things changed for him the older he got, trying to be the man of the house. The only difference was Myriah had a stable environment, just not a steady man, judging by the life she lived if he looked on her Instagram, Twitter or Facebook from time to time.

She had a group of friends that looked to be a bit racy, but he really wasn't trying to find out. He just wanted his son to be straight and for now, things were cool. The only reason he was even probing was, because his boys would tell him things from time to time. The way he saw it that was her man's problem. Not his.

"Now you know we don't have to worry about that, short of a few fights that I know he got in to prove to you he can fight," she said, washing the fruit she just cut up as she glared at him.

Ignoring a potential argument, he said, "Let's talk about this weekend so I know how I want to move around with him."

Keyz tried to remain focused, but she kept moving around to the point that even her breasts were jumping up and down.

Thick ass, he said to himself since she had definitely maintained her shapely full figure. His eyes traveled down to her breasts that were easily a double D that pretty much looked like two mini watermelons wrestling to get out of that tank top.

Keyz shook his head hoping Ish wouldn't go for that type of girl, but if his blood ran through his son's veins, he knew he would. Even if it was just to get his dick wet. Yes, she was a voluptuous woman who kept up her appearance over the years, but she also knew he was coming, choosing not to dress more appropriately. He was all for a woman loving the skin she was in, but that shit was ridiculous.

"What about it?" she asked until she gasped, covering her mouth. "Oh, I'm glad you asked. My sister is over the dance ministry at church and he has to perform tomorrow. Damn, I forgot."

"Dance?" he asked confused. "You mean like some ballerina shit? And what fucking sister?"

"No, Keyz. It's called mime and liturgical dancing, and never mind about my sister," she said, chuckling at how uncomfortable he looked. She didn't plan on introducing him to the family anyway.

In fact, part of her plan was for him to whisk Ishmael in after service started and tell him they could leave as soon as his performance was over. Nana and Papa B loved church too much to get up and leave early just to say bye to Ish. It took her a minute to devise a plan that wouldn't disappoint Ishmael or his aunt Iyana, who was his dance ministry teacher.

"Yeah, Dad. I don't be doing that girly stuff," he said, popping up in the kitchen with his overnight bag. "I dance with my arms and hands moving to the words on the song.

Oh, and with my face covered with this white stuff," he continued.

Rubbing his chin, Keyz pondered on what that looked like, but even more so, he wanted to know why she hadn't mentioned it the night before. He also didn't recall her having a sister all these years, but he shrugged it off, not wanting to stay any longer than he had to since he had plans today and wanted to get started on them.

Especially if the rest of his plans had to be cut it short in order for him to perform at church. Seeing how excited his son was about performing, Keyz decided to go along with it.

"A'ight, lil' man," he said, tossing him the keys to his truck.

"Go sit in the truck. Let me finish up with your mama right quick," he said, glancing at Mryiah who seemed like she was prepared to spar with him. Yes, she forgot but not intentionally.

Once Ishmael was in the car, Keyz decided to give it to her straight just so she knew why he was going to accommodate her request. He wasn't a religious man, couldn't be with the life he lived, but he feared and respected God enough to allow his son to have one.

"You think your ass slick, but you're not," he said, approaching her with a scowl on his face.

Keyz kept his itching hands in his pockets as he tried not to slap the shit out of her. Myriah knew she could never have him, but she took pleasure in controlling his time with his son. He had seen growth over the years, but she was still the same girl who only saw him for what he had, not who he was, and he paid for it anytime he had to deal with her.

"You knew he would get excited about that and that's cool,

but one day you will feel my wrath behind all the silly shit you do. How you know what I had planned?" he belted, standing almost on top of her.

"I don't, and I really don't care since you want to catch an attitude. So do something," she sneered, pushing her body against his just to get under his skin.

Without trying, he became aroused as she rubbed up against his dick, their eyes steadily locked in on each other. Keyz hated that Myriah could still get a reaction out of him when it came to sex. If she could fuck him without feelings he wouldn't mind, but he knew better after all of these years.

There was no need in playing himself or her, so casual sex was never an option. That and the fact that he feared her trying to trap him with a second kid. He'd only want another child if it was with his wife, preferably Iyana.

"I think I woke something... up," she whispered, poking her full, pouty lips out as his dick pressed against her stomach.

Her soft, light brown skin was flawless, as small beads of sweat lightly covered her exposed breast area from the heat in the kitchen. Their bodies were so close that even Keyz could feel the heat emitting off his body, secretly frustrating him because he wanted to put his dick inside her mouth.

"You ain't woke up shit," he lied, pinching her nipples that were full like large raisins, visible through the thin fabric of her tank top.

Damn, I hate this bitch caught me off guard like this, he said to himself, trying to adjust his midsection without stepping back, still twisting her nipple.

Myriah, looking like a lighter version of Toccara Jones from *America's Next Top Model,* had him and she knew it. Biting her lips that were tucked between her teeth, she knew she was breaking him down. She was over wanting him as the man in her life, but she enjoyed rendering him helpless when it came to their sexual chemistry that was almost like none other than *one other* person she fucked with hard.

Backing up, Keyz grinned, realizing how quickly Myriah got in his head. *Simple bitch,* he thought, remembering his son was outside waiting for him. No, he wasn't a toddler, but this was just another example of how being a mother was not always the priority she made people believe it was, if she was willing to fuck while her son was outside waiting in his truck.

"Myriah, my son outside waiting for me, so let me get at'chu later," he spoke coolly, releasing her nipple and willing himself to walk away.

"You mean *our* son," she said slowly, pulling his zipper down on his jeans before he could move.

Her eyes widened as his widened, and his pink, mushroom head popped out of his boxers, leaking pre-cum. His penis, so swollen and firm, bounced up and down in the air before she caught it with her small hand that was now wrapped around it.

"May I?" she whispered, seeking consent to take him in her mouth.

"Myriah, man. I got to go. Stop trip—" he said, before she dropped down to her knees unfastening his jeans, and then sliding him quickly into her mouth. Pulling it out and then bouncing it on her face a few times, she swallowed his entire his manhood as it hit the back of her throat.

"Fuck!" he belted, watching her deep throat him with 10 inches of nothing but dick.

Keyz was mad at himself for not stopping her, fearing that

Ishmael may come back inside, but also mad that she had him under her spell… again, just like old times.

Whenever he tried to pull himself out of her mouth, Myriah would grip his thighs, pulling him in deeper into her mouth, twisting her hands up and down his thick shaft. Struggling even more to stop what she started, Keyz lost it as she spit on his dick, quickly taking his it back into her mouth. She then dragged her tongue up and down until she inserted his balls in her mouth.

Keyz felt his legs growing weak as she jacked him off, while gargling the saliva she produced from sucking on his balls. He held on to the kitchen island, but wasn't sure how much longer he could take it before he busted in her mouth.

Got damn, he thought, ramming his pole roughly down her throat as he locked her head in with both hands. He was so rough, tears ran down her face, as he started pulling on the messy bun he managed to wrap around his fingers.

"Keep your head still, Myriah," he spat feverishly the more she gagged.

Trying to gain control back, Myriah started lightly humming on his member while Keyz threw his head back envisioning Iyana's mouth on him. He then grunted as his orgasm rose, remembering how Iyana tasted in his mouth.

"Ahh. Uh, uh, uh. Mmmm," he grunted, releasing his kids all over her face once he let her head go and pulled out. Instead of being angry like most women, Myriah was glad she still had it until she thought of the love of her life.

"You're a sick bitch, but that head… now that head is a fucking gold mine," he managed to say, catching his breath, before he snatched a few paper towels off the paper towel roll.

The One That Got Away

"Clean yourself up, then give the address to the church," he said after cleaning himself before he walked out the door.

∽

ONCE THEY GOT to his mother's house, Keyz took a quick shower. He hated Myriah was still able to have her way with him, so he needed to talk to Skebo about being the middle man whenever it came to getting and dropping Ishmael off.

"Boy, this one right here shole is handsome with all that wild and curly hair," his mother said, rubbing Ishmael on the top of his head.

"Yeah, he looks just like his mama though, honestly," he said, pushing Ish's head. "Thank God she ain't looking like Cruella with his pretty self," he joked as he plopped down on the sofa.

"Man, Dad, stop that," he pouted before he rested in his grandmother's arms. "Hey, Grandma Lacray. I miss you," he said squeezing her tightly.

"Uh huh. Grandma can't tell, with the way I have to beg you to come over sometimes, but I still love you."

She hugged her grandson back, swaying to music it seemed only the two of them could hear. Lacray was not the best mother, but she made up for it once her grandchildren came along.

If she wasn't dropping them off or picking them up from school when they needed her to, she was taking them to the movies or taking them shopping before she sent them back home to their parents. All of them had children except Sunshine, who was now pregnant with twins.

"Ishhhhh!" the twins yelled tackling their older cousin. Iesha, at age eight, tried to get a hug, pushing KJ off, while Kelon mushed her in the face.

"Hey! Hey! Y'all stop that! Ish will be here for the next few days. Y'all have plenty of time to play, fight and make back up. Now go on upstairs and make sure you have your sunscreen in your backpacks," she directed her grandchildren.

Keyz shook his head not believing that Shower had an eight-year-old daughter and Sunshine was about to be a mother. Keyon having twins wasn't a shock since he was a certified, yet reformed ladies' man. Keyz was glad he only had one instead of two from Myriah, since twins ran in their family on his mother's side. She had six brothers and sisters that lived in Cairo, Georgia. Two sets of them were twins, leaving his mother and Uncle Phil as the only single births his grandparents had.

"How far along is Sunshine, Ma?" he asked, knowing he might not get a chance to see her since she worked and was in college fulltime. Once she knew she was pregnant, Sunshine never looked back, as she wanted to graduate before the twins were born.

"I think about six months. Lord, that girl won't sit still for nothing! If her and Shower are not working on that party planning stuff, she's at the library working on a paper or something. Talk to her, Keyz. I keep telling her she needs to slow down."

No matter how old her children got, Lacray tried to make it up to them with her sometimes overbearing, parenting approach. Although most of what she said was true, Keyz tried to stay out of his siblings' business unless they were in trouble

The One That Got Away

or being taken advantage of by someone. Most times, Keyon was the troublemaker on and off the court.

One was a DUI that was thrown out his first seaons, while the other was a brawl in a bar after he and Chase received bad service in a restaurant.

His sisters pretty much had no drama. If they did, they usually could handle their own, choosing not to involve him because of the lifestyle he lived. After fifteen years, he'd never been shot or been arrested, which was saying a lot about how skillful and smart their organization was. It didn't hurt that they had most of the law on their payroll.

"So what's up with Oneal? He's been coming around?" he asked, deciding to probe just a little. He'd heard from Keyon that old boy and Sunshine broke up, but Keyon was a man's man. He didn't talk another man's business too much, but he let him know that he got with Oneal for how he tried their sister. Keyz was glad because Keyon's handling was throwing hands, while Keyz's way was throwing bodies—dead bodies.

"Well, between me and you," she whispered, looking around, "I overheard her telling Shower he's married. Now baby, I wasn't the best example, but that hurt your mama's heart really bad when I heard that. Sunshine's not like Shower, you know. She hides her pain while Shower will bust a nigga upside his head."

Keyz laughed, but his mother was right. Shower gave no fucks as he would say, when it came to dismissing a dude for misbehaving or not stepping up to meet her needs as a man should. Sunshine, although not a total pushover, always gave people the benefit of the doubt. This time, it's was costing her nine months of pregnancy and eighteen years times two, since she was carrying twins. As soon as he looked up, he saw his mother getting teary-eyed. It didn't happen much, but he knew she secretly beat herself about how she raised her children.

"Shit, Ma. Come here," he said, jumping up to hug her as she stood busily in the kitchen making sandwiches for the kids.

No matter how many times they all told her they forgive her, she would go off on a tangent about how she could have done this or that. There were days she wouldn't even take his money and not because it was illegal money. It was because she felt guilty and was trying to play catch like now.

Even now, she was making sandwiches to take with them, even after he told her food wasn't allowed inside Miami Seaquarium, but Lacray did it anyway. He loved his mother unconditionally and before he allowed her to beat herself off, he'd jump to reassure her he loved her.

"Ma, you did the best you could. I keep telling you that, woman," he said, picking her up in a bear hug as she stopped to dab her eyes.

"Boy!" she screamed laughing. "Put me down so I can finish cutting these sandwiches in half. Shoot, let Mama do what feels right. Never know. Maybe my grandbabies don't want that park food and these here sandwiches got the crust cut off with the good cheese. What they call it?" she asked snapping her fingers. "Gouda cheese! Yes, baby. Nothing but the best for my grandbabies."

Lacray smiled with her hands on her hips, proud of the sandwiches she'd prepared with rotisserie chicken she made the night before. They were not bourgeois, but she enjoyed spoiling them. Sometimes more than she should have.

"Ma, we got money and you know them kids are not going

The One That Got Away

eat it so, chill out. Order whatever y'all want once we get out there," he said kissing her on her cheek.

"Uh huh, all that kissing should be for that girlfriend I ain't never met," she shot back. "Instead of you worrying about these here sandwiches, worry about not bringing a girl over to meet your mama, and another grandbaby."

"That's because I'on have one. Man, fuck them hoes," he mumbled waving his hand off.

"Excuse me?" she asked, raising her eyebrows with her head titled to the side. Keyz's mouth had been filthy since he was a child, but Lacray didn't care how old he got, she made him respect her when it came to that. The twins were just as bad, even though they played like they didn't know they were cursing.

"Sorry, Ma," he grinned, showing his pearly white teeth.

"Sorry my ass. Let's get out of here before I whoop your yella ass and cut off all that damn hair of yours as a punishment. I see Ish not too far behind with that wild hair."

Not smiling, Keyz stood there like "yeah right" before he grabbed his cell phone to see if Myriah had texted the church's address. He was hot she let him get to her again, but it was the price he had to pay in order to be there for his son.

"Oh, Ma? Tomorrow we're going to church. Ish in some dance sh—thing, I mean," he said catching himself.

"Oh, yeah? He must be in one of those dancing groups that's really big at them churches now. Grandma can't wait, and I finally get to meet that heifer that gave birth to him," she said loudly, but not too loud since Ish was in the house.

She never wanted to make him feel that she loved him any less because of his mother, and how she shunned Keyz and his family all these years by not coming around. Even after Keyz found out about his son, his mother only allowed Keyz to come and pick him up from her house, even though they didn't live too far in the Coral Gables area.

"Yeah, I guess so," he replied with no enthusiasm.

"That means as soon as we get back, I gotta go and get the kids something to wear tomorrow," she said, packing their sandwiches and juice boxes in a thermal bag that doubled as a large, flowery purse.

Keyz smiled, looking at his mother who stood 5'5", just a little taller than his sisters. Her smooth, brown skin was soft, showing her age just around her eyes. She wore her thick, wavy mane in a bun, only letting it down to wash and curl it for a church event. With her capri jeans, denim button-down shirt and Michael Kors tennis shoes, she was cuter than most grandmothers at age fifty.

"Ma, you ain't gotta do all that," he said still smiling. "I heard people go to church wearing jeans and sh—I mean stuff."

"The hell you smiling for, boy? And yes, I do. Now don't think I didn't hear that mouth of yours. You do know it's not too late to whip your tall ass, Kaizer," she said wagging her finger at him.

"Now let's go," she announced, walking off towards the stairwell.

"Ish, Ieasha, KJ and Kelon," she yelled, "Let's go! We got another run to make after we leave the aquarium."

"What you need to do is go change them tight behind capri jeans you wearing, Ma. You're about to have me knocking niggas out about my mama and I'm not trying to hear all that 'mind my business 'cause I'm grown' stuff," he said, smacking her butt.

"Smack my ass again and watch me knock you the hell out," she said not caring that she cursed at him.

No matter how tough he was or feared in the streets, his mother treated him the same way she treated the rest of her children. Yes, Lacray was no longer the frail, vulnerable mother she was years before when Keyz had to become the man of the house. She was stronger and wiser and now required they all respect her as their mother.

"Ohhhh, she mad," he laughed before he walked out the door to his truck. He thought of how this day would be different if Iyana was there, but judging from his cell, he hadn't crossed her mind.

"Hmph. All that pussy I ate and she ain't hit a nigga up?" he muttered to himself as they all loaded up in his truck, with him feeling some type a way.

∼

Hours later

"Yo, papi', como esta?" Chico said, picking up on the first ring.

"Fool, speak English," he joked.

"No, you speak English. I'm Cuban, you dumb fuck," Chico shot back. "Anyway, what happened to your ass last night when you left that meeting?"

"Not shit. Just went home and chilled," he said.

One thing Keyz decided not to do was speak on Iyana with his boys outside of what he had already shared. Now, he wasn't ashamed of her, but she seemed unsure of what she wanted since he knew she wasn't used to dealing with a man of his caliber, be it a street nigga or not.

He may have started in the streets, but Keyz took business under the C.U.B organization and his two legitimate businesses, very seriously. Besides, he was okay with keeping her all to himself for now because once she became his girl, any free time he did have would be spent on and with her.

"You lying fucka," he heard Skebo yell in the background.

"Tell his bitch ass to go suck a dick," Keyz quipped. He loved Skebo and Chico knew it. Instead of relaying the message, he put Keyz on speaker.

"Tell his ass yourself. You're on speaker."

"Aye, where Sunshine?" Skebo asked as soon as he knew Keyz could hear him.

"Why the fuck you worrying about my sister? She's six months pregnant *with twins*. You trying to tell me something?" he asked with an attitude.

"Nigga, I know and naw, them not my kids. So the fuck what? I saw her lil' ass the other day at the bookstore. Her nerdy self had about ten books she was trying to carry, dropping them and shit. So I snatched them up and put them shits in her car."

"Oh, I hear you. Good looking out," he said, popping a piece of the rotisserie chicken and Gouda cheese sandwich in his mouth that his mother made earlier.

"Fuck you!" he teased.

Most of the C.U.B crew was scared of Keyz but Skebo had been his boy way before then. Only he and Chico could talk shit to him without consequences. He only showed up when it was time to take a nigga out and it wasn't with his hands. He either did it slowly through a method of torture from cutting, burning or choking, to straight up blowing a dude's melon wide open.

"Naw, fuck you," he said hanging up.

He knew Sunshine was grown, but he wasn't ready for his boy to be running up in his sister. Like a brother or not, Sunshine was his responsibility since the nigga she chose to lay down with wasn't shit. He didn't want to have to kill his best friend for not being a righteous dude when it came to his sister, so it was best he not even go there with her.

Chapter 8

"So you finally remembered you had a man, Iyana?" Sarcasm leaked from each word that came out of Elijah's mouth. Iyana could easily blame him for not coming to the show the night before, but deep down inside, she knew she made a conscious decision to go and see Keyz whether Elijah was right or wrong about not supporting her.

"Well, good morning to you, Elijah. How's Angel? You all had a good night? Mine was fine. Oh, and the show was great," she rambled, purposely, turning the tables on him, as she knew that last part about the show would shut him up.

Sighing, Elijah decided to start over. "Hey, baby. How was the show?" Although he didn't have to take the bait, he did, offering Iyana some relief while she got her lie together.

"It was actually great. The kids got four standing ovations and I was approached by a Broadway actor about possibly doing a show on Broadway," she bragged, although it didn't happen last night. He actually stopped by earlier that week to see his niece perform when he approached her. After being blown away with Iyana's skills and professionalism, he gave her the card for the director of *The Wiz*.

"Whoa...wow...wow, baby. That's pretty awesome!" He genuinely was elated that Iyana was actually getting the looks she deserved given all the hard work she put in into her craft over the years.

"I know. I got so caught up after he approached me, I left my cell phone in the community arts center. I guess we never know how important a cell phone is until we don't have one."

Iyana feeling her heart beat rapidly, began to fan herself as she stripped down preparing to take a shower once she got that lie out. Saturdays were her cleaning and 'going to the market' days and she was behind schedule. Reaching underneath to remove her g-string, Iyana gasped realizing she left it at Keyz' place.

"Baby, are you okay?" he asked sounding concerned.

"Yeah, Elijah. I just remembered I need to grade some papers for a quiz my students took on Wednesday. You know dancing is more than just dancing. We have to teach them the history of it, as well."

"Well, let me let you get back to that," he said no longer sounding upset with her. "I'm sorry, again, baby, about last night. I will make it up to you."

Iyana hated lying to Elijah, but that was a once in a lifetime opportunity that would never happen again. As far as she was concerned, she and Keyz' satisfied whatever sexual attraction they may have had over the years. Stroking a picture of her and Elijah on her bedroom dresser made her realize the history they had. She wasn't quite ready to give that up because Keyz had sucked the lining out of her vagina.

"It's okay, and I won't be long," she said feeling relieved that his anger had quelled.

"Will I see you and Angel today?"

"Yeah, I wanted to take her to the movies or Chuck E Cheese," he said, shushing Angel who screamed with excitement once she heard the plans he had for them.

"Wow," she chuckled. "I guess you are. She sure seems pretty excited hearing about it. Remember, I can't stay out too late. Tomorrow is second Sunday which is Youth Sunday and my kids perform tomorrow."

"Right, right. It is second Sunday. I just might surprise you and bring Angel," he said trying to be supportive, given how delicate things were between them now.

Iyana knew that, but she was okay with him not coming. Besides, she wanted to focus on her kids. Having Elijah there meant everything had to be perfect in her mind, not allowing God's spirit to move. She also had a brief solo no one knew anything about. She felt that she could perform her solo before God with ease if the pressure from Elijah's presence didn't weigh heavily on her.

"Elijah, it's not a surprise if you tell me," she laughed. "Look, let me get going. The sooner I get back, the sooner we all can spend some time together. You know I love Angel as if she were my own, but I need to be in bed by ten. Pastor Wallace got on me about my puffy eyes last week and I can't have that again," she said turning on the shower.

"Alright, baby. I promise to have you back in time for bed. And Iyana?" he spoke softly.

"Yes, Elijah," she said nervously biting her top lip.

"Tell Pastor Wallace you my woman. The only one who should be concerned with how much sleep you getting or not getting is me," he laughed, remembering how he kept her up most of the night last Saturday night.

"Touché, baby. Touché."

∼

"So you're not going tell her?" Sasha asked, smoking as she laid in the bed naked from hours of wild sex with Elijah.

"Tell her what? Seems to me if you're pregnant, your ass wouldn't be smoking," Elijah said. snatching the blunt from her before he pulled on it.

"Really, Elijah? The test is in the bathroom. The first time I mentioned it you were screaming abortion, crying about your little bitch, Iyana, and how us having another baby would hurt her. Then the next thing I know, you got my ass hemmed up in the shower eating this pussy like she don't have one. So fuck you!" she screamed, kicking Elijah in the back.

"Bitch, kick me again. What you need to do is get up and go see about Angel. Your ass was screaming all night long, all loud, and my damn baby probably didn't get no rest. See, it's going on nine o'clock. Ain't she hungry by now?" he asked, walking to the bathroom to shower.

"Look, you just worry about the one that's on the way and let me worry about Angel. I'm sick of all of this. I came to Florida hoping you remembered us and what we had. Not trying to build shit with her and treat me like the side bitch when I was around first. I mean do you see me?" she asked dropping the sheet around her.

Sasha was beyond beautiful. She was built like Kim Kardashian, only she got it honestly, with greenish hazel eyes. She dropped out her sophomore year at Howard after meeting Elijah, choosing to model until she found out she was pregnant. Embarrassed that she never graduated, Elijah told her he couldn't wife her but he would always take care of her, and that he did.

He had even begun to manage her modeling career, booking her gigs all over which allowed him to travel with her and Angel from time to time. Iyana, being the role model girlfriend, never questioned his time spent away from home, but he couldn't deny that he was in love with her. He just hated that he couldn't give her what she deserved, and that was an honest dude. Sasha made it too easy to fall into her pussy and falling is what he did every single time.

"Mommy, is daddy spending the day with us?" Angel asked, popping in right after Sasha put on her robe.

"Good morning, precious," she said, kissing Angel on both of her cheeks. "Well, we have to ask him as soon as he comes out. What would like to do today?"

"Well, Ms. Iyana had a dance show I missed. Can I go play and dance with her?"

It was no secret that Angel adored Iyana, taking her to the park, movies, shopping, and even dancing with her, as they watched videos on television. No matter how much Sasha told her that she was her mother, Angel still asked for Iyana whenever her daddy promised her they could spend time together.

"What did I tell you about asking about that black bitch?" she yelled as soon as Elijah walked out of the shower.

"Ahhhhhhhhh, Mommy. Ahhhhh, don't say that," Angel screamed and cried before Elijah picked her up.

"Get the fuck away from her," he yelled, pointing at Sasha who was obviously hurt that Angel and Elijah loved Iyana.

"Gladly. Fuck you, Elijah," she snapped as she walked out of the bedroom.

Chapter 9

"Awww, Chico! Damn! Shit!" Myriah screamed, clawing at the sheets and anything else she could grab on to, while Chico had her stretched out on all fours.

Unlike Keyz, Chico refused to lay his head in any other city, fearing for the safety of his family after all the dirt he'd done over the years. Yes, he was now sharing his throne with his protégé, Keyz, but it didn't lessen the fact that he remained a target.

Then there was the fact that he not only had Meka, but Myriah also who needed his protection. It didn't matter that no one knew about them. He still felt obligated to make sure she was safe at a moment's notice, so living out of town wasn't an option.

After slapping her ass twice, and watching it jiggle, Chico stopped moving as he rested deeply in her pussy. He could feel the muscles contracting firmly around his pole like a suction cup. Whenever she did that, all he wanted to do was lay in the pussy until money called. Truth is even Meka couldn't stop him from getting money even though Myriah felt she came second to her.

"Damn, girl. I love this shit, mami. I want to marry this pussy. Just give me some time, mami. Shit," he moaned.

Myriah lost it, throwing it back, meeting him thrust for thrust. Chico was playing dirty, but Myriah was obsessed with his dick and he knew it too. She craved it, bouncing up and down while he watched his coated dick plunge in and out of her. She also felt that the more she gave it to him, the least likely he'd go home and desire Meka. Most times, she was right.

"Ahhhh, mami', don't stop! Just like that!" he grunted feeling his nut rising as he held onto her hips tightly.

"Oh. Ah. Ohhh. Ah," she sang once he slowed down, releasing inside of her.

Myriah continued to bounce up and down, not wanting it to stop. She knew Chico had to go, but she wanted to savor every moment they had together. Easing himself out, Chico dropped down kissing her pussy from behind before he slapped her ass again.

"Ouch, Chico! Stop!" she whined, collapsing on the bed. She slowly looked over her shoulder watching his pink, semi-hard penis glisten from her wet center.

"Naw, Myriah. We're cuttin' it close. Ain't Keyz dropping Ish off tonight?" he asked, cleaning himself off, then throwing her a warm, wet washcloth he made for her.

He had a strange look on his face when he asked this, but most times he did. It was a look that Myriah was all too familiar with whenever he became paranoid about something. Him asking about Keyz was one of them.

"Nope," she said, flipping over to clean herself, deciding to ignore the look he was giving her. "He decided to take him to church tomorrow, but gosh, you know why I don't want that, Chico."

Myriah was tired of lying to her family, but Keyz was adamant that he was keeping Ishmael. The longer she stared at Chico, she felt her heart fluttering, wishing all their dirty secrets were out so they could just live their life.

"So what happened when he got here?" Chico asked, raising his right eyebrow, as he got dressed. He heard Keyz's version and laughed about it, but hoped his boy was lying. With an uncomfortable look on her face, she got up and went to the bathroom letting him know he hadn't.

Tugging on the bridge of his nose, Chico shook his head up and down realizing that maybe there was some truth to his Keyz story. *Yeah, I'm wrong, but she still pining over my boy* he thought as she made him cut off all of side pieces except Meka just too secretly be with her. Afraid of him leaving and not coming back, Myriah turned around to tell her ugly truth.

In her heart, she figured he knew anyway once he got quiet. She wanted this to work, so she decided to just tell him the truth. Especially since he still had Meka, who didn't seem to be moving out anytime soon.

"Chico, I—"

Whap!

He slapped her so hard, he sent her down to the floor, leaving a red handprint on her face. The last time he had hit her was after Keyz showed them nude pictures of her clean, shaven vagina after a Brazilian wax she sent to him from the spa. The longer he stared at it, the angrier he became as Keyz pretty much disrespected his heartbeat, although he didn't realize the offense he had committed.

"Chico! You said you would never—" she screamed holding her face, when he punched her two time, drawing blood that splattered on the floor.

Chico loved the ground Myriah walked on, but he was tired of being disrespected for loving the woman who was known as a whore amongst his crew. Besides, she was his first real love. He thought Meka was, but realized it was a relationship out of convenience since he got money with her family. It had to be or he wouldn't have fell for Myriah the way he did.

"Get'cho slutty ass up, bitch!" he yelled, dragging her by her hair to the bathroom.

"Nooooooo. Noooooo. No. No. No," she screamed, holding the top of her head as she felt her hair ripping from the scalp.

"Myriah," he gritted in her ear, still holding her by her hair. "If you scream that shit one mo' time, I'm kicking your fucking teeth out of yo' mouth, motherfucker."

Shaking her head no for him to stop, she coughed while crying uncontrollably. She couldn't explain why she did it other than her not wanting to accept Keyz's rejection yet again. She honestly was surprised he even allowed her to touch him, but it was definitely not something she planned. She only wanted to flaunt how good she looked and see if she could still lure him in, so once he lustfully looked at her, she went for it.

"You understand?" he asked.

"Now stand up and go wash yo' fucking mouth out with

this bleach!" he yelled, grabbing a small bottle she had underneath the bathroom sink.

Fearing for her life, Myriah gently took the bleach bottle from Chico, carefully closing her throat while she threw her head back taking the bleach in. It burned, but she was more focused on not ingesting it. Quickly spitting it out, he snatched her head back.

"Do it again and hold that shit until I say spit it out!" he demanded, glaring at her in the mirror as they looked at each other.

Tossing her head back once more, she poured bleach in her mouth holding it as she lodged her tongue against the back of her throat. After ten seconds, her tongue quivered from burning. Tears rushed down her eyes the longer she held it in. Before her tongue gave way, Chico released her head, telling her to spit it out.

"Ughhhh. Ugh. Ugh. Ugh," she coughed, inhaling the strong fumes from the bleach. She wanted to wash out her mouth with water, but feared being punished if Chico saw that as a way of not accepting the consequences for betraying him.

Reaching around her, he turned on the water, never taking his eyes off of her in the mirror. As the water ran, Chico began to gently rub her scalp, feeling nothing but shame for hurting her. Truthfully, it was the last thing he wanted to do, but he became enraged feeling like she was playing with his emotions. Especially with his friend, his brother.

"Rinse your mouth out," he whispered, rubbing her back as she put her mouth under the running faucet.

After a few coughs, he grabbed the mouthwash placing it in her hand. "Here, baby. I'm sorry, Myirah."

After a few swishes of mouthwash, Myriah held it in her mouth to relieve the overwhelming sting. She could tell Chico blacked out, but he took this to an entirely new level.

The longer she was bent over, the pain in Chico's heart intensified. He loved Myriah and knew she deserved better than what he or Keyz had offered her. If he could just give up his life with Meka he would, but business was business.

The C.U.B was deep in the game with Meka's family tied to the infamous Haitian gang, Zoe Pound. No matter how much he rationalized that in his head, or even attempted to explain it to her, he felt like less than a man. That, and the fact he was failing as a father since as the true love of her life.

"Do you love me?" he asked her, tenderly kissing the back of her head as he gripped her waist.

"Yes," she spoke barely above whisper, their eyes connecting in the mirror. He could see the love, tainted with the blood that dripped from her nose and lips. He was ashamed of his acts, but not of his love for her. He craved Myriah in many ways, but sex with her was mind blowing. He couldn't be in the room with her and not want her.

Pulling out his now erect penis, he tapped it on her lower back. He knew he was wrong, but he felt the need to reconnect with her sexually now that she was clean in his mind. Although illogical, her sins or indecent acts she committed with Keyz, were no more, and she was back to being his woman, his prized possession.

"May I?" he whispered bending over in her ear, feeling her body shaking out of fear.

"I'm sorry, mami," he repeated pushing up against as he dipped down to enter her.

Sadly, Myriah wanted to get back in his good graces, whispered yes before Chico re-entered her slowly. He hissed as he felt her warmth. He wanted to take care of her, even take care of Ishmael who they both knew at this point was really *his* son.

His soft hair and light brown eyes were traces of Keyz. Yes, Keyz was light skinned, but many would ask if Ishmael was biracial or of Hispanic descent and Myriah would just brush it off. If they asked Keyz, he would just say he had pretty boy genes.

Whenever Ishmael would visit his home or hang out at a C.U.B family function, Chico made sure to spend as much time with him as possible, even naming himself the godfather, which Keyz gladly obliged him when he did.

Yet and still, that still wasn't enough. He knew they would be exposed one day, but he wasn't prepared for that. He was running a million-dollar drug empire and he wasn't ready to kill or be killed. Not for something he could resolve another way. At least to him.

"Please have my baby?" he asked, guiding himself in and out of her. "Give me another one. One we can raise together."

He figured that might be the fix since he knew Keyz didn't want Myriah. He could blame it on a drunken night, anything, but not lying to him all of these years. He knew Keyz would be mad, but not for long since they shared plenty of hoes over the years.

He wasn't worried about Meka because she wasn't so innocent herself after reading a few text messages from random dudes about how they hooked up. So either she would accept it or walk the hell away.

He figured if she did that, it was her leaving and not him.

If her peoples wanted to die behind her rash decision to go, he would be ready to go war, but not because he fell in love with another woman.

"Yes," she moaned, gyrating her hips up and down to receive him, as their eyes remained connected in the mirror until he turned her head, kissing her bloody nose and mouth.

The metallic taste from the blood coupled with mouthwash coated his tongue, reminding him yet again the demon he was because of his love for her.

"You just drive me so fucking crazy, Myriah. Why would you do that, mami? That's my fucking brother. A brother I would die for but baby, he ain't checking for you like that. So, let papi fix it. Give me another baby. Let me be the one to give you the world. Fuck Meka. I'll figure that shit out, I swear I will," he begged, pumping in and out of her.

"Promise?" she panted as he watched her breasts bouncing up and down as he dug deeper inside of her.

"Yes, baby," he growled, sucking and kissing on the back of her neck.

Myriah then opened her mouth pulling Chico's waiting tongue even deeper in from behind. She was ready for love, but was he serious this time she wondered. This was their cycle. He would come, fuck, make promises, get mad, fuck again and make more promises. She never questioned his love, only his lies, but who was she but an even bigger liar. So, she took what he gave her hoping, just hoping things would be different next time.

"Uh. Fuckkkk!" he grunted, releasing inside of her with locked knees as he literally stood up inside of her. "That's it right there! That's my motherfucking seed right there!"

The One That Got Away

Satisfied that they were good and, hopefully, had just created a new life, Myriah turned around once he removed himself as they both frantically apologized to each other.

∽

"Welcome home," Meka spoke, sitting in the dark drinking a glass of Pinot Noir.

"Home, maybe. Damn sure not feeling welcomed. What's up? Why you sitting in the dark?" he asked tossing his keys on the kitchen counter, hoping she'd cooked.

"Not shit and no, I didn't cook. Figured you ate plenty wherever you been," she said sitting on the sofa with her legs tucked underneath her.

Meka was a sight to behold, and had been since they day he met her at Waffle House one night after leaving the club. She was with her girls who were laughing loud, obviously drunk, but not her. She was nestled in the corner of the booth quiet and crying. Chico, exiting the bathroom, saw her and immediately wanted to know why everyone was laughing, but pain reeked from her face and body language.

"May I?" he asked extending his hand to her.

"Damn, Meka. You know this fine ass Puerto Rican?" one of her friends belted, eye fucking him while the others laughed.

"Cuban and no, she doesn't," he said with his hand still extended.

Unsure as to why he wanted her, she cleared her throat asking for her friend to let her out.

"Girl, don't go too far. Your food almost here!" one of the other girls yelled as he lightly pushed her to an empty table and chair. The C.U.B crew was in there heavy with different women, but Chico was alone that night. He was tired of waking up to random women and was fine grabbing something to eat before they went home.

He watched this tall, elegant cinnamon-colored woman who looked as if she'd just left a gala in a cream, sheer beaded dress that snuggly hugged her body slightly below her knees. Her short, honey blonde texturized hair was something he wasn't used to, but turned him on the more he watched how graceful she was. Her crew may have been loud and visible, but she wasn't.

"Fuck that food. Eat with me," he blatantly said, catching her off guard.

He reminded her of her uncle and two older brothers who were men of a few words, but demanded respect whenever they did speak. Her family was tied to the infamous Haitian Miami gang, Zoe Pound. Meka was brought to the U.S. being raised by aunt and uncle.

Her older brothers were already here, yet struggled because of their thick accent and broken English. Picked on like most kids who couldn't speak English, Chico immediately knew how they felt experiencing it himself when he first came to the US. After joining the family's criminal enterprise, life seemed to get better for all of them except Meka who was barely allowed to date.

"Man, so it must be fate," he said after he ordered his food, telling the waitress to bring hers to their table.

"Why you say that?" she asked, still sniffling, although he never asked her why she was crying.

"Come on, girl. Look around. Who the fuck you think we are?" he asked not used to people not knowing who he was.

"Honestly, I don't know. Shit, I barely date, let alone go out which is why I'm upset. The one night I can enjoy myself, my brothers fucking with me about what I'm wearing, who talking to me and why. Shit like that is aggravating," she laughed out of frustration.

The One That Got Away

"Yeah, mami. I see what you wearing. The shit is hot. I figured you came from a wedding that served some bad fucking food to end up here, but they not wrong. I got two sisters who will get a nigga fucked up quick for coming at them wrong. Can you blame them?"

"Actually, a bridal shower and fuck them. I'm tired of that. They can be with as many girls as they want and put me in the middle of their drama, but I can't. Whatever," she said dismissively waving her hand. "You see the girl over there with the red, sheer dress on with her breasts on display?" she asked pointing behind him.

Chico glanced over his shoulder making eye contact with her, as she quickly looked away smiling.

"You mean the one that's been eye fucking me since I got here? If so, I see her. That's one of your brothers' ole lady?" he asked, shaking his head as their food was placed on the table.

"Yep, and it ain't about love," she said, gulping down the glass of water the waitress put on the table. "Nah, it's all about power and joining forces with her family which means more shit for my family." Chico understood power, but was impressed that she wasn't as he watched her tossing hot sauce on her steak and eggs.

"Yeah? Then imagine how much more y'all could have fucking with C.U.B.?" he asked, trying to see if she really didn't know who he was.

Chewing her food not flinching when he mentioned his organization, Chico smiled. He wasn't looking for commitment, but she definitely had his attention.

"Hey, Chico? We're about to roll. You're good?" Skebo asked, rubbing his hands together as he admired the brown beauty that caught Chico's attention.

"Are you good?" he asked Skebo, pulling up his shirt to make sure his boys were strapped. This time of night, in the area they were in, there was nothing but jack boys trying to hit a few licks in late at night

165

on the unsuspecting or inebriated crowds that grabbed a bite to eat after the club.

"More than good," Keyz responded, showing one semi-automatic pistol in his waist under his Versace top. "You stay up, and shorty with the blonde hair?"

Turning to face him, Meka gave him the most menacing stare he'd ever seen on a soft, well put together woman. Her first instinct told her to ignore him, but the boss in her said 'fuck it.'

"Looks like you the one who's short," she said, patting her beaded purse before she revealed that she was carrying two small .22s, a pink and silver one.

"Awww, nigga. She ready!" Skebo yelled as Chico sat back ready to fuck her in that booth.

"You'fd ready?" Chico whispered, getting her attention before he tossed a few twenty dollar bills on the table motioning for them to leave.

Ready to be rebellious, Meka and Chico slipped out of their booth barely making it to his truck where he partook of her fruit. He wasn't concerned with being seen as he had illegal tint that every law enforcement officer knew not to pull him over for because of who he was, and bullet-proof windows.

Chico was wild and dangerous, but particular; this was not him at all. He tossed and passed over women all day, but something about her raw and natural beauty coupled with her ruthless edge made him break all of his rules.

Halfway in the back seat, Chico threw both of Meka's thighs on the head of each seat as she rested her back on the second row. The longer he stared, the more he watched her honey run down the crack of her ass as he spoke sweet nothings to her in his native language.

Who is this man that got me about to bust and he hasn't even touched

The One That Got Away

me? she asked herself, breathing heavily as he kneeled down to inhale her womanly scent.

"Mmmmmmm, mami. You smell so sweet," he professed, dragging his nose lightly between her aching center.

Chico's hardened member pressed firmly against his jeans, wanted in, but he wanted to please her first. Especially after hearing how she felt like her wants or desires didn't matter. As Meka's nub tingled from his breath that gently invaded her secret garden, she squirmed willing him with her eyes to taste her.

Chico detected the sense of urgency as her eyes peeked at him over the top of her dress that clung tightly against her thick thighs. Without warning, he indulged like his life depended on what she expelled from her body.

"Ahh. Uhh. Mmm," she groaned from deep within, as he French kissed her satin, slick tunnel.

Meka tugged and pulled at his soft curls uncontrollably, as orgasmic waves drifted from her abdomen down. Lifting her ass, Chico dipped into her heated abyss that hungrily received him.

"Yes! Yes! Yes!" she chanted as she arched her back, unable to see his face, but fully enthralled with the pleasure his tongue and lips gave.

Once she felt the euphoric waves subsiding, as she rested in his hands hoping he wouldn't drop her.

He didn't that night, but five years later, they were two different people. She was power hungry, wanting something Chico couldn't give because he gave it to someone else who saw him as a man. He wasn't sure when he fell out of love with her, but it was getting harder to ignore what he needed the most. Sadly, Meka could careless as long as the money kept coming in and he kept coming home.

Chapter 10

"So my bestie is back and you couldn't call nobody?" Sky yelled like she was on a playground outside, with her usual loud, unfiltered self. "Yi, you tripping. I see how you moving now. All college educated with ya boo thang who think he doing something. Girl, I see you, but I'm going to let you make it because you my girl and his ass temporary."

Sky's rants were a great exaggeration, as over the years they talked at least twice a month, about nothing and everything simultaneously. And whenever they did, it was as if time stood still, as if they had just spoken the day before because that is what true sisterhood was to them.

By this time in their lives, they had hoped to be married with children, but life as they knew it was chasing career goals while still trying to figure out this love thing. Iyana had Elijah while Sky, to Iyana's knowledge, wasn't interested in dating.

Sometimes leaving Iyana to question if Sky was batting for the same team. Sky being Sky was open to a lot of things, but she quickly let her girl know being a carpet muncher wasn't on that list.

"One, tone that all that down. Damn, Sky! You're still loud and, two, Selena said she hasn't seen her only begotten daughter in almost a year. Really, Sky? You know I've been so caught up since I've been back that my black ass didn't even notice it."

"Chile, Selena needs to stop. I don't come home like that because she hates to cook. Like, what I look like coming home just to cook a whole heap of food and whatnot, when I can stay in my humble abode and cook for one?" she quickly replied.

Although Iyana was her only friend, even her friend thought she was a traveling nurse when she really was secretly employed with the DEA. She had an assignment that would be bringing her to Miami in a few weeks which was the real nature for her call.

"Oh, I know. Justin Bieber got you all tied up in his polygamous world. His pale must be packing, baby, 'cause the things you tell me about him and Sasha and the little one, no black woman is going for. Bitch, how are you letting him try you like that repeatedly?" she asked, referring to Elijah requiring Sasha to move to Florida once Iyana decided to go back home to Miami.

"Honestly?" she asked, dreading this topic.

"Naw, bitch. Tell a lie," she quipped. "Of course, honestly. I hope you're not on that sad 'whoa is me shit' because, Iyana, I would date you if I was a carpet muncher. Plus, you're one of the smartest, kindest and most compassionate people I know on earth since Jesus! Do I need to come there and slap a bitch because I'll do it?"

"And lose that wonderful traveling nurse job? Ah, no thank you. It's really not as bad as it looks. He just wanted Angel close by. You know Elijah. I told you he hates his father and he is trying to prove he is a much better dad than the one he's got. I can give really give two fucks about Sasha, truthfully. She stays on her side of town and I stay on mine. I see Angel when he has her and that's about it. The rest of my focus is helping Nana with Papa B, and my career. So if Sasha and Angel can occupy his time while I'm doing my granddaughter duties, so be it. I don't give a shit."

"Awe, shoot, now! Miss Thing has picked up a potty mouth! It's about time. Now let your boyfriend know the bestie is coming so he can get missing for a long, long time," she belted. "But on a serious note, how is Papa B?"

Feeling overwhelmed with the "what ifs" and "how long", Iyana took a deep breath before responding. She was one to never complain, but this was Sky, her confidant, and best friend. If she could tell anyone, she could tell her.

"I'm scared. Most days he's lucid, but when he's not, it's a nightmare. He's combative and mean and confused. He can overpower Nana when he is really irritable, and even when he is not, she can barely rest worrying about him. So, whenever I am on that end during the week at the community arts center, I stop through, cook, do laundry and tidy up a bit."

"Shit, what about Myriah? She's not helping?" Iyana didn't want to talk about Myriah since they had been getting along, but Sky had no qualms about disclosing her dislike for her. Even after she told her Myriah had somewhat matured over the years.

"Being Myriah, but I must say, she is a great mother. Ishmael is really getting the best childhood any child could ask for," Iyana said as her voice trailed off wondering when her time would come.

"Mm hmm, still defending her, but it seems like someone has the baby blues. Don't think I didn't pick up on the lil' shift in your mood when you brought up your nephew. Shit, we still young and we have time. So what's really up?"

"No baby blues. Just wondering where does all of this lead me. I mean five years in and we are no closer to being married or having kids and, truthfully, I think I'm over it. I only think about it when I'm around the kids at church or the center. I sort of wonder how life would be if I went home to my own one day, but we have Angel—"

"Who belongs to him and Sasha, Yi," she replied, cutting her off. "Yeah, you love her, but there's nothing wrong with wanting your own. If anyone deserves to have it all, you do," Sky spoke softly. "So anyway, let's talk. Tell me more about Papa B. I can call up a few of my old co-workers from Mercy Hospital that also do private duty to help out. You know, to give you more support."

After high school, Sky really did become a registered nurse, but grew bored easily like she always did as a child. Watching *Cops* and other shows, she one day hoped she could work in the criminal justice field.

On a whim, after watching a few cops who came in to interview a gunshot victim, she went home and went online and saw that the Drug Enforcement Agency was hiring. After a

The One That Got Away

rather arduous process of interviews, lie detector tests and a physical, she was offered a job and had been with the DEA for four years now. With Iyana being gone and her not having many friends, her emergence into this underground world was easier than she thought.

There were times hiding it from her mother and Julio were tough, especially since he seemed to live on the other side of the law, but she was able to skirt their probing quite easily being the busy body that she was anyway.

"It's okay. It's just... just... like what if he dies? I mean I know one day we all will, but I'm not ready for that, Sky," she said, voice quivering.

"Hey, no talk about death, Yi. He's strong and so is Nana. Let me put in a few calls and I will pay for some private duty care," she said, taking over before Iyana had a meltdown.

"Damn, I see we need a bestie day," Sky said trying to comfort her. "Since I'm coming in a few weeks, let me see what we can get into. Jet skiing, line dancing, that Painting with a Twist shit everyone doing. Hell, we can even go to the Keys for a few days. Ain't that Octoberfest Pride Day event coming?"

"Seems like to me someone's keeping up with the carpet munching events," she laughed.

"Fuck you," Sky shot back.

"No, thank you. This over here is well taken care of. No muncher openings over here. So either you tell me who *she* is or why you don't have a man."

Sky laughed, but shamefully, she fell in love with a guy who she was supposed to be taking down as one of her targeted assignments. His name was Trevor, but on the streets he was

173

known as Shyne. He was the head of one of the biggest gun cartels in the east from New York all the way down to Florida. It started out as a business arrangement.

She was undercover and they knew Shyne's weakness was beautiful women. Instead of trying to set up him buying and selling illegal weapons, they sent in their best, and their best was Sky. No man could deny her and she was one of their sharpest agents. One thing they never factored was Sky and Shyne falling for each other, which was something no one knew about and Shyne not knowing her true identity.

"When I get one, you'll know. This is not about me, though. This is about me trying to spend some time with my friend."

The more Sky talked, the more she laid in her empty bed thinking about Shyne. He was this tall, yet stocky buttermilk specimen, as he took pride in his body, working out almost three hours each day, then on the gun range, faithfully, for at least one hour thereafter.

Even his dreads, due to his meticulous nature, stayed neatly twisted complementing his milk chocolate eyes that seemed to melt her whenever she got caught up in them. After taking her assignment, Sky learned that he was obsessed with guns since he was a kid, watching shows like *Batman and Robin* and even westerns like *The Lone Ranger*. He would come home every day from school with his granny, sitting front and center watching her favorite westerns.

After a quick snack and homework, Shyne and his younger brother would watch a western with her until she allowed them to go outside to play. New York was tough, so they had to go together.

The One That Got Away

Unlike Shyne, his younger brother wasn't into sports or horse playing, so as they got older, he found himself back in the house with granny and their mother after a long day working at the laundromat. Their father, Trevor Senoir, was serving a life sentence for assassinating three of the largest drug cartels' men in the business, before he took over when they were three and four.

Their mother, Monique, never loved again and visited him faithfully at Florence Federal Prison in Florence, Colorado at least once a month. Shyne, who worshipped his father, went with her, while his younger brother had pretty much abandoned the family, moving immediately after high school to Florida with a few college friends.

Shortly after he left, both their mother and grandmother were killed in a car accident. Although tragic, this loss brought Shyne and his younger brother closer together as adults visiting each other a few times a year.

"Sky, you don't have to come to Florida. Enjoy yourself. The same ole stuff is here. Besides, I know how stressful work is. I mean, I been home almost a year and you be so busy. Don't waste it on me. I just had a moment. Let me get myself together," she sniffled, walking into her office as she rambled on, knowing Sky was ignoring her.

She was even more upset with all the assignments she still needed to grade as well as creating the choreography for the next production at the community arts center.

Trying to take time off now just wasn't good for her even though she really did need it. She purposely didn't tell her about Keyz because even *she* didn't know what that was about.

So, there was no need in even bringing it up. Growing tired of her excuses, Sky nearly lost it.

"Look! Shut that shit down, look at your calendar, and see if we can clear a week for ourselves. I'm coming, so get ready and tell Casper I'm coming," she snapped although she was trying to be funny.

"If Elijah knew you called him all those names—"

"He wouldn't do shit," Sky snidely replied, swinging her legs around the bed wishing Shyne was there between her legs.

Sky tolerated Elijah, but she felt Iyana was selling herself short because of her insecurities about her skin color, and never feeling like the girl all the guys wanted growing up. Of course, over time, she embraced who she was, but those insecurities would pop up from time to time, and Sky felt Elijah used that to his advantage.

"Oh, shit. Damn, I miss you," she said smiling. "I almost forgot how ignorant you were. Ignorant but funny, and he wouldn't do shit but ask me how I ended up with the most ghetto Spanish girl as my best friend."

"Fuck him, and what's ignorant is your man thinking his ass not black with that kink in his hair. Don't get me started, Yi. You know once it's on, I can't turn it off. So make sure Casper get missing like a friendly ghost!"

She laughed, tickled with that nickname. "Bitch, stop calling him Casper? Bye, I'm gone. I often wonder why you still have a job with your no filter having self."

"Well, I do, and their ass can get it, too! Don't start with me. You know how I am about you," she laughed.

"Yes, I do, and thank you," she replied quietly with her

eyes closed, envisioning Keyz' mouth on hers and that much-needed vacation.

"For what?"

"Just being you and letting me be me. Love you, bestie," Iyana told her, smiling.

"Uh huh. You acting a little' moody over there, but anything for my bae," she teased.

Sky could tell Iyana needed her and she needed Shyne. The moment she touched town, she was making plans to see him. Not for sex, but to be near him. To hear his voice and feel his body heat. Shyne was tough, but known to be a loner. His closest friend, Gunna, lived in Atlanta, Georgia, only seeing him once a month for business. So even Gunna knew very little about Sky and he wanted to keep it that way.

Slapping her desk, Iyana stood up to shake all of her emotions off. That pep talk she got from Sky is exactly what she needed. She also was going to call Keyz to see if they could meet up. She was tired of being in denial and wanted to see if he really wanted what he said he wanted.

She wasn't sure what he did for a living, but at this point, she didn't care. She was used to being judged and didn't want to be a hypocrite. She figured whatever it was, he would tell her in time.

Yeah, the heart wants what it wants and right now, something is telling me it's Keyz, she thought to herself.

"I got you, bae. So let me finish grading these papers. Check your email later for those dates. Oh, and let's do something exotic in the Caribbean. You know, like Stella?"

"Who the fuck is Stella?" Sky asked rudely. "Trick, you went and got a new bestie besides Rickey's swing low sweet chariot ass? I ain't fucking with no new friends even though Rickey seems hella cool, but I still need to approve him being in the sistah circle."

Shaking her head, "Girl, what circle? Wait, never mind. Check your email one day this week. I need some time to look at my schedule with the center trying to prepare for the next show. I gotta go."

"Yeah, you know, bih. Later."

Hanging up, Iyana laughed, but was grateful for Sky's brazen and protective presence in her life. Any mention of a new friend always ruffled her feathers, but Iyana loved Rickey to the core and wanted both of her friends to get along so well. She figured they'd invite him too, but really needed to make sure Nana and Papa B were good since he went by there from time to time whenever she was busy.

Realizing she hadn't eaten, Iyana decided to take a walk to the government center downtown to grab a salad from this shop that specialized in any kind of salad from buffalo chicken strip salads to jerk chicken salads. She never had to watch her weight but seemed to find herself eating a salad more times than not just because.

Maybe because whenever she cooked, it was a heavy meal for Nana and Papa B, or even Elijah on the days he wanted something special like pot roast or oxtails. Again, he wasn't claiming his blackness but he ate like a black man every chance he got.

"Rickey, if anyone is looking for me, I'm going to grab a salad up the street. You want anything?"

"Bitch, no. Do I look like a need a salad?" he laughed with poked out lips, as he spun around showing off his laced and

The One That Got Away

layered, burgundy pencil skirt and white, fitted button shirt that showed his nice C cup breasts.

"A yes or no will suffice, Rickey. Bye," she waved before leaving out of the building.

Besides Iyana, Rickey was the only other African American dance teacher selected to teach at Miami-Dade College, which is how they met. So they pretty much stuck together outside of the classroom whenever they were at work, which led to a few happy hours afterwards. Before long, they were like Siamese twins except she never brought him around Elijah.

No, she wasn't homophobic, but Rickey had no qualms about telling Elijah about himself. Rickey felt like black men already had it hard for them to be hating on each other. Especially him, living the life as a black woman, fabulously embracing his transgender transformation.

"May I have a number… hmmmm," she said tapping her chin, "A number four?"

"A number four, Asian Chicken salad, and what else?" the cashier asked with her eyes fixed on the man standing behind Iyana.

"A date," Iyana heard from behind as a chill ran down her spine. She didn't even have to see him because she felt and smelled his presence. It was Keyz.

The shock on the cashier's face matched Iyana's, although Keyz was unable to see it. He could tell he had her, as he watched how tensed her shoulders became as she scratched the back of her neck.

Damn, she still scratches the back of her neck? he thought to himself.

"Ma'am, I think the gentleman behind you is talking to you," the cashier pointed out with wide eyes. You could tell she was a young girl mesmerized with Keyz's boss like swag. He was one of the cockiest guys Iyana ever met and she craved his attention whenever he was around. Today was no different, even though it was unexpected.

"She knows. Her ass wanna act slow like a disabled motherfucker," he whispered, placing his hand on her lower back.

"So you let a nigga suck that sweet pussy and just get ghost on him, Cheeks?" he hissed in her right ear. "Fuck that salad and cashier. Answer me before I snatch you up and take you back to my spot." Before she could protest, Keyz dropped a twenty-dollar bill on the counter as the cashier stood in awe, almost forgetting what she was doing.

"Add a number six, Philly cheesesteak salad, and two bottles of water," he said, taking over after she lost her voice.

Rendered almost helpless in her presence, Keyz reached down for Iyana's hand as he pulled her back into his lap at a nearby chair with a table that seated two.

"Ummm, excuse me. We are in public," she countered, trying to get out of his lap.

"Cheeks," he spoke with authority. "If you get your ass up from off my lap, you're going o have problems. Keyz don't like problems. Keyz takes care of problems."

"Keyz?" she asked with a confused look although she was very aware of his street name. In this setting, he wasn't daddy, making her feel some type of way.

"Oh, Keyz that nigga you don't want to meet. In fact, act like you don't know him," he said reaching in to kiss her shoulder that he then caressed with his lips. "Now, I'm daddy," he whispered, causing her to shiver.

She wasn't cold, but the moment she felt his lips against her skin, goosebumps appeared. An image of him taking her right there in front of everyone was turning her on. Keyz didn't know it, but Iyana really was a lady in the streets but a certified freak in the sheets.

She was an oral specialist, as Elijah would call her, bringing a man down to his knees in an infant-like state with her head game. Pleasuring her man got her hot and she was ready to ride him right there.

Rubbing her shoulders with crossed arms trying to shake it off, Iyana sat straight up giving her body some distance from his. If not, she was about to commit an indecent act right then and there.

"Fine," he said running his hand down his mouth and chin with an intense stare at the side of her head. He was used to being chased, not being the chaser.

"Fine, what?" she quipped, immediately staring at him with her piercing grey eyes, which he found out he loved to get lost in that night he had her bent up like a pretzel in his bed, devouring her flower.

"A'ight, I'll fuck with you," he said, gently lifting her up as he stood up next to her.

He knew he wanted Iyana and he also knew she would someday be his, but he wasn't up for it today. He needed to make a few changes with the cigar lounge, holler at his mother about maybe running one of his businesses, stacking his money so he could plan a timeline of when he was getting out the game, then meet up with Ish. That's why he was downtown that day. He needed to get his permits updated with his mother's information and pay his taxes.

With all of that on his plate, he took her rejection as a good sign since he was far from accomplishing that part of his life that she didn't need to see. He never told her what he did, but she also didn't ask.

He figured he'd share once that part of his life was behind him and he could take on a wife and kids like the Cosby's, a family on one his favorite re-run shows. Now, he wasn't naïve. He knew he had a line of enemies, but once he was out, those enemies would be out too; out like dead out with no living witnesses.

"Touchy, aren't we?" she asked, slightly feeling shunned as he stood there now with his arms crossed, his cologne lingering in the air. It was the same smell that emitted from his body the other night, a smell that sent her mind back to where his tongue found pleasure within the folds of her center.

Shit, Iyana. Stop it! she said to herself, rubbing her thighs together.

"Naw, I ain't touched you the way I want to yet, but we're good for now," he said, refusing to give her eye contact.

"Number four and number six with two bottles of water!" the cashier yelled with the hugest grin like a star-struck teenager.

"I'll holla," he said as he stepped up to grab his lunch, thankful their food was separated into two different bags.

Before Iyana could find the words to express how much she wanted him to stay and maybe have lunch with her, Keyz was out the door, leaving her to her thoughts and aching center.

"Well, if you don't want him... I do," the cashier said following him as he barged out the door with the meanest scowl on his face.

"Ugh," Iyana growled, pouting as she grabbed her food.

∽

"UN UH, girl. What's wrong, boo?" Rickey whispered as he peeked into her office no more than two seconds after she sat down to start eating. His eyes quickly shifted to the left and right down the hall to see who could have made her mad since he thought they were the only two there.

"Why does something have to be wrong, Rickey?" Iyana replied, sifting through her salad while her appetite began to wane.

She had been sitting there ignoring Elijah's text messages with hopes of getting at least one of them from Keyz since he departed so abruptly. With each passing minute, those deep-rooted feelings of inadequacy crept their way inside her mind, reminding her of all the reasons she didn't take him seriously years ago. Based on his behavior today, it was just a game to see if she would just let him have his way with her. To her, it was more. Sadly, part of her knew she never gave her all to Elijah because he was competing with a ghost. A ghost known as Kaizer Paul who'd never touched her until recently, and whose touch continued to linger, even in his absence. Before Rickey walked in, Iyana's mind was doing a serious number on her.

Bitch, he doesn't want your black ass. You're just something for him to do.

Why would he want you when he could have anyone? Especially someone who complements him in public and can match his swag.

Iyana, you just lost your real shot of finally being with a man, a real man who doesn't mind being a black man.

You're so dumb. Now he thinks you're a live ass thot playing like a good girl.

Frantically, Iyana went through her phone, deleting any trace of Keyz from her life. There weren't many, but they all meant something to her and just like that, they were nothing. He said he'd holla and even that wasn't promising, so she figured why wait. If he could easily dismiss her now, he could in the future and she wasn't strong enough for that.

"Look, you left here shaking your little ass excited about a damn salad. Now you're back here looking like you lost your Todo or something. Wake up, Dorothy! Wake up!" Rickey belted, snapping his fingers. "Unnn huh. Wake the hell up!"

"Well if I were sleep, I think you just woke up me *and* the rest of the faculty. I'm sure they're back by now. Damn, Rickey. Can a girl eat her salad in peace?" she snapped, now stabbing her salad.

"Girl, fuck their pale asses and that ching chong salad! Now, tell me what happened. Ice Ice Baby, acting up?" he asked, stepping in as he closed the door with sympathetic eyes.

Laughing, although still visibly upset, she tucked her bottom lip and shook her head, trying to figure out where to start. *Like how did they go from that night to him leaving her there alone in front of a stranger like it meant nothing?* she thought to herself. Rickey, unlike Sky, didn't hate Elijah, but he definitely felt like Iyana's main reason for staying with him was because of his Caucasian pedigree that somewhat made her feel validated or accepted by others. Sadly, he knew his girl was a victim of that house negro mentality, and he despised it.

"Look. I'ma need you to stop calling my man anything other than his name. You starting to sound like Sky and shit," she giggled, tossing a forkful of chicken breast in her mouth.

"Oh, the infamous Sky and I finally agree on something, huh?" he smiled, popping his lips. "Thought I was going to have to scratch her eyeballs out, but maybe, just maybe she can be my boo, too."

"Now you're reaching, but honestly," she said like she was in deep thought. "Y'all are actually a lot alike. Scary, but very true."

"Naw, bih. She can't be as fabulous as I am," he said doing the Kenya Moore twirl. "But we shall see. I mean, I even got your lil' poor ass to eat because you one bite away from being *The Walking Dead* around here. Now what happened? Talk to Rickey," he said, planting himself on her office sofa.

Rickey took great pleasure in being loud and ballsy, but when his friend needed him, he knew how to be just that. Especially now that he helped Nana with Papa B one night when she called to say Papa B had gotten out of the house and had wandered off.

No questions asked, Rickey got up and rode around town looking for Papa B as if he were his own grandfather. Iyana, being a nervous wreck, tearfully thanked him, resulting in Nana and Papa B adopting him into the family after that.

"Kaizer P—" she leaned in and whispered before Rickey's mouth shot wide open in a shocked-like state, his eyes bulging out of his head like he saw a ghost.

"What...what did I say? You're scaring me!" she panicked, pushing her salad away.

"Bitch! Did you just say Kaizer? Like Kaizer Paul as in Keyz? As in King Pussy Pounder, fine ass, 'he can get it' Kaizer Paul? The head of the C.U.B crew?" he belted, forgetting to use his inside voice that quickly.

"Wait! I mean—no, I don't think so. Did you say King Pussy Pounder? C.U.B crew?" she asked, almost in disbelief that he was known for his skillful usage of his manhood.

"Did I stutter?" he asked slowly as he leaned forward.

Scratching her neck, Iyana felt uncomfortable even discussing their one-night rendezvous realizing that Keyz had some serious street credibility she could never touch, even if she wanted to.

Damn, Iyana. Get it together, she thought, collapsing in her office chair, disappointed in another missed opportunity.

Realizing his girl was beating herself up, Rickey chose a softer approach. He wasn't suggesting that she wasn't worthy of Kaizer Paul or couldn't handle a dude from the streets, but he knew she struggled with her self-esteem due to her chocolate, dark hue.

He found out one day after throwing out every single compact powder or foundation that was way too light for her. Because he was known to 'beat a face' like a make-up artist, they spent an entire day at the MAC store, purchasing makeup that complemented her skin complexion. So, Rickey knew why she was questioning herself yet again.

"Iyana, baby. I'm sorry," he said reaching for her hand. "It's just you two are from different worlds. Like, I don't think you understand how far his reach is."

"No, no need. I can understand why you wanted clarification. I mean look at me," she said in defeat. "Why would he want little ole me who knows nothing about the streets, let alone couldn't compare to a woman that does?"

"No, girl. Never that," he said clutching his shirt. "Just shocked he got *your* attention. I mean, look at you. You're fabulous... like muah. You run your own dance program, you are a kick ass cook, and you're fine as hell with that tight lil' ass and perky tits you got. Bitch, I would fuck you if I wasn't a tranny!" he laughed, pulling her up as he batted his eyelashes at her.

"Now turn around so I can slap all that ass you got! Yasssss!" he belted as he twerked effortlessly. Watching him pop his butt up and down with ease like he was in the club was hilarious to Iyana, as he did it almost better than her.

"Oh my God! You are so stupid! I can't...I just can't with you! Ahh, mmm. Mm, mm, mm," she said falling back in her chair as she watched Rickey twerk to imaginary music like he was in a twerk contest.

"Shit, I'm tired. You would think with all the dancing we do, a bih can twerk and not run out of breath, but the R to the I to the CKEY is tired like a motherfucker," he said, falling back on the sofa as he fanned himself.

"So anyway. Let's talk. Tell Rickey about King Pus-, I mean Kaizer Paul. Let's talk, darling."

Glaring at him with the right side of her lip curled, Iyana pondered on how much she should share with him, but deep down she knew he genuinely wanted her happy. She also figured since he knew Kaizer, he could give her some tea on what all that King Pussy Pounder was about and anything else the streets knew him as.

"So, let me start from the beginning. My first—"

"Wait!" he said, holding his hand up. "We have twenty minutes before class starts, so give me the quick version."

"I would if you would just be quiet. Damn, Rickey," she snapped back pouting. Here she was ready to share an already uncomfortable topic and he went from the nurturing and supportive friend to the blunt, rushing one.

"Okay, okay. I can see the estrogen at work in here. Let me tap into my feminine side and relax," he laughed, crossing his legs.

"Well, turn your estrogen *all the way up*," she replied sarcastically, fake smiling as she gave him the middle finger before she continued.

"So, I met Keyz back in middle school on the first day of seventh grade. It sort of happened by accident one day, when I was running near the basketball court trying to get to class, and the basketball they were playing with hit me. Instead of apologizing, my ass lost my ability to speak, gawking at him like a retard. Crazy thing is right after I made it to class, guess who shows up, too?"

"Wait," Rickey said scooting to the edge of the sofa. "Ashton Kutcher?"

Pointing to the door she said, "Get. Just go."

"Hell naw. You're going to pay me for this therapeutic service I'm offering. Now Miss Wilkers, please continue," he played, writing on his imaginary notepad.

"Nope, I'm done," she said, throwing her hands up in the air before she stood up.

The One That Got Away

"Too bad. I'm not. So what part of that story actually has anything to do with today, because I'm lost as hell?" he said, looking at his watch. "Oh, you got eighteen minutes now. Carry on."

"Ugh, okay. It was him," she smiled gazing at the ceiling. "But I never saw him after that day until a week ago. Well once, but that doesn't count 'cause he didn't see me. Back to that day... So, anyway, he pretty much got kicked out of class, but before he left, he told me to meet him for lunchtime at the basketball court. It never happened because I never went."

"Why, bitch? Didn't he tell your retarded ass to meet him where y'all met? Girl, was you in ESE?" he asked standing up.

Iyana's eyes quickly shifted to her salad before she tossed it in the garbage. "A lot of reasons, but the main one being, why should I? I was a nerd, lived a sheltered life with my grandparents, could barely put a sentence together and I wasn't his type."

After her harsh admission, Iyana stepped around her desk, avoiding more questions from him. He knew her ugly truth about her self-esteem, so any more talk about her being fabulous was him just being a good friend. She would have done the same for him or Sky.

"Well, your ass was wrong because you standing in here like you lost your BFF but managed to slip in you saw him a week ago. See, unlike you, I was in Advanced Placement classes. Not a lot of shit gets past me," he spat.

"So? You threw him that snatch and now he acting like the average dude on the street once he got what he wanted? See, that's why Rickey baby has no love for these niggas. I gets my coins at work, and then theirs after work by doing very little work," he laughed, snapping his fingers. "'Cause R to the I to the CKEY don't play that, hun."

"Wrong, wrong and wrong," Iyana shot back with a sneaky grin, shrugging her shoulders. "He ummm… had your girl hemmed up in his face and all."

"Wait!" he screamed with one hand on his chest.

"Are you saying he licked the kitty? Sucked the box? Plunges the tongue? Oh my God!" he belted jumping up from the sofa. "Ice Ice Baby gots to go ASAP! Like, did I not tell you how fabulous the stories are about your man's ummm…skillful pounding ability? Girl, is your cat good and waxed 'cause I can't have your name being dragged through the streets that you hiding a fur ball under there."

"Yes, he did, and of course I do. I maintain my regular appointment twice a month," she shot back. "I now know I'm just a pawn in some sick, twisted game he is playing. Like what in the hell is C.U.B? I mean, I can tell he's doing well for himself, but that also means well with having a variety of women at your disposal. Pffft… He doesn't want me," Iyana replied, defeated, with her arms crossed, rubbing her shoulders.

She just couldn't believe she fell into his trap all these years later, while she had a whole boyfriend for the past five years. She felt stupid and ashamed for even allowing him to see her in such a vulnerable state, remembering how he had his way with her.

At least with Elijah, she was a sexual beast, unleashing all her tricks almost like a dominatrix. But with Keyz, there was obviously a role reversal as he took the lead, controlling every act from the way he sucked and licked her to how he kept her there until he was ready to let her go.

"Ughhh," she sighed, slapping her forehead. "It was a stupid decision. I had just had an argument with Elijah who, at the last minute, told me he couldn't come to my show at the center. Frustrated that he won't fucking accept that prejudice bullshit he believes about blacks, I ripped my tights on this damn Pandora bracelet while I was trying to get dressed, and you *know* how much I love this bracelet, making me even more frustrated.

Then rushing to get to the center on time, I decided to stop by Target to grab a new pair and then this asshole in front of me wouldn't let me get into the parking garage to park," she belted full speed not stopping. Rickey, tired of watching her mouth move while keeping up with all the details just sat, waiting for her to come up for air.

"Fuck you, Rickey. I see you over there smirking quietly. See, that's why I didn't want to tell you," she replied dramatically, disgusted with herself.

"No, that's why you need to. Your ass really do need a therapist. I'm doing shit a therapist wouldn't do. You think they want to hear all that? Hell naw," he barked responding to his own question. "But I'm sorry, boo. That's what besties do. We listen to the bullshit a therapist doesn't want to *for free*," he said crossing his legs.

"Whatever. So, Mr. Asshole was none other than Keyz, and before the night was over, my ass was in his face for the *rest of the night*. I'm talking about he was swimming in my shit like an Olympic gold medalist. Then today, I run into him at the salad shop and pretty much brush him off," she stated with regret and confusion on her face.

"Bitch, why? Oh, and therapist don't get to say bitch either," he giggled.

"I mean I wasn't trying to, but damn, Rickey, I don't know what I want. Well, I do, but I don't. Ughhh, I am such a thot!" she whined as she rolled her neck with her eyes closed.

"Well, that will be $125. Where shall I send the bill?" he teased, writing on his imaginary notepad.

"Go!" she yelled pointing to the door.

"Naw, boo. I see why you tired, rolling your neck and all. You been pretty busy playing catch up with Keyz. Ain't shit wrong with that! Damn, Iyana. Live a little and stop playing like you happy with Robin Thicke.

Hell, he sounds boring as fuck and then you barely see him because of his child and baby mama. Listen, I keep telling you he still sleeping with her. My spidey senses don't lie. Go get with the plug, King Pussy Pounder, and have some fun.

Stop with all of this woe is me stuff. And puh-leaseee, know that you are not a thot," he quipped. "A little loose in the heat of the moment, but who wouldn't be? You just got cold feet, girlfriend. I mean, damn! That's—"

"I get it," she stopped him, shaking her head. She knew who he was, but Rickey seemed to enjoy shouting his name.

"That's Kaizer Paul, Keyz, King Pussy Pounder and some other nonsense you said. I get it," he said, motioning for him to get up and go as she opened the office door.

Before she was ready to step out, Iyana stood firm and tall and shook her shoulders off. One thing she took pride in was never allowing the outside world to see her sweat when she was in work mode, and today was no different. On the inside, she felt like her world was crumbling, but on the outside, she was as solid as they come.

"Now, let's go. I got a little less than 10 minutes to get it together. Today I am teaching on Renaissance dance and you know most of them not even interested just like him, but thanks for listening," she said, kissing Rickey on the cheek as she stood on her tiptoes while he stood next to her.

"Nah unnn. Don't be kissing on me," he said pushing her away laughing. "I don't want your man coming for me like I want his boo."

"Psssh," she said pursing her lips. "Yea, like that would really happen."

Grabbing her, he said, "He'd be a fool not to. Now let's give these pale faces our ass to kiss and shake that shit off. I have dates on top of dates to get you ready for. Once I am done, King Pussy Pounder won't know what hit him. He wants you, so get it together. Stop letting all that dark-skinned shit this and street shit that be bigger than what it is.

Hell, even white men checking for the darkest black woman they can find to be, how can I say it? More culturally sensitive with their lying ass, doubling back around to take their Becky's back from the Tiger Woods of the world."

Nodding, she shook her head yes as if she believed every word that came out of his mouth, although she felt like a 'hell no, he don't.' What Rickey didn't know was she didn't plan on seeing him again anyway, so why argue?

Chapter 11

"So we meet again?" Skebo playfully said, running to help Sunshine load up groceries she just purchased for the month.

It was getting harder and harder to maintain all of the things she normally did pre-pregnancy, and shopping for the bare necessities like food was one of them. Although she could easily have dinner at her mother's house, Sunshine embraced being independent while preparing herself for motherhood. Whenever she wasn't party planning and working an event with her sister, Shower, she was either at school or in her humble, quaint two-bedroom apartment, fully decorated, as she awaited the birth of her twin, baby boys.

"You call it meeting. I call it scary," she swiftly replied, as she pushed the shopping cart to her Range Rover.

"So, Skebo. Tell me. Why do *we* keep meeting up like this?" she asked, waving her finger between the two of them.

Smiling, he replied, "Shit. I'on know. Call it fate and shit.

Ain't that what they say? You know, when something's meant to be?"

The more he spoke, the wetter his lips got, as he lightly scaled them with his tongue. Met with silence, he said, "Yea, that's what I thought. Now gon' jump in and let me finish this up for you. It's fucking hot out here and you wanna play."

"Oh, now that I can do," she said, sighing as she opened the driver's door, easing her way slowly into the driver's seat. Skebo watched how big she had gotten, realizing that sooner or later, she wouldn't be able to step up in her truck without assistance. He made a mental note to talk to her about that later.

What Sunshine didn't know is that Skebo had been pining over her for years. Unlike Shower, who was the outgoing one, Sunshine chose to stay in the background. Being one not to care for a loud mouth woman, Skebo often enjoyed her company whenever he came by the house to check on them for Keyz when they were growing up.

Sometimes she would make him something to eat and they would play Spades and even UNO, although he told her he would deny it if she ever told anyone. Once Skebo moved up the ranks in C.U.B, he sort of distanced himself, not wanting to wife any girl in particular, but as of late, his mind drifted to the "what ifs". Especially after he found out she wasn't dealing with her children's father.

After securing her grocery items in the truck, Skebo tapped on the passenger's door trying to stall Sunshine by sitting in her truck. He was never one to chase a woman, but Sunshine wasn't just any girl. She was Keyz's baby sister who was all woman, who held her own, not pitying herself like most women who'd found themselves single and pregnant.

She didn't joke a lot and she did little in terms of having a great a time like most young women her age. At twenty-three, she was in her last year of college and would soon graduate with her bachelor's degree in Accounting.

At 5'6", she carried her baby weight well, although her small, firm breasts were now full, along with her thick thighs and hips. He couldn't help but smile as he watched her tuck her jet black, wavy hair behind her ear that was stuck to the side of her copper-toned skin due to excessive perspiration.

Her chubby cheeks looked like they were made for pinching, which Skebo would do from time to time whenever he saw her. Their mother would often tease both of her girls who were very shapely at an early age, for having baby-making hips.

While Shower embraced it, Sunshine dressed conservatively, hiding her curvaceous, yet toned body. Even at six months pregnant, Skebo was extremely attracted to Sunshine who was wearing a short sleeved, denim button top and white, floral maternity skirt. Her pale, yet manicured toes were cute, although her feet were quite swollen. Noticing that, Skebo wanted to offer her some relief.

"You should let me do something about that," he said pointing at her feet.

Confused, she asked, "Like what?"

"I'on know," he shrugged. "Maybe let me follow you back to the house, put your shit away and rub 'em for you. No funny shit. I promise."

Blushing, Sunshine turned two shades darker, imagining

how weird it would feel to not only have her feet rubbed, but for Skebo to do them. Even after all of these years, he never once touched her, other than a brotherly hug, but even a blind man could see that they were venturing into new territory.

He chuckled, watching her dry off her glasses that seemed to steam up although she primarily wore contact lenses. With or without them, her soft, maple brown eyes gave her that Bambi, the deer, look.

"Fuck, Skebo! Why you do that?" she pouted with a smile.

"Man, because I can. What your little ass gon' do but let me. You know you want me to touch on you and shit. It's just your feet," he teased, showing his flawless, white teeth before he tucked his bottom lip.

Sunshine smiled, then shook her head no. She was very much aware of how her brother and his C.U.B crew got down over the years when it came to passing women, and she was already in a vulnerable place; single and now pregnant by a man who ran and got married on her. She no longer cried about it, but was afraid to let anyone else in, so she hid behind the obvious reason she should say no.

"Do you see my stomach?" she asked, rubbing the top of her stomach, looking over her glasses that sat loosely on the end of her nose.

"Yea, I see them lil' mini monsters you having. Why?" he joked pushing her glasses on her face.

"Boy, stop!" she squealed slapping his hand away from her face. "Why my babies gotta be mini monsters? I swear you say the damndest things. Anyway, as you can see, I've *been* touched. In fact, permanently touched for the next eighteen years at least."

Grabbing her hand, Skebo struggled with sharing his real feelings for her. He fucked hoes on the regular, but for Sunshine, he was ready to take on everything that came with her. Even letting Keyz know he was ready to hold his baby sister down. He knew his time in the streets and running his businesses with Keyz still required his attention.

But fuck it, he thought. *It's now or never.*

"Why you sitting over there all in deep thought holding my hand?" she asked smiling as she felt subtle flutters in her lower abdomen area. It was like her boys knew she was excited or happy about something. That something was obviously Skebo.

"Nothing, gorgeous. Just thinking," he said playing with her fingers.

Afraid to probe even more, Sunshine basked in his touch, leaning back as she closed her eyes. His image was now deeply embedded in her mind as she envisioned how handsome he was and how soft his lips would feel on hers.

Once she sat straight up, she looked at his smooth, caramel skin that was perfect. Almost too perfect. His tatted, well defined arms were the arms of a man who gave just as much as he took, as she knew very well what he did for a living and how he took care of his. Although she should run for cover, she was all in if he was serious, not giving a thought to what Keyz would say.

"What?" he asked, pushing her on the side of her head.

"Stop, Skebo!" she squealed batting his hand away.

"Oooo, you get on my nerves," she winced as she felt one of the twins pushing on her bladder. "I think one of my little ones wants mommy to go bathroom."

She really did need to go to the bathroom, but the nervous

energy in the air made her feel like she had to go right then. *Sunshine, girl, relax. This just Skebo. You can't go pissing on yourself.* Siking herself out, she ignored her rather full bladder, which was bad for her, but she wanted to see where this conversation would eventually go.

"Hey, lil' ones. Mommy talking to your future stepfather. Calm your lil asses down," he said with his mouth now on her stomach, gently biting her hand.

"Boy, don't be cursing at my babies, and who said anything about them having a stepfather?" she asked, twisting up her lip.

"Oh, so you not gone let me do that for you either? First I can't rub your feet and now I can't marry your funky lil' self. Damn, Sunshine. You used to be the nice one."

"Do what, Skebo?" she sighed, realizing this was all a mistake just that quickly.

"Look. I got two babies on the way with a man in the NBA who married a fucking Miami Heat dancing Becky, and I can barely wash my ass most days in between me going to class, doing homework, and working in order to put enough money away for my baby boys. So tell me what you really want. It can't be pussy 'cause you get plenty of that and don't lie, 'cause I know how you and your boys get down," she barked almost in tears.

Irritated, Skebo nodded his head. He knew her situation, but her repeating it offended him like he didn't care, when he cared more than she would ever know. There wasn't a day that went by that he didn't ask Lacray or Shower about her or stalk her Facebook or Instagram page. As for the women he slept with, once she was his, she'd never have to worry about any of them. He respected her and her brother too much for that.

"I'll wash your ass. I really would. I'll get wit'cha," he said quietly, kissing her on the cheek before he hopped out the car. Before he argued with her, he decided to put that situation on pause.

Sunshine sat up, shocked, with her mouth open, before a smile crept on her face.

Damn, this man is really serious about me, she thought, not realizing that he felt defeated with her lack of confidence in who he was as a man.

Yes, he was involved in an illegal organization most of his adult life, but he valued family and was loyal. Almost to a fault, bringing a few youngins on over the years that weren't quite ready to be in the game, but that was who he was. He would help the homeless man by feeding him, or giving him clean clothes to wear, when others would walk over him like he was invisible. Sometimes he wondered if any one of them was his father, not knowing him if he saw him on any given day.

"Close your mouth, greedy," he laughed. "There's more where that came from once you ready to come fuck with a *real* nigga."

As Skebo walked off, jumped in his truck and drove away, Sunshine watched from her rearview mirror until she couldn't see it anymore. She promised herself that if he approached her one more time, she would let him in just a little to see if love was really in the cards for her.

∼

"Hello."

"Sup? Whatchu doing?" Oneal spoke softly into the phone.

They hadn't spoken in a week, but Sunshine welcomed the distance. His call was just a reminder that she made one poor choice on top of all the great ones she made, until the day she met Oneal who shared a dorm room with her brother, Keyon.

"Polishing my toenails. Well, trying to anyway. What's up?" she asked unenthusiastically.

"Mmm. All that fat cat wide open, huh?" he replied lustfully.

Staring at the phone in disbelief, Sunshine was at a loss for words. Oneal had just married his wife, Kennedy, who eagerly flaunted their whirlwind romance on every social media website known to man, but yet and still, her husband was lusting over his pregnant ex.

Disgusted, Sunshine hung up the phone, tossing herself back on the sofa. After making herself some smothered pork chops, homemade mashed potatoes, string beans and skillet cornbread, all she wanted to do was soak and scrub her feet, adding a pink, translucent polish on her toenails.

Shower and her mother would scream if they knew she was trying to save money by not getting a professional pedicure, but Sunshine enjoyed catering to herself whether she had money or not.

Hearing her cellphone ring immediately after she hung up, Sunshine answered it full of rage.

"What the fuck do you want and where is your got damn wife?"

"Hey, baby," her mother timidly responded.

Being a mother of four, she knew how pregnancy could make one moody, but Sunshine's outburst scared her mother, making her almost forget why she'd even called.

"Oh, Mama," she said. "I'm so sorry. I thought you were Oneal. You know I would never disrespect you like that."

"Well, I wasn't sure, but I take it what I heard was true…or not true."

Unable to hide her emotions, Sunshine tearfully wept, confessing to her mother that she was pregnant and alone.

"Now, now, Sunshine. You ain't neva alone. You got me, Shower, Keyon and Kaizer, baby. Let's not forget Chase and my grandbabies. Seems to me you got a lot of folks waiting to love on them babies," she gently spoke, trying to comfort her.

"But, Mama—"

"Mama nothing. Now I know how you're feeling or did you forget? There wasn't a day that didn't go by that I didn't try to justify why I had to have a man up in my house, no matter how he spoke to me. Shoot, in my mind I was doing what I had to do. But that same thinking almost cost me Kaizer," she spoke with conviction.

"I praise God every day I hear his voice and know he's alive, after he robbed and even sold dope to get me to leave them no good niggas alone. That's why I work so hard now, baby. Not to pay bills, but to be there for y'all. Just like I help take care of Ieasha, KJ, Kelon and Ishmael, I'ma take of them two lil' ones you got. Now hush that fuss. You hear me?"

"Yes…yes, ma'am. I hear you," she sniffled, glancing over her stomach as she wiggled her toes.

"Mama?"

"Yes, baby. What is it?"

"Do you think it's wrong if I like someone, but that someone is someone I shouldn't like?"

"Baby, you grown. Well, hell, almost grown, because I swear y'all kids nowadays still growing. I'on see nothing wrong with it, but you gotta have your priorities lined up. Now, I never had to worry 'bout you like that, but you got two mouths to feed. I'm a woman, but if liking someone may hinder you from reaching your goals, maybe now is not a good time. Why you ask?"

"Ughhh, you're right," she said sitting up to make herself a plate.

"Well who is it, Sunshine? I mean, you asked for a reason. So talk to mama," she pled, knowing it was Skebo considering how he looked at her every time they were around each other, or the way he checked in on her.

"Ahhhh, never mind, Mama. Never mind. Let me go eat. I cooked some smothered pork chops if you want some, and a few sides."

"Mama shole do. Let me send Kaizer over there to grab it," she said hanging up before Sunshine could protest.

~

It was Thursday night and the C.U.B crew was deep in King of Diamonds. At least once a month, they all came together to just chill and throw a few dollars away. Their empire went from crack cocaine, to now cocaine and an assortment of pills from Xanax, Mollies and Ecstasy. Once they linked up with Meka's family, they even started buying and selling guns which was Keyz's thing.

The One That Got Away

It wasn't less hazardous than selling dope, but he was less visible in the streets, which was perfect since he was giving himself two more years before he was completely out of the game.

Cameo's song "Candy" was playing, letting the crowd know that Candie Coated Thighs was up. They hadn't been there long in their regular VIP section. It was the regular crew with Chico, Keyz, Skebo, Kaleela and now their boy, Tone, who moved quickly up the ranks, coming in with that pill game. He knew how it moved quickly amongst the athletes and white college kids, adding almost $500,000 a month to their payroll.

After Shona couldn't handle being number two, she ducked off from the crew choosing to fuck with Meka's brother. Chico lost no love since she was actually the third chic in the food chain, getting dick after Myriah and Meka. Kaleela, being a nigga at heart, chose not to choose sides, getting money instead. Every now and again, Shona would come through and hang with the crew, but tonight wasn't one of those nights.

Their favorite waitress, CoCo, was working tonight. She had a thing for Skebo, but he never took her serious, knowing a few of the crew had hit back in the day. True, it was years ago, but he just couldn't get past it and would have to kill a nigga for talking greasy out his mouth about his ole lady. So to avoid that, he casually fucked her and threw a few dollars her way to pay bills since she had a sick granny at home that raised her.

"Bring us out the usual," Skebo whispered in her ear as she bent down showing her breast to him and her ass to his boys. CoCo was a stacked, caramel chic that stood at 5'4", looking cornbread fed, with thick thighs and an ass that could be seen long after she turned a corner. She had a baby face, lightly covered with freckles, and a mole on her top lip that she darkened with eyeliner so it would pop against her full, juicy lips.

Although she wore her hair in a high ponytail at work, she rocked Peruvian weave that was 30 inches or more. Tonight, her red button up top hugged her so tight, her breasts looked like a miniature booty sitting on top of her chest. Yes, CoCo could get the attention of most men, but not Skebo. All he wanted was good service and a lap dance or two.

"What?" he asked. staring at her as she still stood in front of him with her hands on her hips.

"What happened to you the other night?"

Keyz, Chico and Tone laughed watching CoCo question their boy like she ran his movements. Little did she know, he was also hitting her homegirl, Sparkle that worked as a bartender there. Sparkle was an obedient mutt as he called her. She fucked, sucked, and let him do him with no questions asked, understanding the arrangement they had.

She had even let Kaleela, one of the girls in their crew, in on a threesome, although Skebo just watched. He wasn't fucking no one inside the crew like Chico, but he'd fuck with them from time to time depending on what the girl was working with. The only person that spoke up was Kaleela.

"Bitch, the fuck you standing here for? I came to see Candie's ass and you fucking up my time. Move around," Kaleela said, mean mugging her.

"Chill, Lee. Hoes gotta get dick, too," Tone said admiring

The One That Got Away

CoCo. "Shit, I'd hit that if he don't. Skebo?" he asked pointing at her.

"Nigga, when you had to ask if you can hit some random shit another nigga hitting. Man, fuck her. She better go do what the fuck she supposed to do before her ass won't be getting anybody no bottles in this motherfucker tonight."

Skebo was really mad because Sunshine had been ignoring his calls. He went by her apartment a few times after that day, doing exactly what he said he would do—rub her feet. She even let him kiss her and rub on her booty, but nothing beyond that.

Skebo didn't care what she thought, because she was wifey once she stopped playing. He knew Keyz might trip, but he didn't care. Like he didn't run who Keyz fucked with, Keyz had to accept he wanted his baby sister. He knew it would come with its challenges, but not so soon and definitely not from her baby daddy.

One night, Oneal called kind of late talking about a loss the Heat had to the Lakers. Instead of her letting it go to voicemail, Sunshine took the call and went in her bedroom. Feeling disrespected, Skebo left, blocking her number for a few days. He figured that was the lesser of two evils because he really wanted to curse her out and fuck her baby daddy up the next time he was in town.

After a week, he started missing their morning talks and chats throughout the day and he was ready to give her an ultimatum. Imagine his surprise when he got to her spot and Oneal's truck was not only there, but she refused to answer the door.

He mentioned it to Keyz, who didn't know they were

kicking it, to see if she was dealing with her baby daddy, but Keyz told him he didn't know. After CoCo pissed him off even more, he decided to go by there after they left the strip club.

Stomping off, Candie approached their area ready to come up because she knew how the C.U.B crew did it. Before she could even decide who she wanted, Kaleela waved her over and whispered in her ear. Kaleela was short, red and mean, but very pretty.

Too pretty, so she walked around with a scowl on her face wearing men's clothes a size too big. Tonight, she was clean, dressed in an all black, Balmain outfit and boots that went halfway up her calves. Her braids, freshly done, were covered with a fitted, black hat covering her glossy eyes from the blunt she was smoking. She was ready for a private dance but figured she'd wait for their bottle to get back.

"Bring all that ass over here and sit that shit right here," Kaleela said patting her lap. Candie, looking like Remy Ma, clapped her ass in Kaleela's face before she bent touch to her toes. Her red g-string knited deeply between her pussy lips hid nothing, as Kaleela sat up and stuck her face there.

"Shit, Candie. Let me fuck you tonight?" Kaleela asked, not caring who heard her. Bouncing to the beat of the song, Candie's ass popped up and down on Kaleela's face as she stuck her tongue out, licking whenever her ass cheeks came down on her mouth.

"Damn, Lee!" Chico yelled. "You about to have shorty cumming right here. That's my nigga! Yeah!"

"Fuck that! Her ass about to have me cumming," Tone yelled, stretching his legs apart as he caught a boner watching

The One That Got Away

Kaleela blow in her ass. "Lee, we might have to go get us a private room. You down?"

"Fuck you, nigga. She'on need no dick. I got this shit. You see all these hoes out here? Find yo' ass one, then, bitch."

"Man, fuck you! We just got here and you licking ass 'bout to spend all your money on one hoe." Tone wasn't mad, but the longer Candie twerked and bounced her pussy for Kaleela, the more he had to get his own action.

Keyz was always on chill mode whenever they went to the strip club. His regular, Lollipop, had quit a few months back, so he just came for the company and to wind down. He wasn't pressed for pussy and if he was, he had a few he could call up. At this age, he refused to pay for pussy unless she was his ole lady, and he didn't consider that paying for pussy. That was maintaining your bitch. What got him was how quiet Skebo was after he ran CoCo off.

"Fool, what's up with you popping off on CoCo? She ain't fuckable no more? What, that pussy done got too loose for ya? Tell me something," he asked.

"Fuck CoCo. Who the fuck she think she is putting a time-clock on when the fuck I see her and shit? Bitch, you not my girl and you damn sitr wouldn't be in here showing your ass and tits and shit in front of my boys.

See, that's the problem with these hoes. You fuck them real good, throw them a few dollars and if you do it more than once they start believing you trying to wife their ass. For what? So I can stick it to only one pussy that prolly ain't faithful anyway?"

Keyz nodded his head, listening to his boy. They had known each other almost their entire life and he knew when his boy was lying. Especially now. Whenever he lied, he would sniff like he had a cold. It was subtle but noticeable. If he hadn't been doing it all of his life, Keyz would have thought the nigga snorted powder.

"Nigga, you do know when I know you're lying and motherfucker, you're lying. And don't think I don't know you been laid up with some shorty. I'on know who she is, but your ass was running lights and shit to get to her anytime we wrap up a meeting or finish up business. Yeah, nigga. I know."

Skebo shifted in his seat watching CoCo, as she brought two bottles of Patrón, a bottle of Cîroc and Remy XO. Keyz watched how she slammed them down on the table, almost splattering ice from the bucket on them.

"Bitch, you wanna play," Skebo snarled, standing up as he brushed his Polo shirt and jeans off. He'd never hit a woman, but the thought of Sunshine laid up with her married baby daddy made him want to kill somebody.

"Aye, man. We good. CoCo, baby, take the rest of the night off. Tell Steve I got you tonight on that payroll shit. My boy tripping," Chico stood up, placing his hand on his chest.

No matter how easily enraged he could become, Chico was nothing but a gentleman in the streets when it came to women. It wasn't a front. He truly was attentive and nurturing, only a lunatic when it came to Myriah because that was a situation that seemed to get the best of him time and time again.

Nodding with tears in her eyes, CoCo stomped out mouthing 'bitch ass nigga' to Skebo before she took off.

"I wasn't no bitch ass nigga the last time we fucked and I moved some shit around in her uterus. The hoe was crying for days talking about take her to the ER because she think she

The One That Got Away

got a bladder infection. More like a dick one because my cousin, Teshon, told me that bitch be down to the clinic like she works there," he huffed, refusing to sit down.

"Damn, Skebo. That's cold putting her business out there and shit," Tone said, slapping the ass of the Spanish stripper named Selena. Her ass looked just like Jennifer Lopez, but with dark black hair.

"Fuck you, and worry about that Zika or Eboli shit you gone catch from fucking with them Spanish bitches that live out there on Miami Beach. Nigga, watch the news. Them shits done took over out there on MB."

"Damn!" Kaleela yelled. "Candie, let's go. These motherfuckers messing up my lap dance and shit. Keyz and Chico, get your boy or send his ass home. I can't even get high and suck a nut out a hoe around him. Fuck!"

"Bye, guys," Candie squealed walking off, with Kaleela on her ass like they were attached.

"Shit, I'm out. I shouldn't have come anyway," he said, dapping his boys up.

"Without a drink? Shit, that Remy yours. Better take that motherfucker. I'on drink that, and Chico gone suck on that Patrón all night. Fuck Tone. His ass just gone smoke like a chimney."

"Well, at least pussy in my face while you three homos sitting aaround like we not at a fucking strip club. Fuck Zika," he said, motorboating Selena's titties while slapping her ass.

Grabbing his bottle, Skebo took off and headed to Sunshine's. He was never scared of prison and tonight wasn't any different.

"Yeah, let that bitch made ass nigga be there and see what

the fuck I do," he said to himself, running a light before he jumped on the highway.

All he could see was him splitting Oneal's dome the minute he saw him. Sunshine was his. He didn't care whatever else thought. Within twenty minutes, he was at her condo. It was two in the morning. He expected her to be sleep but he could tell a light was on.

He saw an unfamiliar car, but familiar or not, he was seeing her tonight. Running up the stairs, he pulled out his .9mm and banged on the door.

Boom! Boom! Boom!

Looking through her window, he could see a male figure but he couldn't tell who it was but it didn't matter. He was ready to catch a body and he didn't care whose family was about to grieve, as long as it wasn't his. His aunt was old and frail, but lucid. Other than her and a few cousins, Skebo's family was C.U.B, and now Sunshine and her twin boys once she had them.

"Shine!" he yelled, calling her by the nickname he gave her. "Open up this fucking door, Shine. I'ma fuck that nigga up in there!"

Looking back through the window, the figure was gone and the living room and kitchen were empty. Calling her cell, he decided to let her know the consequences of not opening the door. After two unanswered calls, Skebo was about to shoot her lock off until he heard someone unlocking the door.

"What the fuck are *you* doing here?" he barked, barely catching a peek at Sunshine who was visibly shaken, breaking his heart.

Chapter 12

"Really, Elijah? Again?" she asked, looking at the ceiling in tears. "Yep. Uh huh. Yep, I understand. Well, tell Sasha to get better. Tomorrow is fine. Okay, love you too."

"Fuck him," she whispered as she sat and had lunch with Myriah at the restaurant off the water called The Banana Boat. Throughout the week, they played live music and even had a chartered boat come and take guests down to the ocean near the back of the restaurant.

At night, the boat converted to a party boat complete with music, drinks and lots of dancing. Since dancing was their thing, Iyana invited Myriah up just to spend some time with her to see what they were going to do about Papa B.

"Elijah cancelled, again?" Myriah asked, finishing off her coconut shrimp, fries, and cole slaw. She didn't mean to eat so much, but she was becoming an emotional eater which made her more emotional once she realized she ate way too much.

"Yep. Something about Sasha got sick and needed to be rushed to the hospital," she replied angrily. "I mean she supposedly got her own man, but mine always seems to come to the rescue."

"Seems like he is quite available when she needs him, sis. You may want to see what that is about," Myriah said, knowing all too well about living a secret life.

"You know what, Myriah? I don't even care anymore. I guess I'm just waiting for him to admit he's over this and move on. We barely fuck when we used to fuck two to three times a day and when we do, instead of him staying over, he goes home when he works from home."

Myriah could see her sister getting teary-eyed, admiring her soft, grey eyes that seemed darker based on her mood. She shifted in her seat remembering how she hated that Iyana got their father's eyes and she didn't.

If that wasn't enough, Iyana got their mother's dimples and she didn't. Short of her peanut butter complexion and thick body, Myriah always felt Iyana had it all until she would listen to her drudge up the mean kids from her past, and now Elijah. Guilt washed over her realizing that she wasn't the best big sister, so she did and said as much as she could now to make up for it.

"You ever think about mommy and daddy?" she asked Iyana as she stared off into the ocean, watching the small boats pass by.

Pushing her blackened salmon around, Iyana shook her head no, somewhat embarrassed that she barely remembered them because they died when she was only three years old.

"I do," Myriah admitted. "I often wonder would life be

different if they were here raising us, you know? Like would we still be sitting here talking about men that don't give a shit about us. I mean think about. You don't ever wonder why I don't bring Ish's father around?"

"I guess because you don't want the headache if he's not trying to see him. I mean, who wants to see their child get rejected over and over again by a man who created him but left him? I wouldn't. See, our parents were taken from us. They didn't choose to leave us behind."

"You sure about that?" Myriah asked furrowing her eyebrows.

"Uh, yeah. Don't you remember how they died?" Iyana asked wondering what that was all about.

"Yeah, I do, but sometimes shit is not as it appears in life. Like this whole Elijah thing. I'm telling you there's more, so do your research because shit is not always as it seems," she said getting up.

"Well, I gotta head on back. I let Ish hang out with some friends from school, but I don't let him stay the night. You know the cops see a little black boy walking down the street or riding a bike in a neighborhood he shouldn't be in, and they putting bullets in him. Not mine, so let me go."

The shootings of African American men by cops was increasing day by day all over the country, but Miami was no stranger to it, and Myriah would kill a cop before her son made the eleven o'clock news.

"Awe, tell Ish we missed our weekly call. He usually keeps Auntie in the know, but I think he's into girls now," she fake pouted.

"That and basketball, but you know he loves the dance

ministry. So, stop that. I'll tell him to call you," she said, bending down to give her a kiss before she pulled on one of her Bantu knots.

"Child, they are coming out today. Me, Rickey and Sky have a Caribbean trip coming up in a few weeks, and I want to wear my hair down before then because you know how wild and thick it is when it's loose."

Myriah stood and observed Iyana's natural beauty as she wore an orange Givenchy sundress and gold strappy sandals that complemented her chocolate skin. She loved her sister, but just couldn't find the words to say just how much, or why she treated her so poorly over the years.

"What, girl? I got a booger in my nose?" Iyana asked, twitching it around before she wiped it with a cloth napkin.

"Nothing Reese's Peanut Butter Cup," she laughed. It was also his way of not having to remember their names.

"Dang, Myriah," she smiled, feeling mushy inside. "You used to hate that name. Remember when you used to ignore him and call him ole man under your breath? My lil' black ass used to be scared of you until I realized you was just mad at the world."

"Iyana, don't do that," Myriah said softly, chewing the inside of her jaw.

"Do what?" Iyana asked, confused. Here she thought they were having a bonding moment and Myriah was getting all serious.

"Call yourself black. If anything, we are all black. God just gave you a little more because you're just that special to Him, sis. Hell, I'm glad just to be in the 'cup' with you. Guess it's a good thing the chocolate part is on the outside because I like that part the best."

Iyana smiled, jumping up to hug her sister. She wished they could get the years back they lost bickering and fighting or not speaking at all, but she would take what they had any day over not speaking at all.

"Oh, and tell Sky that we need to talk. I kinda feel like she and I need a do over," she said, grabbing her purse.

"Ummm, that's gone be hard, sis. But let me see what I can do. Now, Rickey is all in, if it's a good time for him, whether he likes you or not, but Sky... well, you know how she is. She's Sky. Maybe I can convince her to have dinner with us before we take off for our trip."

"Yeah, do that." She dropped a fifty dollar bill on the table before she headed out to beat the afternoon traffic.

Iyana admired Myriah's beauty as well. She was always the bigger of the two, but she was well put together, wearing high boyfriend jeans and a fitted Guess t-shirt, making her look like a teenager with her Coach tennis shoes.

Waiting for the waiter to close their bill out, Iyana received a text from an unknown number.

Unknown: *I need to see you.*

Iyana: *Do I know you?*

Iyana looked around to see if maybe someone nearby was playing a joke on her. She never received random text messages, but lately she had been getting calls from someone who would never say anything once she picked up. It happened at work and on her cell phone. She was rather freaked out, mentioning it to Elijah, who promised to look into it for her, but never did.

Unknown: *Cheeks…*

Shit, she thought jumping up out of her seat, knocking over a glass of water.

"Oh, I'm sorry," she said to the waiter, wetting up their bill. "I really am. Can you just take this and keep the change? It's my fault. No need for you to print a new bill."

Smiling after receiving such a huge tip, the young waiter took off before Iyana could change her mind.

Iyana: *Yes?*

Unknown: *Meet me at Rocky's, the hookah bar in Fort Lauderdale. Just give the valet your name.*

Feeling antsy, yet excited at the same time, Iyana couldn't respond fast enough. She hadn't been getting any action lately with Elijah and had been beating herself up for deleting Keyz' contact information.

Unknown: *Cheeks, you coming?*

Iyana: *Omw.*

Driving like she was in a high-speed chase, Iyana whipped in and out of lanes, as The Banana Boat was in Palm Beach. The good thing is both establishments were off of I-95 South, allowing her easy access to get on and get off the highway. Dabbing her MAC lip gloss and checking out her freshly threaded eyebrows, Iyana was glad she chose to dress chic yet casual for the lunch date with her sister.

Pulling up thirty minutes later, Iyana gave the valet her name and was quickly escorted into the kitchen area of the hookah bar. She wasn't much of a party goer, but she was hoping they could enjoy one smoke together.

Once seated at a private table overlooking the kitchen, Iyana was fascinated with the ins and outs of how quickly food was prepped and served. Especially since it was happy hour.

"Mr. Paul will be out in a minute. Would you like a beverage, a glass of wine or mixed drink?" a petite, blonde waitress asked in almost too tight of a vest and a short black skirt.

She must be some eye candy for those white college boys, she said to herself, surprise that she was even working there. *And why am I here? Does he pay for this space back here?* she asked herself.

The longer she sat there, the more uncomfortable she felt, until she realized she was being watched. It was him standing by the door, looking so fine she was ready to fuck him right there in front of everyone on the table in front of her.

He was casual, but definitely making a statement in his black, Versace jeans and button, fitted top with black Giuseppe high top sneakers. His tatted arms, looking bulkier than before, looked soft and smooth all the way to his manicured nails. His hair, still wild, drove her crazy, although he'd let his sideburns grow out just a little giving him more of an untamed look that made him even more irresistible.

Yes, I could fuck him now and go home to glory, she said to herself, not realizing that she was eye fucking him until he approached the table and spoke.

"You wanna do this here or back there?" he asked pointing to the back.

After a surge of nervousness hit, Iyana caught herself speechless once she realized he was reading her mind. She could tell he wanted her just as much as she wanted him as his jaws tightened waiting for her to speak.

"I—I—I don't know what you're talking about," she lied, scratching her neck.

Bending down, he whispered in her ear, "You know that's some bullshit, Cheeks. Now I been watching you since you sat down and as soon as you saw me, your lil' ass started squirming. Yea, tell that pussy daddy's home to collect what he left. Let's go."

Before she could protest, Keyz' had whisked her away into his office which was nicely decorated with brown, Italian leather furniture, a lavish bathroom equipped with granite countertops and a hot tub along with a bed that dropped out of the wall once he pressed a button on a nearby remote control. Within seconds, the lights were dimmed and they both were out of their clothes until he stopped hovering over her perfectly sculpted body that belonged to him.

"Why? Why are you stopping?" she asked, watching his thick pole bouncing up and down between his legs, lightly hitting her thighs.

"Tell me why you never came that day?" he asked looking like he was in deep thought.

What in the hell? Is he serious? she questioned herself. *What day is he talking about?*

"The day we met, that day. Why didn't you come? Did you know I waited for you? Hell, I even went back after school mad as fuck, thinking my lil' ass made some kind of fucking connection with you."

A million thoughts ran through her mind trying to think of an answer he may be satisfied with, as long as she didn't have to tell the truth, the ugly truth that was creeping its way in now.

"Naw, none of that confused shit either. Don't overthink shit because your ass knows. Stop fucking with me."

Iyana detected his feelings was hurt which was the last thing she ever wanted to do to anyone. It was pretty much the reason why she hadn't broken it off with Elijah. She was used to being the one rejected, dumped, and walked off on. That was her role and she was comfortable with it, no matter how strange it sounded to the outside world.

"I guess," she started.

"No, don't guess. Why?" he demanded, breathing heavilymlike he was angry with her. His muscles and jaws twitching like he wanted to release his pent-up frustration on her.

"Because, why would you want me? Like, look at me. I look like a freak. A little, black mouse. A fucking dot and all that other bullshit your friends and everyone else called me," she huffed, trying to get up before she broke down crying in front of him.

Wrestling her back on the bed, Keyz stared at her so long her eyes began to hurt, trying to focus on what he was thinking because he hadn't spoken a word since her outburst. Before she asked him if he was satisfied with her answer, he bent down, gently kissing her face from her forehead to her nose to her chin, then her mouth.

"Keyz," she said when he broke their kiss.

"Shhhh," was all he said as he took his time becoming acquainted with her entire body, kissing her down her neck, shoulders, arms, torso, thighs down to each finger and toe.

Nothing was left untouched except her throbbing center that was leaking between her legs. Iyana was being tortured, trying to return each touch and kiss, but he wouldn't allow her, instead, holding both hands over her body tightly until she let him move about freely.

"I waited for you," he whispered then kissed her before he slid in her body.

"Ah!" she yelled trying to adjust to his girth that was overpowering her small, snug tunnel.

Sensitive to her size, Keyz didn't move as he basked in her warmth, taking her mouth again. He'd never hurt her and was waiting for her to let him know he could continue, until he felt her wrapping her legs around him, clenching his member vaginally as she whispered sweet nothings in his ear.

It was as if they had made love for the very first time in their lives. With him, Iyana allowed him to lead and with her, he wanted to show her just how perfect she was for him.

"Mmmm," she moaned as he picked her up with him inside of her, before he lay back down waiting for her to take off.

Once she slid down to the base of his shaft, Iyana's mouth opened in awe, feeling all of her climatic nerve endings coming alive. Unable to control herself, she bucked up and down on him willing him to give himself to her, and that he did, tugging and pulling on her breasts which he wanted to feed his babies.

"Cheeks," he said, his voice cracking like he could barely speak.

"Uh huh," she said almost in tears each time his curved pole snaked its way into her body.

"I'm about to cum. Can daddy let it go now?" he asked, slowly stroking her feeling her fleshy tunnel grip his firm pole.

Knowing what he was asking, Iyana whispered yes, grabbing his mouth hungrily while he rammed deeply inside of her until he couldn't go any deeper.

"Arrghh! Fuck!" he screamed, with Iyana erupting right behind him, biting his shoulders.

"Damn, girl! You bit the shit out of me!" he laughed, as she panted in his ear somewhat embarrassed that she was in this vulnerable place again, only seeing him the second time after all of these years. Her body, tensing up, got his attention.

"What's wrong?" he asked, hurriedly sitting up, still inside of her.

"Nothing," she said, casting her eyes down.

"Cheeks, don't fucking lie to me. What's wrong?"

"Was all of that true? You know, what you said to me today?"

Watching her dark, brown skin glistening from their body sweat, Keyz got angry that she had to question him. The fact that he was fucking her without any protection knowing she had a man and sharing something no one knew about because he'd never admit he waited for a girl, ran him hot.

"Why the fuck I gotta lie, Iyana? You know you really need to wake the fuck up and understand what happened not just today, but years ago," he yelled pulling out of her.

"What happened? You and your friends made fun of me? You mean that?" she snapped back, remembering the laughs and jokes.

"No, what we felt," he said pointing to her heart. "The chemistry, the connection. And for the record, I beat the shit out of them that afternoon for fucking with you. One thang about Keyz, he don't let anyone fuck with his and before you were mine, I still didn't. So after today, stop fucking playing the victim.

I need to play catch up and learn a lot of shit about you,

like your favorite color and shit, what you like to do when you not fucking up my mind running around this shit, who the hell you hang with besides that loud ass Spanish girl, and anything else a nigga supposed to know about his woman.

And me, well, I'm a member of one of the most notorious drug and gun trafficking crews in Florida, but I own this fucking hookah bar and a cigar lounge because my ass won't be dying in a fucking prison dealing with that illegal shit forever.

I have one son whose ten years old and, no, I don't fuck with his mother. I got a brother and a set of twin sisters. I love seafood, I play and watch basketball, I hate to sleep alone although I do every night, and I have never had a birthday party. So after today, call up my sisters, Sunshine and Shower, and help them plan my 30th birthday party coming up in January. Cool?"

Feeling like she was run over by a truck, Iyana sat there trying to process everything he said. *Who is this man?*

As if he read her thoughts, "I'm yo' nigga. Can't nan bitch on the street lay claim to me. That shit you may hear in the street about King Pussy Pounder is true, but I just retired that shit 'cause I just made love for the first time in my life. Any questions?"

Keyz never spared a woman's feelings before today, and he wasn't sparing hers now. Everything he spoke was true because it was now or never, and he couldn't see letting her go after she gave herself to him.

Scratching her neck and looking down, she shot back up remembering what he said about that bad habit of hers.

"Yes," she said softly. "Why me?"

"Why not you? Shit, look at you, and your name has never been popping in the streets. Keyz wanted you then. Keyz wants you now. You in?"

Smiling so hard that her cheeks hurt, she nodded, forgetting she had a man until Keyz reminded her.

"Now call ole boy and let him down quickly. In a few weeks, I'm moving you out that shit where you live. Yea, I know it's not far from one of my spots."

"One?" she shot back with an attitude, feeling played from that night.

"Iyana, I run an organization. I rest my head in many places, but my home is right here in Fort Lauderdale. I know where you work, so find something that can get you there in less than an hour, but you're moving.

Ole boy can't step foot where mine lay her head at. Now don't fuck with me or he gon' take a dirt nap for a long ass time. Understand?" he asked getting hard again, ready for a second round.

"I understand," she smiled remembering not to break eye contact.

After that day, Rickey and Iyana began house hunting and she barely saw Elijah. She conveniently avoided him, working late hours at the community arts center before going to Keyz's spot in Fort Lauderdale.

Funny thing is Elijah didn't seem that concerned with their limited contact, making her feel that Myriah's words were true. Not caring enough to find out, she spent the next month playing catch up with Keyz and planning his party like he instructed her.

The only time things seemed to be a little off is whenever

she asked about his son. Keyz, being overly protective, told her that one day she would meet him but he wanted this time to be just about them. Truthfully, he was embarrassed to tell her how he toyed with his son's mother over the years.

He also didn't want Myriah to run her off at the moment, since he never had a steady girl to introduce to his son. Deep down inside, it bothered her, but she decided to trust the man she felt totally complete with. Even if their worlds still had not fully collided yet.

Chapter 13

"Agent Ramirez, are we good? Do you think you can get what we need on this next trip?" her superior, Lt. Shaw asked. He was worried that their asses would get chewed out by his superiors if she didn't get what they needed to shut Shyne and his organization down. They had been on it for almost a year and Lt. Shaw had concerns that his agent may not be able to get the job done.

"Of course, sir. Why wouldn't we? Some targets are easier to crack than others. Haven't I always gotten the job done?" she asked irritated that her skills were being questioned.

"Yes, you have. So go in and do what you do best. We already have the room wired and and a tactical team ready to move in once you alert us. Copy that?"

"Yes, sir," she said hanging up, angry with herself.

"Fuck, Shyne! Why?" she cried hating that the only man she truly loved could go to prison for life because of her.

She tried resisting how attractive he was, but that wasn't

what drew her in. It was his story about his childhood and how he had no family after the death of his grandmother, except his brother who rarely came around.

He told her of the days where they would steal to avoid their grandmother working long hours trying to buy them the basics, from food to clothes for the winter time. He rarely showed emotion, but once they met at a gun range, she lied telling him about an abusive boyfriend.

Shamefully, he begged for her number, checking in with her every day until their calls turned into stolen moments where she secretly flew to spend time with him in New York. Now here he was, begging a woman he really didn't know to marry him.

"Oh my God, bitches! This resort is so nice! Iyana, girl, you did that!" Rickey squealed as the Uber driver dropped them off in front of their resort in Ochos Rios, Jamaica.

"Call me bitch one more time," Sky laughed, although she took a liking to Rickey from the time they met in Miami the night before they flew out.

"Bitch, what?" he asked slapping her on her shoulder before he kissed her on the cheek.

"Oh, he likes you, Sky. He kissing you already," Iyana said smiling, as she motioned for them to follow the bellman to the registration desk.

"Welcome to Jamaica!" three women sang, dancing with cups of rum punch in their hand as they placed them in their hands, encouraging them to dance.

"No, thank you. Wrong team," Rickey said, throwing his shades on with his rum punch in his hand before he walked off.

"Oh boy. As if they didn't know that," Sky giggled, whispering in Iyana's ear.

They were all dressed comfortably in shorts and tank tops with flip flops, ready to go in their room to change into something for the water. Sky told Iyana she upgraded her room before flying in so she could have a better view, but she really wanted a room on the other side of the resort.

"Shit, I'm tired. You know my flight from Seattle with that layover in Dallas really gave me jet lag. Then you two kept me up all night. You two fine with me catching a nap for a few hours?" Sky asked, hoping that Shyne was in the room waiting for her. She sent him the information the day she changed her room type.

"Well, I guess since you put it that way."

Sky could tell Iyana was disappointed, but she was thankful Rickey was there. Initially, she thought he would be a distraction, but she actually liked him and felt he could fill up some of that down time with her girl when she wasn't around.

"Girl, go. I got her. Her ass needs to loosen up and grab another rum punch. Run along," he said shooing her off with a kiss.

Rushing off the elevator, Sky couldn't wait to see Shyne. It had been two months and she needed to feel his body against hers. Knowing the layout of where the wires were, she snatched him quickly into the bathroom, throwing him into the hot tub while she attached pre-recorded conversations to the wires.

That was another tactic she'd learned that the DEA knew nothing about, taking advantage of the underground world of spies that were defunct from their previous organizations like the FBI and CIA.

"Damn, Sky. Your ass fucking snapped my neck yanking me in here," he said, admiring her voluptuous, thick thighs, breasts, and freshly shaved pussy.

Sky was toned, but curvy, never once trying to lose a pound. She took great pride in her appearance though, hitting the gym every day for two hours.

"Shut up and eat this pussy," she said, sitting on his face in the hot tub. Like an obedient dog, Shyne devoured her budding clit that welcomed his hot mouth.

Sky didn't know what she liked the most, his head game or his exquisite stroke game which made her want to murder the entire DEA for fucking with the greatest stroke game ever to exist in the game of fucking. Without fail, Shyne greased his face up, deep sea diving his tongue between Sky's slippery pussy.

"You's a nasty bitch," Sky seethed, bouncing on Shyne's face, as he gripped her like he hadn't eaten for days.

Pushing her down without warning, Shyne rammed his erect shaft inside of her, daring her to scream or complain. She had been teasing him for weeks, sending him all types of videos and pussy shots of her fucking herself. He told her that as soon as he could he was going to murder the pussy, and he did just that. He murdered it.

Lying in bed, both smoking a freshly rolled blunt, Sky began to plot out how to just give herself up to Shyne and go rogue just to be with him. He wasn't a rapist or pedophile, two things Sky probably could easily kill a man for. He simply earned a living doing what the U.S. and other countries did legally manufacturing and selling weapons. The only difference was Shyne bought and sold them on the black market, then learned how to manufacture them himself over the years.

Why should he be punished for something the government did every day? she questioned herself.

"Why you so quiet?" he asked, rubbing her hair as she lightly stroked his penis wanting more. "I could go another round, but I can tell when something's wrong. Talk to me. Is it work?"

"It's always work. That shit ain't new, so no," she said sitting up with his semi-flaccid penis in her hand. Instantly she wanted to taste him, but wanted to deal with the elephant in the room.

"Shyne, what if I told you a secret? A secret no one knows about. Not even my family or Iyana. A secret that if shared, lives could be changed. Hell, even destroyed?"

"Shit, Sky. What if the moon was purple and Lucky Charms are real motherfuckers that walk the earth at night when the rest of the fucking world sleeping? 'Cause that's what that shit sounds like to me.

Ain't no fucking way you got a secret that powerful that your ass ain't told no one. Shit, yo' mouth stay on go even when a nigga sleep," he laughed, dragging her down on top of him as he kissed the top of her head.

"But... but what if? I'm just saying," she asked not letting it go.

"Well, let's see," he said lifting her face up by the chin. "Would this secret cause me to lose you or vice versa?"

His eyes were steady and his breathing was even. Whenever he got that serious, his mind was trained to take in everything in his immediate surroundings, assessing for threats that could take his life. He never once questioned Sky's loyalty, but this hypothetical question was gnawing at him once she posed it a second time.

"Maybe, maybe not. I'm just saying. Would you rather take that secret to the grave and run off with me, or possibly trust me if I say I got you? Even if it looks like you lost me."

By this time, Shyne had sat up, uncomfortable. Not wanting to pop off on her, he decided he needed some air.

"Look, this conversation is creepy as fuck," he said, grabbing his cell that just went off. He forgot to call his brother back earlier this week to tell him he was traveling. Outside of a few trusted members of his crew, only his brother knew when he was not tucked away at home.

"Let me go this take this shit outside. And Sky?" he asked pulling on some sweatpants and a t-shirt.

"Yes, Shyne," she responded too quickly, standing up in front of him as she searched his eyes.

"To answer your question because I fuck with you the long way, I would take my chances saying fuck the world and run off with you."

Reaching down, he delicately cupped her mouth, kissing her, before he stepped out to call his brother. Sky, feeling confident of what she had to do next, decided to move on it and do it quickly before he came back.

"Yeah, Rickey. What's up?"

"Really, Shyne. Nigga, it's been three days since I called. I was about to hop my black ass on a plane as soon as I left Jamaica, to come to New York and fuck you up. Now you know I don't do New York except for you. Why you playing?"

"Calm the fuck down, Rickey. I'm not one of them bitch ass niggas you play," he said, taking the elevator down to the main bar to get a drink.

"Oh, trust me. I know, but you know how I get. Other than you, who do I have, Shyne, if something were to happen to you?"

"Rickey, man. I hear you and did you say Jamaica?" he asked ordering him two shots of White Hennessey.

Before he could respond, the cellphone dropped. After trying to get him back twice, Shyne decided to go back to the room to really see what was up with Sky, leaving the door slightly ajar, he heard her whispering.

"Lieutenant, I'm good. No, he stepped out," she whispered facing the balcony that overlooked the water.

Trained to walk like he was walking on cotton, Shyne slipped up behind her after carefully reaching for his pistol he had tucked under his pillow. Before Sky could move, she felt the barrel of his weapon to the back of her head.

Chapter 14

"Look, I'll get wit'cha later. I'ma be out of town a few days, but I promise to make it up to Ish."

"How do you plan to do that, Keyz? You know he loves church and didn't even let you know how much it hurt him that you didn't make it the last time. Now here you go, about to miss another Sunday that you could have seen him perform," Myriah complained.

"Look, I spent all day with my shorty and my peoples. How I spend my time with my lil' man is how the fuck I want to. Damn, I swear if you ain't the most miserable bi—look, I gotta go," he said hanging up the phone.

"Myriah?" Chico asked while they drove to meet up with their connect in Palm Beach.

"Yea, I try to respect her because she's Ish's mom, but shit came up and I sent him to church with my mama. How the fuck she expects to manage a whole, grown ass man that don't want her?" he asked, not really expecting an answer.

It was the third Monday of the month and time for them to re-up. Knowing they needed to keep the streets flooded with their product, Keyz decided to go along for the ride since Skebo had been missing lately. Keyz was worried, but was giving him some time to work out whatever it was that was going on. Business was good, so he figured he'd hold him down for now until he was ready to talk.

"So anyway, you thought more about what we talked about?" he asked, changing the subject.

His boys were used to him ranting about Myriah, so there wasn't much Chico would say that he hadn't said already. Keyz also noticed Chico either defended her or would sit quietly, not speaking on it, like it wasn't his place to speak. Keyz took that as a hint to only speak on her when necessary as of late. Little did Keyz know, Chico was fuming every time he called her out her name or mentioned his son, knowing deep down inside he wasn't his.

"Keyz, man. I'on like shit like that," he grinned. "You know me. Like, I'm used to doing shit for other people and paying for their parties and whatnot. All that popping bottles and hoes shit don't even faze me, honestly. Why we can't just celebrate your young ass?" he teased.

"Fool, I'm about to be thirty, which is a clear sign that we *both* need to start thinking and moving differently."

Kaizer was planning his 30th birthday party for January, which was three days before Chico's 34th birthday. They were both Aquarians who possessed many of the same attributes, including their ability to love hard and be somewhat overbearing. Neither celebrated their birthdays growing up, but Kaizer decided that it was time to start engaging in normal stuff in life, like birthday parties, going to church and even settling down. He chuckled to himself when Iyana was the first person he saw himself settling down with.

Looking at him from the side as he cut his eyes, Chico said, "Nigga, what you over there smiling about?"

Shrugging, "Not shit."

"That not shit must be the shit because you love to keep a mean mug on your face. Have bitches falling all over your pretty boy ass," he teased.

"Yea, maybe, but there's this one that can knock any and all them bitches clean off once she stops playing," Keyz said seriously.

"Oh yea? Who?" Chico asked, now interested to see who had his boy wanting to settle down.

"Remember that chic from midtown? The one who called herself cussing a nigga out for blocking the parking garage?" he asked, smiling once again as he thought of her.

"I remember that night, but not her. You fucked and keeping it on the low?"

"Something like that," he replied, choosing not to share all the details because his boys would know how fast he moved on her.

"Yea, I knew some shit happened the way you left KOD like you got a curfew," Chico laughed.

"Never that. I just know what I want and it's not these loose coochie bitches out here thinking a nigga want his dick sucked and fucked all the time. Shit, I need a woman that knows how to stimulate this...first," Keyz said tapping his temple. "The kind at the end of the day, who knows how to bring all that chaos in my world to a halt just by standing there, being at home and waiting for me. The kind that keeps up with politics and shit or cultural stuff. Not that fucking reality TV and definitely not a bitch into labels, unless the name on that damn purse is our fucking name. I mean she can like and buy nice shit, but not worship it. Know what I mean?"

Chico was quiet, but he was listening as his boy spoke. Everything Keyz spoke was real and what hurt him the most is he had that woman in his life. He just couldn't share her right now with the world.

"Yea, I hear you, Keyz. I want that shit, too. Just not with Meka's ass. She got that mean pussy, look good and will hold me down around the house, but she don't want it. Not that Huxtable life or even that Bonnie and Clyde shit we probably could have.

She wants to be Bonnie *and* Clyde 'cause of her fucking family. I ain't complaining though because C.U.B still eating with 'em. Just calling it how it is until I'm ready to move off from her, or her ass up and move the fuck around."

"Well, Chico, do something, but only when you ready because this right here," he said pointing around as they were riding through the hood "won't be where I eat much longer. The shit I'm on won't get me locked up or dead. Just pussy at home day in and day out with some kids. You know, shit like that."

"Awww, man!" Chico laughed. "Just a few years ago, my ass was telling you about women and life, and now you trying to school me. Yo, you funny, but I hear you. So, tell me more about this party shit."

"Nigga, whatever," Keyz replied smirking. "So Shower and Sunshine gone do something for us at the hookah bar. My girl

The One That Got Away

will help out. Guess you can meet her then. You know with my mom taking over management, they been running her raggedy ever since trying to get my mom to put in shit like a stripper pole," he laughed.

"Got damn Sunshine and Shower," Chico laughed, shaking his head.

He remembered how feisty and sneaky they were growing up, although Sunshine really was quiet the older they got. Gone were the days where Keyz ran dudes off since they both were pretty independent having babies and all. Keyz stayed in his lane for the most part, but most dudes knew not to disrespect his sisters.

"Yea, man. You know they got that party creations company they started last year and they making a killing," he smiled. "I'm talking about five to six grand a month sometimes on baby showers, bridal showers and other girly shit. My girl is amazed, damn near trying to get me to invest in that with them."

"Yeah, I hear you bringing up your girl. I like that. Especially since their asses fucking with her. They both done grew up on me, huh?"

"Shit, on me you mean, but the only one I'm worried about is Sunshine. That fuck nigga she pregnant from ain't disrespecting her, but his punk ass ran off and got married. The only thing holding me back is the bitch nigga in the NBA.

Gotta catch him slipping during off season, but when I do, his ass gon' be resting for a long ass time. Fuck that. My nephews straight for life. They'on need his bitch ass, but he still tried my baby sister. What made me even madder is I been told Keyon to stop fucking with that square ass dude, but you know him.

Any dude that have hoes for days is a dude Keyon wants to hang with. From what I hear, his ass done calmed down after Chase was about to leave him, but I know my baby brother. If it looks like pussy, smells like pussy and tastes like pussy, its pussy and he just gotta have it."

"Oh, trust me. I hear Meka and 'nem on that social media shit asking me about him and Chase. Fuck I look like monitoring what another nigga doing unless he fucking my ole lady?" Chico asked like that was the lamest shit any nigga could do.

"That part," Keyz said agreeing with him.

"So, you know Skebo feeling Sunshine. He ain't said shit, but every time one of us bring her up, his ass waiting to see what we gone say. Now, me personally, think my brah is a stand up dude, Keyz. I mean, he ain't never lied to nain woman about her being his main."

"True, but he ain't asked me shit about my sister," Keyz replied, tightening his jaw. "So until then, he better stick to these streets and fuck them hoes. Sunshine ain't one and ain't gon' never be one."

"Man, that's your boy," Chico said sitting up, looking at Keyz like he was crazy. "Hell, I'm your boy. You think either one of us would fuck over one of your sisters? Man, tighten up, Keyz,"

Keyz was no longer that little boy, robbing and hustling to make a come up, and Chico knew the more he changed, the more shit was about to get real for all of them.

"True," was all he said as they approached their connect's house.

~

"Ishmael! Ish! That's you?" Myriah yelled from the kitchen.

This month was National Hispanic Heritage month and Ishmael's teacher, Ms. Johnson, really had the kids all riled up about ways they could recognize it in class. Of course, they could have opted for drawing a picture or dressing up in Hispanic native garbs, but they chose food, from fried plantains and burritos to red beans and rice.

At first, Ishamael wanted to make tacos, but settled for beef empanadas, something he ate all the time from the local Spanish bakery near their house. She planned to surprise him by making them from scratch while he was at the community arts center with his aunt. Since Iyana's return, she had been spending quite a bit of time with him, from the mime ministry at church and now the center.

"Not, Ish, mami," Chico yelled as he walked in using the key she gave him for times he came in late at night.

"Mmmm," Chico moaned as he bent down, kissing her on the back of her neck as she rolled the dough for the empanada.

Upset that he had been ignoring her for the past few days, she tensed up, locking her neck to the side to minimize the touch of his lips. She was growing tired of this charade where she had to be his secret, not only to Keyz, but to Meka as well.

"Baby?" he whispered. "I'm sorry."

Moving around not wanting to talk, Myriah grabbed the ground beef, onions and peppers from the refrigerator, and pulled out her large frying pan. She often would cook out of necessity, but this special project came as a pleasant distraction for her aching heart. She wanted Chico so bad, but she knew in her heart that being second best in any man's life was the norm.

"Let daddy make it up to you," he whispered, leaning his chin on her shoulder as he inhaled her body scent.

Ignoring him, Myriah feverishly started chopping the onions and peppers before she was interrupted by Chico's hands, gripping both of her wrists. Overwhelmed with pain and frustration, Myriah couldn't take it anymore.

"Stop, Chico! Just fucking stop!" she cried tossing her knife down, facing him. "You full a shit, Chico! Just full of it. Why, baby? Why can't we just tell them? Tell them he's your son. Tell them we want a family. Tell them I want to have more of your babies. Why, baby?" Myriah was begging and crying, almost uncontrollably as he stroked her pained face matching how he felt.

"Because…shit, My," he said drawing back from her the more she cried, "Keyz is family and shit and we waited so fucking long. It's been like…eleven years, yo. Like, I guess I have accepted it."

"Bullshit! You didn't and you don't accept it!" she screamed, poking him in the chest. "You give him a higher cut to take care of your son! Your son! Then put a gotdamn handcuff on who I sleep with but still fucking Meka when my ass was around *wayyyy* before her! That ain't fair!"

Pushing up on her full of rage, Chico grabbed her neck as

he slid his hands down her leggings until his fingers touched her pussy.

"So that's what you what you angry about? Huh?" he gritted. "You wanna give this nigga my pussy, My? Shit, he already claiming MY SON! Fuck!" Chico yelled, slapping his head three or four times as he gripped her neck tighter and tighter.

For the life of him, he couldn't understand why he let it go this far except admitting that he was afraid of losing his boy because he took away his title as a father.

Watching him, Myriah began to shake as her ability to breathe was getting harder and harder. She loved Chico almost more than anyone in the world except Ish, his son, but she was tired. She wanted out. As she felt life leaving her body, she gave in to it not wanting to hurt anymore.

"Kill me...just kill me," she managed to speak as her lips turned blue.

Slightly releasing her throat, he took her mouth wanting to feel her tongue and mouth become one with his. Wanting her to focus on what he was able to give her right there in that moment, he slid his fingers deep into her vaginal lips, lightly probing her clitoris.

"Baby, stop. You know you are my princess. Just...just give me some time to figure it out," he whispered, his mouth still on hers.

"But...but you said you wanted me. You want Ish," she croaked as he loosened his grip while releasing himself.

"Shit, baby. I'm sorry," he whispered, picking her up as he sat her on the kitchen counter to feel her slick walls against his manhood.

"I do. I just don't know what to do anymore," he spoke softly in her mouth, catching how warm and wet she was for him.

"Ssssss," she hissed as he went back and forth inside of her.

"I'm sorry. I'ma do better, Myriah. I'ma do better," he said, dragging his tongue up and down her bruised neck, marked by his finger imprints.

Defeated, Myriah took what he gave her like she always did, thrust for thrust without saying another word. Her heart was broken and, again, Chico got what he wanted. Sadly, the moment he left she was going to plan her suicide. She was done…forever.

∽

"Oh, Lord. Who it this calling this late at night," Nana muttered trying to catch the phone before it woke Papa B up.

Today was one of the roughest days Nana had since Papa B was diagnosed a year ago. As promised, Sky secured and paid for a home health aide to come to the house daily to assist Nana as needed, be it cooking or cleaning or just sitting with him so Nana could take a nap.

Even when Iyana attempted to pay by depositing money in her account or sending it through PayPal, Sky would send money to cover Papa B's home health aide care. Being stubborn, Iyana decided to not only book but pay for their girls' trip to Ochos Rios, Jamaica right before Christmas.

While they were gone, Sky had paid for around the clock care, still trying to have one up on Iyana. All Nana wanted was her husband back healthy, or even a little rest, but tonight she could see that was impossible.

"Hello," she whispered watching Papa B who stirred slightly when she moved.

"Is this the Jamie Wilker, the mother of Myriah Wilkers?" the unknown caller asked.

Panicking, Nana sat up clutching the phone, praying this was a prank. She knew the life Myriah used to live, but after becoming a mother, her granddaughter had made almost a 180-degree turnaround, short of her and Papa B not seeing eye to eye like she'd been praying for.

"It is. I'm her grandmother. May I ask whose calling?"

"This is Dr. Ryan calling from Jackson Memorial Hospital Ryder Trauma Center. Myriah—"

"Myriah, what? What about Myriah?" she jumped up waking Papa B up.

"Now what the hell going on around here? Is that Sheryl? Didn't I tell her ass that if the lights catch her and she ain't home, we ain't letting her in the house? I don't care if Jesus made the call for her!"

By this time, Papa B was up looking for his house shoes so he could go to the door and tell her to come back tomorrow. That was his usual routine whenever Sheryl would come home late from a rally, protest, or sit in.

Nana and Papa B had created a modern-day Rosa Parks as she sat in their lap day in and day out hearing stories related to the Jim Crow laws. At first, they were fully behind her, but once her life was in danger, they begged of her to find safer ways to protest, like writing letters to the local mayor or even governor.

"Ma'am? I'm trying to tell you, but—"

"Baby, it's not Sheryl! Now get back in the bed!" Nana screamed almost losing her mind.

"Dr—Dr. Ryan. Tell me what's wrong with Myriah. Please," she begged once she realized he couldn't get out of the house or turn the stove on. Since his last episode, the locks were all open with a key only, and the stove's knobs were off unless she was cooking.

"She was found in her bathtub by her neighbor once they found water running out of her front door. Apparently, she attempted to commit suicide. She has two large lacerations across each wrist, but we got her here just in time.

Can you come? We understand there is a child involved and before we contact the Department of Children and Families for abandonment, we wanted to reach out to her first of kin."

"I'm coming, I'm coming, I'm coming," she ranted, looking around for anything to put on. "Give me twenty minutes, please! Just give me 20 minutes! I gotta get my husband dressed, too."

"Ma'am?"

"Mrs. Wilkers. I'm the grandmother and great grandmother of Ishmael Paul. Is my grandson there?" she asked, throwing on a house dress, sweater and sandals.

"No, ma'am. He's not. He's with a neighbor," the doctor advised offering her some relief.

"Papa B! Come in here and put on your shoes! Come on, now!" she yelled, grabbing his orthopedic tennis shoes he loved so much. Instead of listening, he was in the living room yelling at the television watching *Family Feud*.

The One That Got Away

"That damn Steve Harvey sho nuff is ugly, baby! Ahhh, haaaa. Ah, ha, ha, ha," he laughed, slapping his leg.

"Lord, give me strength! Doctor, I'm on my way," she said hanging up to get Papa B out of the house and in the car.

She wasn't sure if Ishmael was home with her when it happened, but she didn't let her grandbabies go into foster care and she wasn't prepared to let him go either. Especially since no one knew who and where his father really was.

"Naw, baby. Damn, Sheryl. I'm not bailing her out of jail again. Don't you see Steve Harvey on? She will be just fine. Nope, not doing it. Can't go," he said giving her a hard time.

"Bernard Dwight Wilkers!" she yelled. "Get your butt up and put your damn shoes on right nah or I'm leaving your butt right here! Do you hear me?"

Shaking like she was about to lose the last bit of patience known to Job. It was as if God heard her and he snapped out of it, putting on his shoes as she grabbed his jacket.

"Okay, baby. I'm sorry. Let's go get Sheryl."

"Okay, let's go," she sighed, not even calling Iyana to alert her of what was going on.

Within twenty minutes, they were at the hospital rushing in to get to Myriah. Papa B was cursing and yelling about how Sheryl needed to close her legs and "sat down somewhere" while Nana frantically waited for the receptionist to tell them where to find Myriah.

Nana's heart collapsed, remembering that she was in ICU after the receptionist told her where to go. All around her, she saw young girls with babies on top of babies, and old people who appeared to be alone, in need of great help. A feeling of

247

despair came over her the more they walked, and Papa B rambled on until they got to the ICU area.

"Yes, may I help you?"

"Yes, yes, yes. We are the parents of Myriah Wilkers. I got a call from Dr. Ryan. Somethin' about my baby girl being rushed to the hospital and a suicide attempt. Oh, Jesus! Please!" she wailed, holding Papa B's hand, whose face was fixated on the nurse behind the nursing station.

"Baby? Why you ain't tell me Sheryl work at the hospital now? Hey, Sheryl. You shole done made Papa B real, real happy," he said, grinning, like he was seeing his daughter who had died over twenty years ago.

"Papa B, now. That ain't—"

Nana could see a resemblance, but lately, Papa B had been speaking of Sheryl more and more, scaring her each time, since their daughter had been dead over twenty years. The nurse, obviously aware of his diagnosis, took over, giving Nana time to get herself together.

"Yes, Papa B. It's me," the nurse replied, smiling ushering for Nana to go and see about Myriah. "Let's catch up over here until mama comes back. Is that alright?"

Without incident, Papa B embraced the nurse as she came around the nursing station. She felt nothing but compassion once she assessed how overwhelmed Nana was, realizing that she was the parent of the young woman who came in about an hour earlier, in bad shape. That, coupled with a husband with declining cognition, was more than the strongest person could handle.

"Rachel!" she yelled to the other nurse behind the station. "I'm headed to the cafeteria for a few. Okay?" Nodding her

The One That Got Away

head yes, Papa B gladly went along with her, asking her questions about her "new" job. Nana was thankful, rushing off to see about Myriah.

Beep, beep, beep, beep...

The sound of all of the machines Myriah was hooked up to seemed to be keeping her alive. Because it was a suicide attempt, Myriah's room had its own private nurse monitoring it at any time. Upon entering the room, the nurse asked Nana to step out.

"Hi, I'm Elaine. She's stable, but sleeping now. Dr. Ryan can give you more information on what he did to stabilize her," she said, trying to comfort her during her time of distress, even though there was more.

"Ma'am, because she tried to kill herself, once we discharge her from here, she will be transported to our psychiatric unit for further assessment. She is only in here because of the nature of her injuries. We had to give her a blood transfusion due to the loss of blood. Although she was lucid, she was very fragile, insisting we call you and someone named Chico. Are you aware of who he is?"

Trying to take it all in, Nana missed the question about Chico until Dr. Ryan walked in, who was briefed by the nurse. Judging from Nana's salt and pepper hair and soft, wrinkly skin, Dr. Ryan knew she had seen better days and was easily in her mid, possibly late 60s.

"Mrs. Wilkers? Dr. Ryan," he said shaking her hand.

"Thank you, thank you so much for calling me. Tell me about my baby," she begged, getting worked up again.

"As nurse Elaine advised, she's stable but we have another issue. She's pregnant. According to the blood work, she's about eight weeks. We believe the father is someone by the name of Chico. Before we sedated her, she asked for him continuously," he finished, rubbing Nana's arm who stood in a trance-like state.

"Look, Dr. Ryan. I don't no nothing about no baby or nobody named Chico. I got one grandson, Ishmael, and as soon as I know what's going on with my baby, I gotta get him."

"Well, I have his number if you wish to call him. He's been calling all night based on her missed call history. Since she identified you as someone that could make decisions for her before we put her under, I will bring you her phone."

Nana walked slowly in the room, approaching Myriah, who seemed to be at peace until she looked at her badly wounded wrists.

"My God. My child was trying to leave us all. Oh, baby, why would you do that?" she whispered, kissing Myriah on her forehead.

"Ma'am, here you go," the nurse said, handing her the cellphone. "He just called. Dr. Ryan has to make a few more rounds, but I will give you some privacy."

"Thank you. I need to step out and check on my husband. So, let me call him back now."

Walking in a daze, the cellphone rang over and over. Nana wasn't sure who Chico was, but she felt that maybe he had all the answers to Myriah's dark life. Yes, she was a great mother, but Nana knew since she was a little girl that Myriah was troubled, often coming to her defense.

She was afraid to ask her why she hated Papa B so much, but instead, she tolerated her behavior, keeping her at bay which was much easier after the birth of Ishmael.

"Lord, if I ever needed you, I needs you now. Lord, I needs you now," she said, deciding to answer the cellphone.

"He... hello," she stuttered.

"Myriah, baby! What's up? Why you ain't been answering and shit," he yelled like he was about to lose it.

Unsure of how to respond, Nana held the phone for a few seconds trying to piece tonight's events together, when she knew the answer lied on the other end of the cellphone.

"Sir? This here is Nana, Myriah's grandmother. She's at Jackson... she tried to kill herself tonight, but they tell me she's been asking for you."

Before she could say more, the line went dead. Remembering she needed to check on Papa B, she threw the cellphone in her purse before she started reciting her favorite scripture, Psalms 1. Over and over, she allowed the word of God to soothe her troubled spirit, as she found Papa B sitting in front of the nursing station, quietly eating some ice cream.

"Mama," the nurse said. "Papa B is going to sit here quietly until you're ready to go. He told me what our favorite ice cream was, so I got the cafeteria to give us some. Ain't that right, Papa B?"

"Yeah, Sheryl, baby. This right here is good, Nana. Want some?" he asked, lifting his cup of Butter Pecan ice cream to his wife.

"No, Papa B. I'm fine. Give me a few minutes. I gotta run to the ladies' room."

Rushing off, Nana went to the hospital's chapel to spend some time with God. He was the source of strength that got her through the good and bad times, from the death of her only child to the declining health of her husband, and now this. She knew that if God did it then, he could do it now.

～

"Baby?" Chico whispered as he sat next to Myriah in the hospital.

He never feared much of anything in his life until he heard that Myriah was almost gone. Rushing out of the strip club, Chico told Keyz and Tone that he had to go the hospital. Before they could ask why, he took off driving almost 100 miles per hour trying to get to her.

His car, illegally parked in a handicapped spot, was almost left running, as he jumped out without turning it off until security yelled at him. He didn't care if his car got towed. All he cared about was her and Ishmael.

"Myriah, baby," he wailed, collapsing on her body until nurse Elaine came in the room.

"Sir, please. She's resting," she whispered, placing her hand on his shoulder. "I don't want to have to ask you to leave."

Jumping up, Chico looked at her as if she was the enemy, knowing he was the reason Myriah was lying in that bed with death lurking at her door.

"Fuck that. I ain't doing shit. I'm staying right here until her ass gets up and comes home with me!" he yelled, hitting his chest. "And where's my son? Why you in here monitoring me, can somebody tell me where my son is?" he yelled, punching his chest. "Huh? Where is he?"

"Sir, he's safe with a neighbor. Look, she's fighting—

fighting for her life. Can you calm down, please? I want you stay because she was asking for you, but if you don't calm down, I will have to ask you to leave," she pled, sitting him back down.

"She really was? Me? Chico?" he asked in disbelief, always hoping that she loved him as much he loved her.

"Yes," the nurse smiled. "And I'm sure you want her out of here because in less than seven months, you two will be welcoming a little one into the world."

Full of emotion, Chico stared at Myriah in awe. All the dreams and talks they had of them being a family ran through his mind. There were days where he would get lost in her presence, dreading to go home or rushing to get there unnoticed by his crew.

He felt like this was a sign, a sign from God to live in their truth. Turning around to thank the nurse, Chico got the shock of his life when he saw Keyz standing at the door.

> To be continued

**If you've gotten this far, check my catalog.
https://amzn.to/35py0NZ
And please be so kind to leave a review.**

Thank you so much!

> # Steel Roses Bleed Too
> ## A PARANORMAL ROMANCE

By
Tisha Andrews

Chapter 1

Hearing the soft hum of Blue's engine caused Rose to smile. Each hum, each gentle vibration of her Mustang was like a current of goodness, because of him—Diesel. Their connection was beyond some moth to a flame cliché bullshit. It was kinetic, addictive, no matter how strange it looked to others. That shit was *real*. So real, he and Rose had to be touching each other every time they saw it each other just like now.

"So, we're just going to sit here, listening and smiling at the sound of the car, baby girl?" Diesel asked, feigning for her. Whenever he called her that, he wasn't in a playing mood.

He had to have Rose and right then.

"I was just checking… you know, for a nagging sound," she whispered, tucking her lips to hide her smile. She really was too embarrassed to admit each time she listened to that hum, she thought of him, she wanted him, she craved him.

Say it, Rose. Just say it, he said to himself, hearing her thoughts.

No matter how hard he tried, he couldn't help it. Her thoughts were like his lifeline to her heart, her soul, as Rose still battled with being all his. He scooted over just a little and a little is all it took before their skin touched and them both melted, the sweat peppering on her skin. Then her smell was beyond intoxicating. A combination of coconut from her skin and hair to the sweet, sweet smell of her pussy—his favorite scent.

"Baby Girl," he whispered in her ear, as she shuddered. "The only nagging sound is going to be the sound of me in your ear… and between your legs," he told her his face now in the crook of her neck.

He wasted no time either. His quick hands finding their way underneath one thigh. He gave it a light squeeze, as he nipped her ear and told her how good and sweet *his pussy* smelled. She hissed and he licked her from her ear all the way over to her mouth where his lips caught hers. With ease, he slipped his tongue into her mouth and she groaned—she fucking groaned.

He didn't need to hear her thoughts after that. He knew what the hell she was thinking. Her body told it all, and just like her car, she motherfucking hummed.

"Shit," she grunted lowly. "We're going to be late and people can see—" This was their one night out as a couple. With school and both working, time out was a rarity. But even now, he'd rather enjoy her love, the love between her legs as they sat in her car.

"Fuck them people," he growled, hungrily sucking on her

lower lip, as she smiled. While she blessed him with the prettiest, gapped-tooth smile, he leaned down and put her thigh in the crook of his arm. "Rose," he whispered, as she closed her eyes. "Thank you."

As soon as she opened her eyes, it was like time had stopped. Folks outside were still, mouths mid-open, kids running with one leg extended under a trance he'd casted. Rose's eyes grew wide, while she attempted to speak.

"What the fu—"

"Shhhhh, focus on me," he coached her. Besides, her memory would be swiped clean as soon as they were done. He quickly went back to work, taking her mouth once again. A mouth he found great pleasure in. It was her personal sweet haven of kisses. Kisses he could live off of for the rest of his life, while he worked her center. It was warm and slick. Her essence soon covered his fingers as he slid them in between her fatty, satin-like folds. Diesel worshipped Rose's pussy and yet, they still had never had sex.

"Baby, what are we doing?" she panted, her skin flushed. "I thought we were…oh shit," she groaned.

"What you want me to do, right?" he challenged, hoping she would be bold enough to agree.

"Ye—yea," she stammered, his fingers busily gliding up and down her pussy, an occasional dip into her love.

Slowly lifting one leg, he placed it across his shoulder, as Rose fell back against the door. It was tight in there, but just enough room for her to bless him with an eye full of pussy. He groaned lowly, as he felt himself swelling even more.

He thanked the Etan gods she wore this floral, coral sundress that made her look like she was laying in a garden, just for him. In no time, he had a mouth full of pussy. Her yelps, groans, moans and requests for him to keep going were like fuel, as she gassed him up.

Rose had even gotten used to his speed, speed he'd try to hide around her that now, didn't even seem to matter. With one hand flicking her mound, and the other spreading her folds, Rose bloomed like the flower she was... in his mouth.

Gone was the guarded, bossy girl that refused to let any guy distract her from her quest of becoming a doctor. Especially since Diesel didn't make it easy for her. He was there, always there. Even when she slept, unaware he was there. She was like a toy he was fascinated with and him with her. They were forever... connected.

It was infectious.

It was maddening.

It was dangerous. So dangerous, that when her back stiffened and she cried out his name with her still in his mouth, he cried. Diesel literally cried. When he did, she cried too, stroking the waves on top of his head that bobbed between her legs. It was the most beautiful and pleasurable sight Rose had ever experienced.

"We still have time?" she panted out, really wanting to ask him to do it again and again. to

"All the fucking time you need, Rose," he whispered in her pussy and she groaned.

"Then keep going," she panted.

He kept going too, totally unaware that someone outside was moving around unlike the humans that couldn't under his trance... and watching.